Mission Detroit

Chuck Beach

Solstice Publishing - www.solsticepublishing.com

Mission Detroit

Chuck Beach

Dedication

To my three wonderful children Nick, Jen, and Carey. You make life worth living. To my grandson, Mason. You are the new chapter. Make it worth reading.

Introduction

The book is a fictional story that takes during World War II. It centers around two Nazi spies and saboteurs who were inserted into America in 1943 by a German U-Boat. Their purpose is to sabotage the production of the Rolls-Royce Merlin engines intended for the P-51 fighter and PT Boats.

Certain conversations would have been carried on in German. These are related in English but bold italicized print.

Chapter One

"**B**ring *the boat to periscope depth,*" ordered Captain Fritz Wolfe in the conning tower of the Nazi submarine U-42.

"*Bringing the boat to periscope depth, captain,*" said the sailor from the darkness. A couple of minutes later the sailor added, "*Periscope depth, sir.*"

"**Up periscope**,*"* barked Captain Wolfe. The periscope went up, and Captain Wolfe unfolded the 'T' handles and looked into the viewfinder. He slowly went around in a clockwise direction until he had made a full circle, all the while looking through the scope. "N*ote in the log. We are approximately five kilometers off the coast of New Jersey, it is November third, nineteen forty-three, at 2300 hours.*"

"*Yes, captain,*" responded a sailor somewhere in the darkness of the bridge of the U-42.

"*Care to take a look?*" Captain Wolfe asked the Nazi SS officer standing next to him.

"*Yes, I would,*" replied Eric Smoltz as he stepped forward to take control of the periscope. Looking through the scope, "*My compliments, captain. We are right on schedule.*"

"*I would suggest you make ready your landing party. You will be departing in one hour.*" Wolfe said to Smoltz.

"*Of course.*" Smoltz stood back from the periscope, raised his right arm, "*Heil Hitler.*" Wolfe returned the salute. Smoltz made his way toward the front of the boat. He turned left into the small compartment known as the officers' mess. Lieutenant Adolph Richter was already inside. Richter had all of their equipment laid out on the table.

"We depart in one hour, Richter. Let's go over what we are taking."

"*Yes, sir.*"

"NO!" barked Smoltz. "English only from this point on!"

"Yes, sir." Richter responded. "Sorry, sir. Here is your waterproof case. Check the contents. You are now Christopher Hagen. You have a birth certificate, Social Security card, driver's license, ration cards, and draft deferment card. There is a copy of your engineering degree from Penn State. Also a wallet containing pictures of your parents and brother, and one thousand American dollars. There is a letter of hiring from Packard Motor Company addressed to your home in Pennsylvania."

Smoltz opened the case and checked the contents. "Those forgers in the Fatherland do remarkable work, don't they? Have you checked over your documents, Richter, I mean Mr. Phillip Brown?"

"I have checked my case several times, sir. I have everything here, and it is in good order."

"What else, Phillip?"

"Here is a list of our contacts in Michigan."

"Do you have it memorized?"

"Of course, sir."

"Then destroy it."

Richter, AKA Brown, put the paper in his mouth, chewed it up, and swallowed it.

Smoltz, AKA Hagen, pointed to a duffle bag on the table, "Are the detonators and explosives in that bag?"

"No, sir. The explosives are in the larger bag and the detonators are in the smaller bag."

"You need to stop calling me sir."

"Sure thing, Chris," joked Brown.

"Do you have your cyanide capsule, Phil?"

"Yeah, it's sewn into the lining of my coat collar."

"Good. I have mine sewn into the lining of my hat. We should start moving this gear to the conning tower. We leave in a few minutes. Let's do one final quiz of our background stories."

***

Captain Smoltz was the perfect Nazi. Taken from his home at the age of twelve, he was one of the first indoctrinated into the Hitler Youth Program. For ten years, he was fed the Nazi doctrine of the German super race and world domination. He excelled in every physical and mental challenge he was given. His father was born in Germany, educated at the Massachusetts Institute of Technology (MIT) and was a professor of mechanical engineering at The University of Munich. His mother was a beautiful, doting German housewife. When he went away to the Hitler Youth Camp, he spoke perfect German and English.

Professor Smoltz taught in Germany for several years before Adolph Hitler came to power in 1933. The professor had witnessed first-hand the ravages of the Depression and the punitive effects imposed on Germany by the Treaty of Versailles. He, along with millions of others living in Germany at the time, thought Hitler would be able to bring prosperity back to Germany, so the professor became a member of the Nazi Party.

As young Eric Smoltz developed into an adult, he became exactly what the Nazi propaganda machine was looking for. He was a six-foot-two blonde-haired, blue-eyed Adonis. Joseph Goebbels was touring the Youth Camps when he spotted Smoltz and used photos of him in several propaganda posters. The posters caught the eye of none other than Heinrich Himmler, the leader of the infamous Nazi SS. Himmler thought Smoltz was perfect for the German Diplomatic Corps for use in English-speaking countries. Of course, it was just a cover for his SS spying activities. When World War II broke out in 1939, Smoltz was put in charge of several covert spying missions in England. On his last mission, his cover was blown, so he was brought back to Germany. He went through intensive training in the American version of the English language.

Lieutenant Adolph Richter was the product of a wounded World War I German soldier and an American nurse. His mother became pregnant with him just as the war ended. She married Corporal Richter and returned from a French hospital to Germany with him. As a boy, Richter was placed in a machinist training program. He excelled in the program and graduated with Master Machinist qualifications. In his spare time, Richter had a successful career as an amateur boxer. He caught the attention of several SS officers when he beat one of them in the ring, which qualified him for a berth on the 1936 German Olympic team. Mrs. Richter was very diligent in making sure her son was proficient in German, French, and Americanized English, which turned out to be excellent training for the Nazi spy program.

***

Germany invaded Poland in September of 1939, and England and France declared war on Germany. Two months later, Richter, having proved himself as a good Nazi in Poland was smuggled into France, where he conducted undercover espionage. Information that he gathered and sent back to the fatherland was instrumental in allowing the Germans to successfully invade France and force the British to retreat from the European continent at Dunkirk.

Himmler approved a plan to send agents to America to slow the production of the Rolls-Royce Merlin engines. Smoltz and Richter were selected for the assignment. Once they were assigned, the forgers went to work crafting support documents for their background cover stories.

***

"You lived on Maple Street right off DeSoto in Pittsburgh, isn't that right?" Smoltz asked Richter.

"Yeah, that's right."

"I know that neighborhood. There's a big blue house on the corner of Maple and DeSoto, isn't there?"

"No, the big blue house is one street up, at the corner of Pinehurst and DeSoto. Weiss's Market is on the corner of Maple and DeSoto," replied Richter.

"Very good, Richter. We must know even the smallest of details. So tell me, isn't than market owned by a Jew?"

"Yes, it is."

"NO, NO, NO!" Smoltz whispered emphatically. Always answer in English."

"Yes, of course. That slip won't happen again," Richter answered.

"How old is your brother, Richter?"

"My name is Brown, and I don't have a brother. I have two sisters who are both still in high school."

"What are their names and birthdates?"

"Sue was born on December 4th, 1927. Pam was born on November 14th, 1929."

"Now you ask me something," Smoltz said.

"How old is your brother, Hans?"

"My brother's name is Henry, and he's seventeen. He's going to join the Marines when he graduates from high school next year."

"Good. You didn't fall for the trick in the question," Richter offered.

"Details, we must know even the smallest details, my friend. So tell me, are your sisters good fucks?"

Richter jumped to his feet, balled up his fists and exclaimed, "Get up, motherfucker! I'm going to knock your teeth down your Goddamn throat!"

"Very good, Mister Brown. Way to stay in character as a hot-headed American who thinks with his emotions and not with logic."

"Thanks, pal," Brown said as he sat down.

***

"*Bring the boat to periscope depth*," ordered Captain Wolfe.

"*Yes, captain*," responded the sailor seated at the console. A few seconds later he said, "*Periscope depth, sir.*"

"*Up periscope*," ordered the captain. When the periscope reached full height, the captain lowered the handles and looked in the viewfinder. He circled slowly to his right until he made a complete circle. "*All clear. Make ready the launch party. Surface the boat.*"

U-42 broke the surface of the water and a hatch to the deck opened. Smoltz, Richter, and two sailors passed the launch party's equipment to the deck. A sailor pulled the cord and inflated a small rubber raft. He threw the raft over the side and held it in place with a rope as the rest of the men loaded the equipment and gear into it. Captain Wolfe joined the party on deck.

"*You are about one kilometer from the beach, Captain Smoltz*," Wolfe said.

"*Very good, Captain Wolfe*," Smoltz responded.

The raft loaded, Captain Wolfe shook hands with Smoltz and Richter and wished them good luck. Smoltz stood at attention and gave the Nazi salute. "*Heil Hitler.*" Captain Wolfe returned the salute. The two spies got into the raft and began paddling toward the beach. Within a minute, the U-42 slithered beneath the waves and disappeared out of sight. The Nazi spies were now on their own.

***

Just as the German meteorologists had predicted, it was a cold, windy, moon-less night, perfect weather to sneak into America undetected. The Nazis battled three to four-foot waves. They made landfall on the shore of a New Jersey State Beach. The beach, closed to the public hours earlier was deserted. They dragged their raft up the beach to where the dunes began and vegetation began to grow. The two men began to dig a hole to bury the raft. Suddenly, Smoltz was hit in the face with the beam from a flashlight.

"Halt!" someone yelled from behind the light. "Stand up, slowly!" the voice commanded. The two men complied. The man folding the light walked toward the two men. When he got close enough to see, the Germans realized the voice belonged to an American sailor. The sailor was in uniform: a pea coat, white spats on his boots, a white sailor's cap, and an armband that read 'SP,' which stood for Shore Patrol. The sailor held a rifle at his hip, pointing it at the two men.

"What are you doing here?" the young sailor nervously asked as his eyes darted about, hoping to see his partner.

"Fishing," Smoltz replied.

"Fishing?" questioned the young sailor. He briefly shined his flashlight on the contents of the raft. "How do you fish without any fishing tackle? Get your hands up." The sailor pointed his rifle at Smoltz and said, "Let me see some identification, and bring it out slowly."

Smoltz reached in his coat and produced his forged identification papers. The sailor reached out to take the papers from Smoltz. As he did, Richter saw an opportunity and struck the sailor on the jaw with a hard right fist. The sailor fell to the sand, unconscious.

"Shit!" Smoltz exclaimed, nervously pounding his right fist into his open left hand. He was afraid their mission was compromised before it began "We can't leave him here. He'll report us for sure."

"We can't take him with us, either,"

"Then you know what has to be done, Richter."

Richter pulled a switchblade knife from his pocket and opened it. The cold-blooded Nazi knelt down, put one hand over the sailor's mouth as he'd been trained to do, and slit his throat. Both men stood and watched the young sailor bleed to death. Richter stabbed the rubber raft several times to deflate it. They wrapped the sailor's body in the now-flat raft, dragged it into the hole and buried it in the sand. Richter pulled a branch from the shrubbery and rubbed it over the hole to blend the other sand with the fresh-dug sand, hiding the hole. Smoltz crawled up the sand berm to look around, making sure there was nobody else around. Convinced the coast was clear, he scrambled down the berm back to Richter.

"Is the car here?" Richter asked.

"Yeah, right above us."

The two men gathered their gear, scrambled up the sand berm and ran to a car parked in the parking lot of the deserted state park. Smoltz reached on top of the left rear tire of the 1935 Ford and found a set of keys, right where the mission plans said they would be. Smoltz unlocked the trunk, where the spies found two Thompson submachine guns, two Colt .45's and about fifty pounds of explosives. There were also several changes of clothes for each of them. The men hurriedly loaded their equipment, got into the car and drove off. As Smoltz approached the exit, they observed a parked vehicle off to the side. Inside the car were a man and a woman. As he approached the vehicle, its headlights came on briefly and went back off. Smoltz turned off the headlights of the Ford, then turned the lights back on. When Smoltz's headlights washed over the other car, the man in the car was holding up the SP arm band from the second sailor who had taken an interest in the parked Ford earlier. His interest had cost him his life as well. Signal completed, Smoltz headed out the exit and made a right turn onto the highway. The two spies were on their way to Detroit.

***

Nick and Debbie Stark, along with their two daughters, were gazing out the living room window in the suburbs of Detroit, watching the first major snowfall of the year. As the big flakes floated and danced their way down, everyone entertained their own thoughts. The children were excited to play in the snow. Slip and slide, make forts, and have snowball fights. Debbie was thrilled that there would be snow for the holidays. Hopefully it would last so they could have a white Christmas.

Nick Stark couldn't help but think that he had to get up early tomorrow. He would have to shovel the snow from the driveway, so he could drive his Chevy to work at the FBI office downtown. He thought to himself, *Damn snow! It always causes extra work.* He had no idea how much extra work was headed his way from New Jersey in an old Ford.

Chapter Two

Hagen and Brown turned off of 8 Mile Road onto Pelkey Street. They pulled into the driveway of 2026 and turned off the engine of their Ford. They had arrived at the safe house the Nazi spy network had set up for them in a quiet residential suburb of Detroit. A heavy blanket of snow covered the ground, the residue of the storm that struck the east coast and cost them an extra day's travel from New Jersey. It was about 6 o'clock Saturday morning, November, 6, 1943. Both men got out of the car, stretched and yawned. They were tired from their straight-through drive; they had taken turns driving while the other slept, stopping only for fuel and food.

Hagen walked to the front door of the house. His steps made a louder-than-normal crunching noise in the fresh snow. The blanket of white seemed to muffle all other noise in the quaint neighborhood. Strangely, when a sound did occur, it was acutely magnified in the otherwise silent dead of winter. Hagen reached into the mailbox mounted on the front of the white clapboard house, where he found the key, again just as the mission plans that he and Brown were so thoroughly briefed on back in Germany said he would.

Hagen unlocked the front door and went inside, Brown a few steps behind him. Once inside, they discovered they were in a two-story, two-bedroom house with an unfinished attic and a basement that had a small workshop. Brown went into the kitchen and was pleasantly surprised that their handlers had stocked some groceries for them. Hagen came into the kitchen.

"Phil, let's go get our gear from the car. Make sure nobody sees those guns."

Brown was drinking from a milk bottle. After two or three gulps, he put it back into the refrigerator. "Okay, let's go."

All the gear was brought inside. Hagen took the bedroom on the left, Brown took the one on the right. Brown unwrapped the guns from a blanket and took Hagen his Thompson and Colt .45.

"Here, Chris, these are yours."

"I'll put mine it the closet for now, but we need to find a good place to hide them."

"Of course. I'll look in the basement later."

"No, do it now. While you're down there, light the furnace. It's cold in here."

Brown went down the stairs to the basement to find a large coal-burning furnace in the middle of the room and a pile of coal in a corner. He put several shovels full of coal into the furnace and lit a fire, just like he had done hundreds of times back home in Germany. Brown stood in front of the open furnace door warming himself for a few minutes. He closed the door and began exploring the rest of the basement. In the workshop, he found that the handlers had left him all the tools he needed to make bombs. In one of the false-bottom drawers was a large supply of detonators. Another contained timer devices for his bombs. The third drawer contained six hand grenades. On a shelf was a large box labeled nails. Inside the box were twenty boxes, one thousand .45 cal. cartridges, for the Thompsons and the Colts. Under the workbench was a large wooden tool box that looked like a good place to hide the guns.

Upstairs, Hagen had gone up into the attic, where there was a lot of old furniture piled up. Hagen was looking for one thing in particular. He found the old steamer trunk he was looking for and dragged it out. Inside, carefully concealed in the false bottom, was a wireless and a code book he was to use to contact their handlers. He put everything back the way he found it and went back downstairs.

Brown was seated in the living room. The house came furnished, but sparsely like one would expect from a bachelor house.

"Chris, let's go up to that diner that was open on 8 Mile Road. I'm starving."

"Yeah, good idea."

***

Hager and Brown walked into the nearly empty diner. It was built to look like a railroad car, but it wasn't. The duo took a seat at the booth in the far corner. Hagen took a newspaper from an abandoned booth and began to thumb through it.

The waitress brought the men coffee and took their breakfast orders. When she was out of earshot, Hagen leaned in and speaking low, said, "Phil, there's an article in the paper about the Coast Guard responding to an explosion off the coast of South Carolina yesterday."

"Does it say anything else?"

"Yeah. They're convinced that a Nazi U-boat exploded underwater. There were no survivors found, but from the debris field they are certain it was the U-42."

"No survivors huh? Good, that means nobody to tell of our mission."

"Where did you put the bomb?"

"Under a couple of torpedoes, like we discussed."

"Excellent. Good work, Phil."

"Thanks. Pass the cream, will you?"

The two men ate their meals without showing a hint of remorse over sending seventy-five of their fellow Germans to the bottom of the sea.

Chapter Three

The two Nazis finished their breakfast and returned to the safe house. "I think we should unpack," Hagen said as he kicked off his shoes. "After that, I'm going upstairs to contact our handlers on the radio. Why don't you go out and shovel the snow off the sidewalk like a good citizen?"

"Oh, hell, yes! It would be my civic duty," Brown replied sarcastically.

"Put your pistol under your coat, just in case the wrong people intercept my broadcast."

"Yes, captain."

The two men unpacked, then Hagen went upstairs and pulled out the steamer trunk. Taking the radio from the false bottom, he set it up. He clipped a wire to the exposed electrical wires to act as an antenna and sat down to compose a message and code it. In the meantime, Brown went down to the basement for a snow shovel. He went outside through the side door to the driveway and started his civic duties.

Upstairs, Hagen was ready to broadcast to their handlers. He turned on the radio and tuned it to the pre-designated frequency. His message was, 'The fleece on the sheep is white. The tail of the dog wags.' Those cryptic sentences meant that they had arrived at the safe house and were awaiting orders. The return message read, "The wallpaper has pink flowers." Hagen wrote the message down and turned off the radio. The longer the radio was on, the greater the chances of discovery. He took the code book and discovered that the return message said, "You will be contacted tomorrow." He burned the message in an ashtray and tore down the radio, returning it to the secret compartment in the steamer trunk. He slid the trunk back and put a couple of old wooden chairs on top of it. Hagen went back downstairs and sat in the living room, in front of the window. He lit a Lucky Strike, sat back and watched Brown shovel the snow.

Outside, Brown paused to wipe his brow. It was hard work, shoveling a foot and a half of wet snow. A car pulled to the curb closest to Brown, facing the wrong direction. The driver cranked the window down and said, "Hey, you the new neighbor?"

"Yeah, I guess. One of them, at least."

The driver extended his hand out the window, saying, "I'm Michael Kushner, I live in that house." He pointed to the house next to the safe house.

Brown walked up and shook the man's hand. "Phil Brown. Nice to meet you."

"You from Detroit, Phil?"

"No, me and my friend are from Pittsburgh."

"What brings you to Detroit?"

"We start work at the Packard plant on Monday."

"Well, that's good. Stop by sometime for a drink. I'll introduce you to the wife and kids."

"That sounds great, Michael."

Michael parked in front of his house and went inside. Brown went back to shoveling snow. He thought to himself, *Shit! A fucking Jew.*

Brown was almost done with shoveling the sidewalk when a pretty girl in her twenties came out of the house on the other side of the safe house. She came up to Brown and said, "Are you the new neighbor?"

"Sure am. My name's Phil. What's yours, gorgeous?"

"I'm Judy, Judy Nowicki," she responded, giggling.

"Nice to meet you, Judy."

"Likewise."

"So, tell me, Judy, do you live there alone?"

"Oh, no, I live with my brother. He's a Detroit cop."

"Well, I feel safer already, knowing that."

"Brrr, it's cold out here. I'm going back inside. It was nice to meet you, Phil."

"Sure thing. See you around, Judy."

Judy ran back to her house and went inside. Hagen, watching through the front window, thought, *Fuck, these Americans are nosey.*

Brown kicked the snow off his boots and went inside the house. He took off his coat, sat on the living room couch and lit a cigarette.

"What did those people want, Phil?" Hagen asked.

"The neighbors. They wanted to introduce themselves."

"What about them?"

Exhaling smoke as he talked. "The people over there are fucking Jews," he said, pointing toward the Kushner house. "The cute little thing on the other side is a Polack, and she lives with her brother, a Detroit cop."

"Shit. We'll have to be careful around them," Hagen replied.

***

Across town, Nick Stark finished shoveling the snow from his driveway. He went inside, cleaned up and put on his suit.

"Have fun at work today, darling," Debbie Stark said as she walked into the bedroom and kissed Nick on the cheek. She moved around in front of him and straightened his tie.

"Babe, it's Saturday. You know all I'm going to do is sit around and hope the phone rings."

"Anybody else going to be there?"

"No, just me. It's my turn in the barrel for Saturday phone detail."

"Well, maybe some spy will call or something."

"You read too much Dick Tracy, honey." Nick kissed Debbie and left for the office. Nick got in his car and headed downtown. He pulled into the parking garage of the Penobscot Building, the tallest building in Detroit. The elevator took him to the 23rd floor. Once inside the FBI office he took off his coat, and made a pot of coffee. When his coffee was done, he sat at his desk and read the newspaper he'd brought from home.

The FBI Field Office in Detroit was rather small, with only eight agents assigned to it. They mostly did background checks for high-security jobs at the factories. All of the car factories in Detroit had been converted to manufacturing items for the war effort. 'The arsenal of democracy,' as President Roosevelt called it.

Agent Stark was starting to get bored when the special phone across the room rang. Startled, he jumped up and ran to answer it. The other end of this phone line was connected to the 42nd floor of the building, which was completely occupied by the U.S. Army Signal Corps. They were there to assist the FBI.

"Special Agent Stark," he said as he picked up the phone.

"Yeah, Nick, this is Kelly on the top floor."

"What gives, Kelly?"

"A few minutes ago we picked up a coded message on one of the lower frequencies coming out of the northeast part of the city."

"Could you pinpoint it?"

"No, they weren't on long enough."

"What was the message?"

"The fleece on the sheep is white. The tail of the dog wags."

"Did they get an answer?"

"Yeah, a return message came from Windsor, Canada, and it said, 'The wallpaper has pink flowers.'"

"That make any sense to you guys, Kelly?"

"No, but I thought I'd pass it along anyway."

"Thanks, Kelly."

Nick logged the conversation into a special log book by the phone. Sitting back, he thought to himself, *Shit, could this be some real espionage? Things might start to heat up around here.*

Chapter Four

Sunday morning, Brown went out to the car to fetch a pack of cigarettes he left there. On his way back he spotted a copy of The Detroit Free Press newspaper, picked it up and went back inside. Hagen was at the kitchen table drinking coffee and smoking a cigarette.

"Hey, Chris. Did the handlers say how they would contact us?"

"No."

"Well, you better look at this." Brown handed Hagen the newspaper he had found on the front porch. Hagen opened it to the front page and discovered that someone had underlined specific letters in the articles. "Interesting. Get me a pencil and some paper, Phil." The two transcribed the letters onto some paper. When they put it together, the message read in German, "*My chicken is red. It lays brown eggs.*"

"What the fuck does that mean?" Brown asked Hagen.

"I don't know. Let's go upstairs and decode it."

In the attic, Hagen sat cross-legged on the floor with his back leaning against the wall. Brown sat across from Hagen, smoking his Pall Mall and waiting for the results of the decoding. When he was done, Hagen dropped his hands into his lap. Leaning his head against the wall, he related, "We are to take the bridge into Windsor and meet our handler at the southwest corner of Memorial Park. He'll be wearing a green hat."

"What time?"

"Noon today."

"We better get going, then."

"Yeah. Leave the guns here. They'd be hard to explain if we get detained."

***

Halfway across the bridge to Windsor, Hagen and Brown were stopped at the checkpoint. Manning the checkpoint were a U.S. Army Military Policeman and two Canadian Solders. When they got to the front of the line, the MP approached the car. Hagen rolled down the window and the MP said, "Identification please, gentlemen." Hagen and Brown handed over their driver's licenses.

"What's taking you out of the country today, fellas?" asked the MP.

"We're going to have some drinks with an old buddy," Hagen quickly answered.

"That sounds good. Have one for me, Mac, it's friggin' cold out here."

Brown leaned toward the driver side window and said, "I'll have one for you too, pal."

"That sounds even better." The MP handed Hagen back the licenses. "Have a good time, boys." He waved to one of the Canadians who lifted the crossing gate. The two Nazis drove across the bridge and into Canada.

***

Hagen pulled the Ford into a parking stall at the west end of Memorial Park. It was ten degrees outside, so the park was practically deserted. There were a few kids playing hockey on the frozen pond. About twenty-five yards in front of the car was a man seated on a bench wearing a black and red checkerboard wool coat and a green stocking cap.

"You stay in the car, Phil. If anyone or anything looks suspicious, honk the horn."

Hagen got out of the car and walked toward the man. The snow on the walkways in the park was already shoveled, so it didn't take long to get to the man.

"Would you prefer a hamburger or a hot dog?" Hagen asked as part of the identification process.

"A hot dog with lots of sauerkraut," the older man replied. Having passed the identification, Hagen sat down on the bench.

"I trust you found your accommodations satisfactory, Mr. Hagen."

"Yes, very. Are you the handler?"

"What do I call you?"

"Handler would be good. That way, if you ever get caught, you can't give them what you don't know."

"Any change in the mission, Mr. Handler?"

"No. Report to Packard tomorrow, ready to go to work. You will do nothing toward the mission for the next few weeks except look for places to set your bombs."

"Why a few weeks?"

"So they get to know your faces and are comfortable with you coming and going around the plant."

"Brown is not going to like the wait. He is an impatient man."

"Do I need to remind you that you are in charge? Keep him in line."

"Yes, sir."

"Don't expect to hear from us until after the Thanksgiving holiday. Then I will expect a full report. Of course, you can contact me on the radio if anything urgent comes up."

The two men shook hands and abruptly parted. On the way back to Detroit, Hagen explained to Brown what had transpired at the meeting.

"Fuck!" Brown exclaimed when he heard the timeline. Pounding his fist on the dash of the Ford, he said, "Weeks living next to Jews and Polacks! I don't like that."

"Those are the orders, Brown. No one cares if you like them."

"Yes, sir."

***

Hagen and Brown pulled off of the highway around 7:30 on Monday morning and drove into the parking lot behind the Packard Motor Car Company. With thousands of employees, it was not surprising that it took them a while to find a parking spot and when they did, it was toward the back of the lot. Now they were faced with a long walk to the entrance gate.

"Damn, this is a big place," commented Brown as they walked.

"Yeah, three and a half million square feet is a big place," Hagen replied.

Figure 1: Packard Automotive Plant

Brown pointed out the large company logo and motto painted on the side of a building.

"Ask the man who owns one," Brown said, reading the motto out loud. "I will if we ever get there. This is a fucking long walk."

They reached the gate and Hagen checked in at the guard shack. He showed the guard their letters of hire and asked where to go. The guard directed him to the second floor of the building directly in front of them. Outside, Brown was making observations. The main gate was about forty feet wide. Two twenty-five foot towers flanked the gate in addition to the ground-level guard shack on the left side of the gate. He observed that the guards in each tower had Thompson submachine guns slung over their shoulders. There were also machine guns protruding from each tower. Looking down the fence line in both directions, there were additional guard towers spaced about every one hundred yards. The fence was chain-link, about twelve feet tall and had several strands of barbed wire on top.

Inside the personnel office, Marilyn Short had the men fill out some additional paperwork. She also took photographs for their ID badges.

"Stop by on your way out today and pick up your permanent badges. In the meantime, put on these temporaries." Looking behind her, she said to the young man seated at a desk, "Gary. Can you escort these men to Building Ten and introduce them to Bill Shore?"

Chapter Five

Over ten years ago, Bill Shore sat on a stool of an outside diner on Woodward Avenue, drinking a cup of coffee. He was looking for a job in the July 12, 1932 newspaper. Times were tough in Detroit because of the Great Depression. Bill was a master machinist who'd lost his job at DeSoto about a year ago, when they laid off almost their entire workforce. Bill was able to pick up temporary jobs here and there at small local shops, but now he was out pounding the streets, looking for work again.

A man dressed in work clothes sat down on the stool to Bill's right. Bill was so engrossed in the Help Wanted section that he didn't notice who it was until the man said, "Hello, Bill." Bill looked to his right and immediately recognized Eddie McKay. Bill had worked with Eddie at DeSoto before the lay-off.

"Eddie, how are you?" Bill exclaimed as he extended his hand for Eddie.

"I'm great, Bill. Finally landed a job. I see you're still looking."

"Congratulations, Eddie. Yeah, I'm still looking. Times are tough."

Eddie leaned in closer to Bill so the other men at the lunch counter couldn't hear him.

"Bill, Packard is hiring men for their motor department. I talked to a guy in personnel named White. He said if I knew any other highly qualified men, to send them to see him. I don't know anybody more qualified than you, Bill."

"Gosh, thanks, Eddie," Bill said, looking at the clock on the wall. "It's only one o'clock. I'm going to see this Mr. White right now." Bill threw a dime on the counter to pay for his coffee. Bill and Eddie shook hands, with Eddie wishing him good luck. Bill got on the first streetcar headed downtown.

On the way home, the streetcar dropped Bill off in front of the corner market. He went inside and spent his last three dollars on a steak dinner with all the trimmings, some beer, and flowers. It had been a long time since he and his wife Florence had a really good meal; much less something to celebrate.

***

Building #10 at the Packard Motor Car Company housed the engine manufacturing department. In the 1930's, Packard manufactured posh luxury cars for the world's wealthy, people who didn't seem to be affected by the Depression.

Figure 2: 1934 Packard V-12

Packard's were held in the same high regard as the Cadillacs and Duisenberg's at the time. The thing that set Packard above the rest was the strength of its engines. The Packard V-12 engine was legendary for its reliability, strength and long life. The reputation of the Packard engines would be the major factor in the awarding of the $130,000,000 contract to produce the Rolls Royce Merlin engine. Production started in 1940, with the first engines sent to England to power a variety of their aircraft. In

1942, production switched to a two-stage supercharged version that was used in the North American P-51 Mustang, and the U.S. Navy PT Boats.

Figure 3: Rolls-Royce Merlin engine.

Figure 4: North American P-51 Mustang

Figure 5: Patrol Torpedo (PT) Boats

***

Bill Shore began his career with Packard on July 13, 1932. He began by machining crankshafts for the legendary V-12 engine. Bill was a perfectionist, and it didn't take long for people to recognize that he produced high-quality machining. In 1936, the United Auto Workers Union came to Packard, and his fellow workers voted Bill in as their first shop steward. Packard management also saw good things in Bill. In 1938, they made him an area supervisor, followed by a promotion to department supervisor in 1939.

***

Bill was leaning over a wooden table talking to another man about a set of blueprints. The man acknowledged what Bill had told him and walked away. Bill then turned to the three men who were behind him.

Gary, the kid from personnel, said, "Mr. Shore, these are the two men that have hired on."

"Thank you, Gary," Bill said, extending his hand to the first man. "I'm Bill Shore, the department supervisor."

"Nice to meet you, boss. I'm Phil Brown."

"Hello, I'm Chris Hagen, sir."

"No need to call me sir, Chris. Around here we're all on a first-name basis. So tell me which one of you is the machinist we so desperately need."

"I'm a machinist, Bill," offered Phil Brown.

"Did you bring your tools with you today, Phil? I really need to get you up and running on the new two-stage superchargers."

"Bill, I'm just a simple machinist. What's a two-stage supercharger?"

"Well, Phil. Think of a supercharger as a big air pump that forces extra air into the engines. That allows us to force more fuel to the cylinders, and that means a lot more power and speed. The second stage kicks in at high altitude, where the air is thin. When these engines go into the P-51 Mustang, it will be the fastest, highest-flying fighter plane in the world. The boys at North American Aviation tell me that when the P-51 is equipped with extra drop tanks, it can escort our bombers all the way to Germany and back. We like to think around here that what we are doing will help kick the Nazis' asses and speed up the end of this damn war."

The two Nazis exchanged a blank look at each other.

"What about those tools, Phil?"

"Oh, yeah. They're in the car, but we're at the very back of the parking lot. I could never carry them that far."

"Not a problem," Bill said as he turned to write a note on a pad on the wooden table. "Give this note to the guard at the front gate. You'll be able to drive right up to that big rolling door over there and unload your stuff. I'll meet you over there and introduce you to your area supervisor, Eddie McKay."

"Great," said Brown. As he walked by Hagen, Hagen handed him the keys to the Ford.

"Chris, you're the engineer, right? Take a look at this blueprint with me. We need some help redesigning one of the engine cowlings."

***

Phil Brown walked out to the main gate and gave the guard his note.

"Where're you parked at, Mac?" asked the guard.

"All the way at the ass end of the lot."

"Jump in my Jeep. I'll give you a lift."

Rather than move the car, the guard helped Brown load two heavy tool chests into the back of the Jeep. They drove back to the factory, in the yard, and up to the large rolling door in Building #10. The guard honked his horn and the door opened. They drove inside and the door closed behind them. The guard helped Brown unload the tool chests, saying, "Okay, Mac, you want to unlock these things for me?"

"Why?"

"There's a war on, Pal. I need to make sure you're not bringing in a Tommy gun, a bomb, or some other unwelcome shit."

"I guess driving my Panzer tank to work tomorrow is out of the question, huh?"

"Real cute, pal. Real cute."

Chapter Six

A loud whistle blew at the Packard factory at noon, telling the workforce that it was lunchtime. Eddie McKay came up to Brown and said, "Come on, Phil, I'll show you where the cafeteria is. Did you bring a lunch?"

"No, not today."

"That's okay, they sell hot lunches. The meals are hot, but they ain't that good. You be the judge. My money says you'll be bringing a lunch pail tomorrow."

"That bad, huh?"

"Like I said, you be the judge."

Eddie McKay led Brown out of Building #10, across an open area and into the building that housed the cafeteria. Inside, Brown was surprised to see that there were tables and benches that could seat about five hundred people.

"I'll be at that table there, with some of the boys from our department. I'll save you a seat and introduce you around. You get the hot meals in that line over there."

"That's not a very long line, Eddie," Brown observed.

"Like I said, you be the judge."

***

Five minutes later, Brown sat down next to Eddie. On his tray was some meatloaf with mashed potatoes and gravy along with some corn, a slice of cake and a cup of coffee. Eddie introduced him to the guys. He shook hands with the men he could reach and waved to the rest. Bob Rice sat directly across from Brown and inquired, "What do they charge for a plate of that stuff now, Phil?"

"I paid fifteen cents."

When Bob Rice popped off with, "Enjoy," there was a slight giggle from the other men at the table. Everyone watched as Brown put salt and pepper on his meatloaf.

With much anticipation from everyone at the table, he took his first bite. After wrinkling up his face and gagging the whole mouthful down in one big gulp, he gasped, "My God, what is that?"

Through the laughter at the table, Bob Rice volunteered, "We don't know for sure. But we think it's dog food that wasn't good enough for the Army to buy." Another round of laughter ensued, and Brown joined in laughing too. Soon Brown got up, went to a garbage can and scraped the meat loaf into it. He returned to the table and said, "Man. I can't eat that shit." He finished the powdered mashed potatoes, corn, cake and coffee. While eating, he carefully listened in to the small talk among the men, hoping to pick up bits of information that might be useful to his mission.

"How was the rest of your meal?" asked Eddie.

"Well, the potatoes need help, the corn was okay, the cake was pretty good, and this is a damn good cup of coffee."

"Yeah. They do make a pretty good cup of coffee. They leave it on all day. You can bring a thermos over and refill it anytime you want." Eddie informed him.

"Now that's really good to know," Brown offered, thinking that knowledge just might be useful for his mission.

"Hey, Eddie, who's that guy in the suit sitting at the front table with Bill Shore?"

"Oh. That's Mister Reed, the plant manager. If he ever talks to you, address him as Mister Reed. He isn't on a first-name basis with us working stiffs."

"Okay. Got it."

The whistle blew again at 12:45. The room emptied as the people made their way back to their work stations.

Brown was setting up his machine to run another part. At one o'clock the whistle blew again. Eddie was standing close by so he asked him,

"Hey, Eddie, do I have to eat another one of those lunches?"

Eddie laughed and said, "No, that's the whistle for the second lunch. We can't fit everybody at one lunch period. Oh, I forgot to tell you. There are four cafeteria buildings on the property. You can eat at any of them. You know, in case you meet a Rosie the Riveter. You can sit with her instead of us stinky bastards."

"That's also good to know, Eddie."

***

At five o'clock, the factory whistle blew twice, signifying the end of the work day. Hagen and Brown began their hike back out to the Ford. The trip was a little harder due to the six inches of snow that had fallen throughout the day. When they got to the Ford, it took them a few minutes to scrape the snow and ice off of the windows. They sat in the Ford and waited for the traffic to clear, and the car to heat up.

"Did you learn anything today that might help our mission, Phil?"

"Yeah, Chris. We need to stop and buy lunch pails. If I have to eat that cafeteria food, I'll starve before we can do anything."

Hagen laughed and agreed, "Yeah, I know. Wasn't that shit horrible?"

"Aside from that, I noticed this morning that the guards don't search anybody or their lunch pails going into the plant. But when the guard went through my tool chests, he was very thorough. He even checked for false bottoms."

"Interesting," Hagen said. "Sounds like the way to get our explosives in is lunch pails or on our persons."

"I think. It'll take some time to bring in enough to do any good, but didn't Mr. Handler say we weren't going to make a move until after Thanksgiving?"

"Yes, he did. Good observation. Anything else?"

"Yeah, there are four cafeteria buildings at the plant. I can eat at any one of them, and I can also refill my thermos with coffee during the day at any of them. That'll give me a chance to wander around and check things out."

"Excellent," Hagen proclaimed. "I've got some information, too. At the front of Building #10, by Shore's office, there are five completed engines crated up and waiting for shipment. They wait until there are twenty engines ready to go out. Then they bring in a railroad car, load them up and send the whole batch to Texas, where they make the P-51's."

"I don't get your point, Chris."

"Well, I think if there was a way you could put some presents from Hitler in those crates, they'd blow in the rail yard and not the factory."

"And they wouldn't suspect us. Good thinking, Captain," Brown interjected.

"Yeah, I thought so. Come on. Let's get a couple of lunch pails."

***

Around 6:30 that evening, Hagen was in the living room listening to the news on the radio. Brown was in the kitchen, preparing dinner. Suddenly, the front doorbell rang. Hagen and Brown looked at each other in complete surprise.

"Who the hell's that?" Brown questioned.

"You get the door. I'll get my pistol," ordered Hagen.

Brown opened the door. Standing there, holding a chocolate cake in both hands, was Judy Nowicki, the girl from next door.

"Hi, Phil. I made you guys a housewarming gift."

"Judy! Come in, please."

Hagen stashed his pistol in a dresser drawer and walked into the living room as Brown was helping Judy off with her coat.

"Chris, meet Judy. Judy's our neighbor, and she's baked us a cake as a housewarming gift."

"How sweet of you, Judy. Phil, you're right. She's every bit as pretty as you said she was." Judy blushed a little, but soon her attention was attracted to the smell of dinner in the air.

"My gosh, is that Polish sausage and sauerkraut I smell cooking? That smell reminds me of my grandmother's house."

"Well, you must join us then. We insist, don't we, Chris?"

"Come on, Judy have a seat at the dining room table."

"You sure you have enough?" Judy asked as she was sitting down.

"More than enough. You two get acquainted while I finish up."

"So tell me, Judy, are you Polish?" The Nazi SS captain wanted to know.

"Polish descent, but my family's been here for generations. What about you, Chris? Isn't Hagen German?"

"German descent, but like you, we've been here a long time. All American, through and through."

"Here it is," Brown said as he brought in serving plates.

"Wow. This really smells good." Judy remarked. When she finished her first bite, she said, "Phil, this is so authentic, it tastes just like what my grandmother used to make. Have you ever been to Poland?"

"Oh, gosh, no. Born and raised in Pittsburgh. I got the recipe from a lady in my old neighborhood." That was nothing but a lie.

"That was absolutely delicious, Phil. You must give me the recipe."

"I will, but first we must have some of your cake. I'll get us some plates and some coffee." Brown cleared the dinner plates into the kitchen. He returned with the coffee pot, three cups, and three dessert plates. Handing Judy a knife, he said, "Here, Judy, you do the honors while I pour the coffee."

Judy cut two large slices for the men and a smaller one for herself. Brown took a bite, making a conscious effort to hold the fork in his right hand. "Judy, I'm only going to give you my recipe if you give me the recipe for this wonderful cake."

"I agree, this is delicious," added Hagen, talking around a mouthful of cake.

"Thank you, fellas."

The night ended after Judy helped Brown with the dishes. As Brown was helping her on with her coat at the front door, he said, "Say, Judy. Maybe we could see a movie or something sometime?"

"I'd like that, Phil. You know where to find me. Right next door." The two bid each other good night. Brown closed the door and sat on the living room couch.

"Looking to get some Polish pussy there, Phil?" Hagen crudely asked.

"Well, the thought had crossed my mind. I'm also looking to get some information on her brother, the cop."

"Phil Brown. It is truly a pleasure to know a man who can think with both heads at the same time."

Chapter Seven

Hagen and Brown each grabbed a beer and went down into the basement. While Brown retrieved his explosives from their hiding spots, Hagen stoked the furnace with several shovelfuls of coal. Snow was falling again, and it was destined to be another cold night in Detroit. Brown took out the large box of explosives they had found in the back of the Ford the night they landed. Taking the switchblade he always carried, he cut open the box. With a mighty overhand blow, he thrust his knife into the large block of explosives. Hagen jumped back a couple of steps and shouted, "JESUS CHRIST! Are you fucking crazy?"

"Relax, Chris. This stuff will only go off if you set it off with a detonator."

"What is that stuff?"

"It's called plastique. Look, see how I can cut it into small blocks? That's the beauty of this stuff."

"You scared the shit out of me. I thought we were dead for sure." Visibly shocked, Hagen took a long drink of his beer. "Beauty must be in the eye of the beholder."

"Here, this is about a pound, take it," Brown coaxed.

"It feels like child's clay," Hagen observed.

"Exactly. At Youth Camp, they showed us how to mold it to cut metal beams, fell trees, or just plain blow the shit out of something."

"How much of this stuff do you need to blow up a railroad car with twenty Merlin engines on it?"

"I think fifteen or twenty pounds would do the trick."

"Would you set it off with a timer?"

"Yes. Here they are." Brown took out a timer and showed it to Hagen. "There's only one problem with these."

"What's that?"

"I can't set it for longer than twelve hours with these. When I set it, we need to be absolutely sure that the engines will be out of the plant and on a railroad car within twelve hours. Otherwise it'll go boom inside the plant, and that'll bring around a lot of people asking a lot of questions."

"So we need a shipping schedule. I'll snoop around Shore's office and see what I can find. Do you have any ideas on how you're going to get the bomb inside the crates, Phil?"

"No, not yet. I have some snooping around to do too. Have you told Handler about our plan?"

No. I'll go up and radio him for another meeting."

***

Hagen went up to the attic. He set up the radio and transmitted, *"The chicken is in the basket. The baskets are on the table.* That meant he wanted to have a meeting with Mr. Handler for mission changes. A minute or so later Hagen received a message that read, *"More wallpaper with pink flowers is on order."* Checking the code book, Hagen discovered that the message meant, "You will be contacted in the morning."

***

The following morning Phil Brown was up early and went outside to clear the snow from the driveway and again found the Detroit Free Press on the front porch. He opened the paper to the front page and noticed that specific letters of articles were underlined in pencil again. As he was standing there, a rumbling noise coming up the street broke the otherwise white-blanketed silence. Curious to know what was making the noise, he waited. Down the street came a large dump truck spreading rock salt on the street to melt the snow and ice. *Interesting. In the Fatherland, we would just get a bunch of Jews to shovel the streets,* he thought to himself. He took the newspaper inside and gave it to Hagen.

"Chris, can we leave earlier today? There's a foot of new snow outside, and I'd like to park closer so we don't have that long hike to the gate."

"Good idea. Have you made our lunches yet?"

"Yep. The lunch pails are on the kitchen counter. Please don't eat that nice big slice of plastique in yours," Brown chuckled through his laughter. Brown went back outside to finish shoveling the snow. Hagen went upstairs to decode the newspaper message.

During the drive to the Packard plant, Brown asked Hagen, "What did the newspaper message today say?"

"We have another meeting with Handler this Saturday at noon."

"Same place?"

"Yes."

"While we're in Canada, do you think we could pick up some liquor? It's cheaper there."

"You're starting to think like an American, lieutenant."

***

By Thursday, each of them has been sneaking one-pound blocks of explosives into the Packard plant for the past three days. Brown had the explosives wrapped up in an old sweater in the bottom of his locker. Other than that, they'd spent the last few days just trying to blend in at the plant. They both kept their eyes and ears open for any information that might help them in their mission.

The day before, Brown had watched out of the corner of his eye as a boxcar backed into the large door in Building #10. Two Military Policemen got out of the boxcar and headed toward the cafeteria building next to Building #10. Meanwhile, a forklift loaded twenty crated V-1650 engines into the boxcar. In a few minutes, the MP's came back, coffee cups in hand. One of them put a padlock on the boxcar door and a wire seal on the lock. The boxcar was pulled out of Building #10 and disconnected from the railroad engine. The engine drove off, leaving the boxcar parked, locked and sealed on the rail track outside of Building #10. When Hagen and Brown went to work Thursday morning, the boxcar was gone.

***

That evening. Hagen and Brown pulled into their driveway on Pelkey Street. Hagen went directly into the house, and Brown was getting groceries out of the trunk when Judy walked up. "Hi, Phil, got a minute?"

"Sure, what's up?"

"A bunch of my friends are going to Belle Isle on Saturday to ice skate. I was wondering if you'd like to go with me?"

"I'd love to, Judy, but I'm supposed to go somewhere with Chris. Come inside for a couple of minutes and I'll talk to Chris. I'd much rather spend my time with you than him." The two shared a laugh and went inside the house.

"Hey, Chris!" Brown yelled out. "Can you come here, please."

Hagen came into the living room and said hello to Judy.

"Chris, that booze run to Canada we were going to do on Saturday, do you think you could handle it by yourself? Judy just invited me to go ice skating with her."

"Of course. You kids go and have a good time. I'll need to take the car Saturday, though."

"That's not a problem." Judy related, "We can hitch a ride with my friend Grace and her boyfriend. Is that okay with you, Phil?"

"That would be great. I can't wait."

From where they were standing in the living room they could see a police car pull into the Nowicki driveway and turn off its lights.

"That's my brother coming home for dinner. He can't wait, either, so I'm going to run. Come over to my house at ten Saturday morning, okay, Phil?"

"I'll be there with bells on, Judy,"

***

Judy left, and Brown served their dinner at the kitchen table. "Chris, can I use the car tonight?"

"Sure. Why?"

"I'm going to that Montgomery Ward's at Seven Mile Road and Gratiot to buy some ice skates."

***

"Can I help you, sir?" inquired the pretty teenage sales girl at Wards.

"I'm looking for ice skates."

"Right this way," the clerk announced as she led Brown to the aisle where the skates were. "What size?"

"Oh, ah, size forty-six."

"What!" The sales clerk remarked, having never heard of a shoe that big.

Realizing he just screwed up, he quickly said, "Oh, silly me. That would be a European size. The last time I bought skates was in Switzerland before the war. I need a size twelve."

"Here you are, sir. Will there be anything else?"

"Yes, ski pants."

"Right this way."

On the drive home, he couldn't help thinking how much he was looking forward to spending Saturday with Judy.

Chapter Eight

Friday morning in the Motor City, Special Agent Nick Stark checked into work at the FBI office downtown. Michael and George, also Special Agents in the Detroit office, were working the graveyard shift and looked exhausted when Nick said good morning to them.

"Say, Nick," Michael said. "The boys upstairs picked up another coded message coming out of my end of town. There was a return message that came from across the river in Canada. It's all in the log book. Could you call the code-breaking section in Washington and pass it along to them? I'd do it myself, but I'm just too beat. I need to go home and get some sleep."

"Of course, Michael. Go home and get some rest. I'll take care of it." First things first, though; Nick put on a pot of coffee. While the coffee was perking, Nick called Washington to report the coded messages.

"God damn, that coffee smells good," said Steve Johnson, Nick's partner, as he walked into the office. "What's new, buddy boy?"

Nick handed Steve the log book on his way to pour himself a cup of coffee. Nick returned to his desk and silently hoped there would be something to do today other than pushing a bunch of paper around.

***

Hagen and Brown reported for work at the Packard plant. Each had a one-pound piece of plastique in his lunch box. Brown wrapped the two new pounds up with the rest in the old sweater and put it in the bottom of his locker. He made a mental note that there were now eight pounds of plastique in the locker. He figured it would take twenty pounds of the stuff to do an effective job on a boxcar full of heavy engines.

***

Just after ten o'clock, Hagen went into Bill Shore's office carrying his completed blueprints and notes for the engine shroud he'd been asked to design. The plans called for the part to be stamped out of sheet metal. The 100-ton vertical press at the far end of Building #10 would be used for the job.

Bill Shore had a habit of keeping track of daily events on his desk calendar. A quick glance told the Nazi saboteur everything he needed to know about the next engine shipment. The engine assembly crew would be working on Saturday, and a boxcar was set to arrive at 2:00 pm on Monday. The railroad would take the loaded boxcar from the plant property at 7:00 pm. Hagen thought to himself, *Thank you, Mr. Shore. You're making this easy.*

The factory whistle blew when it was time to go home. Hagen made it a point to go by Shore's office on his way out of the building and saw twelve V-1650 engines crated up. Brown and Hagan met at the main gate and walked out to the parking lot. No snowfall today, so it was an easy walk. During the drive home, Hagen shared with Brown what he'd discovered in Shore's office.

"Do you think we can be ready for Monday, Phil?"

"I think so. I have a couple of ideas. You want to hear me out and tell me what you think?"

"Sure, Phil, go ahead."

"The way I see it, I need to get another twelve pounds of plastique into the plant on Monday. Then I need a way to put all twenty pounds of plastique and a timer under that boxcar when it's sitting on the rail spur next to the building."

"Okay, what have you come up with?"

"I need to get some fabric and make a belt with big pockets in it. I can wear it under my coat and then use it to hide the plastique in the undercarriage of the boxcar."

"So you're talking something like an ammo belt or bandolier?"

"Exactly, Chris, that's exactly what I'm talking about."

"Let's stop and get you some fabric."

"Can you sew?"

"I'm pretty good. Stop at Montgomery-Wards, I saw some fabric there the other night."

***

"What can I help you with, gentlemen?" the elderly sales lady asked when Hagen and Brown walked up to the fabric counter.

"I need some canvas," Brown replied.

"Oh, son, there's a war on. We haven't had any canvas in a long time."

"It doesn't look like you have much of anything."

"Well, we have some nice lace." Hagen and Brown looked at each other and shared a chuckle.

"No, I'm afraid that won't do, ma'am. Do you have anything else?"

"I have some pretty heavy tablecloth material."

"Could we see that, please?" The saleslady bent down and retrieved a large bolt of material from under the counter.

"It's red and white checkerboard pattern. That should be festive." Feeling the weight of the fabric, Brown went on to say, "That's fine. I'll need three yards of that, some needles, thread, and a thimble."

"That will be four dollars, please," the elderly lady stated when she finished ringing up the purchase. Brown handed her a twenty-dollar bill.

"Oh, goodness. I hope I can break that," the saleslady muttered as she checked the bills in the register. "Do you mind a lot of ones?" Brown took sixteen singles and put them in his pocket.

***

Hagen and Brown finished their dinner, after which Hagen took a cup of coffee into the living room. He settled in to read the newspaper and listen to the news on the radio while Brown took a beer and went down to the basement. He threw a few shovels of coal into the furnace, then he took out his recently-purchased material. He cut off twenty one-pound blocks of the plastique. Spreading the material out on a card table, he moved the blocks of explosives and the timer clock around as he designed his deadly new garment in his head. Ten pockets to each hold two pounds of plastique seemed to work out best. With long strips on each end, he could tie it around his waist like a belt and hide it under his coat. Brown wrote down some measurements and started cutting up the material. Taking a long drink of his beer, he began to chuckle at the thought of his red and white explosive carrier.

After some time sewing, Brown's mind started to wander. He thought about how much he was looking forward to spending time the next day with Judy. It had been a long time since he had been in a social setting with a woman. He also started to reminisce about his days in the Hitler Youth. He often thought those had been the best years of his life. The war and all its ugliness had changed him. He had loved the comradeship and the way it made him feel special. After all, the Hitler Youth was the future of the Nazi super race. He really loved it when the youth group was taken to the Austrian Alps in the winter, where the children were taught how to ski and ice skate by the best winter athletes Germany had to offer. The children were also taught winter troop movement, camouflage, marksmanship and explosive techniques. What great times those had been for eager young minds.

***

A few minutes before ten o'clock on Saturday morning, Brown was on Judy's porch, ringing her doorbell. He had with him a couple of blankets and his lunch pail with several sandwiches and a thermos of coffee. His new skates were tied together and draped around his neck. He wore a blue Penn State sweatshirt and a pair of sweatpants over his new ski outfit. He had around his neck a strand of sleigh bells he had bought at Wards. Judy answered the door.

"Hi, Phil. Come in." Once inside she noticed that he had brought some stuff with him. "Put your things down on that chair." Once he put everything down in the chair Brown stood up, spread his arms wide and jumped up and down. The sleigh bells rang and tinkled. Judy broke into hysterical laughter. When she finally caught her breath, she said, still giggling, "You crazy, wonderful man! You did come with bells on!" Feeling a wave of emotion for Brown, she walked over, gave him a kiss on the cheek and backed away, "What's in the lunch pail, Phil?"

"Oh, I took the liberty of bringing some sandwiches and coffee."

"How sweet of you. But come into the kitchen. I've got something to show you."

Judy opened a large picnic basket on the table to reveal fried chicken, potato salad, French bread, assorted cheeses, wine, a thermos of coffee and a thermos of cocoa.

"Wow, Judy. That looks and smells great. I guess it'll be okay to leave my sandwiches here." Their laughter was broken off by the sound of the doorbell.

"It's Grace and Bob!" Judy exclaimed as she ran to the front door and immediately opening it. "Come on in, guys." Judy held the door open while Grace and Bob stomped the snow off their boots before coming inside.

"Hey, you ready to go?" Grace asked Judy while hugging her.

"Yes, but first let me introduce you to my neighbor, Phil. Phil, meet Grace and Bob. Grace is my best friend, and Bob is her boyfriend."

Brown stepped forward and shook both of their hands, "Hi, nice to meet you." Grace and Bob returned the salutation.

"You guys need any help with your stuff?" Bob inquired.

"Oh, no. You guys go on out to the car and we'll meet you there." Judy replied. Then she walked into the kitchen to get the picnic basket. Halfway into the living room, Brown intercepted her and took the basket out of her hands.

"Please, allow me," said Brown as he put one hand at his waist and bowed to Judy.

Judy giggled and ran to get Brown's things off the chair. When she picked up the blankets, the sleigh bells fell to the ground, ringing and jingling.

Judy held her hand in front of her mouth to keep from laughing. "Do you want to leave your bells here, Dancer? Or is it Prancer?"

Brown didn't have the slightest idea of what she meant. He did understand that 'yes' meant the bells stayed here, so he gave a big smile and nodded. Judy pulled the door closed and led the way out to Bob's car. Brown lagged back a little because he was trying to see if he was prancing. He thought to himself, *Am I dancing or am I prancing? What the hell does that mean? Crazy Americans.*

Chapter Nine

Around 11:30 on Saturday morning, Hagen left Detroit and headed toward Canada over the Windsor Bridge. It was a nice sunny day, but the temperature was still in the 20s. When he stopped at the checkpoint, he was a little bit perturbed at having to roll the window down and let out the nice warm air in the car.

An MP approached the car,

"Identification, sir." Hagen thought he recognized the MP's voice from last week. He couldn't be sure, because the soldier had an olive-drab scarf wrapped around his face. When the guard spoke, bellows of puffy white steam flowed out of the scarf.

"Hey, Mac. I remember you from last week. Yeah, you and your friend were going to have drinks with a guy. What takes you to Canada today?"

"I'm going to buy some booze," Hagen offered as he put his license back in his wallet.

"Well now," the MP said, leaning in close so only Hagen could hear him.

"I'm working the inbound side this afternoon. If you think you might have any overweight problems in the alcohol department, see me. We can always work something out."

"That's very good to know. I'll keep that in mind." The MP waved to the Canadians, who raised the crossing gate. Hagen drove into Canada and found a little coffee shop near Memorial Park. He went inside and got himself a large cup of coffee and two donuts to go. Not having eaten yet, he gobbled the donuts down on the rest of the way to the park.

Hagen pulled into a parking space. There was nobody in the park other than Mr. Handler, sitting on the same bench that he had been last Saturday. Reaching into the to-go bag, Hagen took out his cup of coffee. When he took the paper lid off, steam rolled off the top of the cup, even in the warm car. Hagen took a couple sips of coffee, got out of the Ford and walked toward Handler. He hadn't gotten very far when he realized he had forgotten his hat. His ears and face started to sting in the unmerciful cold.

"Hello, Mr. Handler," said Hagen when he got close to the bench.

"Please sit down and tell me why I'm freezing my balls off to have this meeting with you."

Hagen sat down. "Richter and I have a plan and we want your approval."

"Go ahead, explain."

"Every two days or so, there are enough engines assembled to fill a boxcar. They bring a boxcar right into the plant and load twenty engines on it. Then they lock and seal the boxcar and park it on the spur next to the building. A locomotive takes the boxcar away during the night. Richter says he can tie a twenty-pound charge to the undercarriage of the boxcar while it's still on the spur. With a twelve-hour timer, it will blow up somewhere else, and they won't suspect the bomb was planted at the factory."

"How are you getting the explosives into the plant?"

"Richter has made a bandolier of sorts out of tablecloth material."

"What color tablecloth material?"

"Red and white checkerboard."

"That's very funny," Handler said as he slapped his knee. "When are you going to try this?"

"Richter says he will be ready for the next shipment, which should be on Monday."

"Good. You have my approval to try this once, but you need to be working on destroying the factory, not just a few engines at a time."

"Of course. Richter and I have been mapping out places to plant charges. Richter wants to know if you can get some bandoliers that would fit about ten of these? Hagen reached in his coat pocket and pulled out a block of wood.

"Forgive my ignorance, captain, but what the fuck are you going to do with ten blocks of wood?"

"It's not going to be wood. Richter cut this to show you the size of a two-pound block of plastique. Make sure this block of wood will fit into each pocket."

"Oh, I see. I'll see what I can do.

***

Hagen had never been happier than he was to get back into the Ford and crank up the heater. He blew his breath into his hands and cupped them around his ears. They hurt a little at first, but once he'd rubbed his ears a few seconds, the pain went away. He put the old Ford in gear and drove to the nearest liquor store. The little bell above the door went ding-a-ling.

"Can I help you, mate?" the burly Canadian asked from behind the counter. Hagen thought, *English is a strange language. Every country that speaks it does it just a little differently.*

"You sure can, pal. I need a case of Crown Royal, a case of vodka and a case of schnapps."

"I'm afraid I'm going to see some identification, please."

Hagen handed the man his Michigan Drivers License. "What's the problem?"

"Well," the shopkeeper started. "You're an American. They are going to charge you a big levy when you go back. They only allow four bottles duty-free, and I have to fill out a report on who I sold it to." Hagen reached into his pocket and peeled off two twenty-dollar bills and put them on the counter.

"Is that enough for you to not do that report?" The Canadian thought what the hell, he only worked there, and forty bucks was more than he made in two weeks.

"Hell yeah, mate. Let's ring it up and I'll help you to your car with it. I'm going to throw in a couple of cases of Pabst, too. On the house."

The shopkeeper loaded the booze on a two-wheeled cart and pushed it to the back of Hagen's Ford. Hagen opened the trunk, and the two of them loaded up the liquor.

"Thanks a lot, mate." The Canadian shook Hagen's hand and Chris headed back toward the bridge.

***

As Hagen had hoped, the friendly MP was working the line to get back into the U.S. Hagen pulled the Ford to the side and waited for a slow period. Finally, with a break in traffic, the MP came over to the Ford.

"What's up, Mac?"

"Well, soldier, I need you to look in my trunk. I think I'm a little overweight."

Hagen opened the trunk and the MP stuck his head in to access the situation.

"Let's see here. A case of Crown Royal, a case of vodka, two cases of beer and what is this schnapps shit? "You ain't a fucking Kraut, are you?"

"It's for my Austrian grandmother. Do I look like a fucking Kraut?"

"Naw, I guess not. I tell you what, Mac. You look like you are two bottles of Crown Royal and two bottles of vodka overweight."

Hagen reached into the cases and took out the four bottles requested and handed them to the MP.

"Here, soldier. Do you think you could dispose of these for me?"

"Absolutely." the guard affirmed as he put a bottle into each pocket of his trench coat and cuddled the other two under his arm like a football. "See me anytime you have an overweight problem."

***

Grace knelt on the front seat of Bob's car to face backward and talk to Judy and Phil.

"Where do you work, Phil?"

"I'm a machinist at the Packard engine plant."

Bob made eye contact with Phil in the rear view mirror.

"Sweet. You must be working on the Merlin engines," stated the red-haired, freckle-faced Bob.

"Yeah, I'm working on them," was a little sarcasm that nobody understood. "What do you do, Bob?"

"My sweetie is going into the Army on Monday," Grace interjected.

"Oh, yeah. Where do you think they'll send you, Bob?" questioned Brown.

"I'm sure they will send me to fight the Krauts. I speak pretty good German."

Brown turned to Grace and said, "How is it you two know each other?" He was pointing back and forth between Grace and Judy.

"Oh, we both work part-time at the phone company." Grace then put her right thumb to her ear and extended her pinky finger. "Operator, how may I help you?" she quipped as a mockery of her job .

Brown picked up on the joke right away. He put his thumb to his ear, extended his pinky and returned, "Yes, can you tell me about Belle Isle?"

" Judy, he is just so cute! You tell him I'm going to talk to my Bobby." Grace patted Judy on the leg before she turned around and slid close to Bob.

"Okay, then, you tell me, Judy," Brown said.

"All I know is that Belle Isle is an island in the middle of the Detroit River," Judy stated.

"How big is it?" Brown wanted to know.

"My brother said it's about a thousand acres. I guess that's big, isn't it?"

"Yeah, that's pretty good size." Brown offered. "What's on the island?"

"Not much this time of year. Everything is closed except for the ice skating ponds. In the summer time, they open the midway with rides and carnival games. Lots of great food places along the midway. Oh, there's a big Ferris wheel and a roller-coaster. There's also a zoo and a yacht club open in the summer. I like the museum out there, too. It's a pretty place in the warmer weather."

"Do we have to take a submarine out to the island?" Brown joked.

"No, silly! There's a bridge." Judy answered and at the same time gave Brown a little love tap on the shoulder.

The drive took about twenty minutes. Bob found a parking spot close to the large skating rink. They unloaded their stuff and carried it a few feet to an unoccupied picnic table close to the pond. Brown swept his arm across the table and benches like a snow plow to clear the eight inches or so of snow off them. He unfolded a blanket on a bench for Judy and Grace to sit on. The girls sat next to each other facing away from the table. Brown leaned against the table, pulled off his sweat pants and laced up his skates. Judy was bent down, lacing up her skates when Brown came around the table and stood in front of her. Grace gave her a nudge with her elbow. When she straightened up, her face was about six inches from Brown's crotch. The very tight ski pants left very little to Judy's imagination.

"Phil, can you help me lace up my skates, please?"

"Oh, sure," Brown said as he knelt in the snow and started lacing Judy's skates.

Judy looked to her right at Grace, and they both started to giggle. Phil got up when he finished, took both of Judy's hands and helped her to her feet.

"So, Judy, are you any good on ice skates?" Brown enquired.

"Well, no, not really. How about you, Phil?"

"I get by."

Phil put his left arm around Judy's waist and held her right hand cupped to his chest. He helped her walk about ten feet and step onto the frozen pond.

"Hold me up, Phil. I don't want to fall on my rear."

"That would be a shame. You have such a nice rear, at that."

Judy smiled and elbowed Brown in the stomach. "You sly dog. I bet you say that to all the girls."

"No, just the ones with nice rears." Then Brown took three or four gliding skating steps and the two went propelling across the ice rather quickly.

"Oh! This is fun!" Judy shrieked.

"Yeah. I love skating. I love the stinging cold air in my face, and I feel free on the ice." Brown barely finished his sentence when he had to squeeze Judy harder around the waist to keep her from falling.

"Can we go faster, Phil?" Three or four more strides from Brown's powerful legs now sent them across the ice about as fast as a man could run. "Oh, my God. I love this, Phil."

Brown smiled when Judy laid her head on his shoulder.

"I'll have to teach you to skate so you can do this by yourself."

"Why? I like this just fine." Judy cuddled in closer to Brown, and the two circled the large ice pond cuddled together. Every so often Brown would take a couple of strides to keep their speed up. Judy would have fallen a few times, but Brown steadfastly held her up. Judy was beginning to like being in his strong arms.

Several yards before they came to their picnic bench, Brown slowed their speed. Still holding Judy's hands, Brown went out in front of her. Skating backward and with both at arm's length from each other, Brown smiled and warned, "I'm going to let you go now. Just skate toward the table." Brown let go of her hands.

"No!" Judy objected. She managed to stay up for a few feet, but finally gravity took its toll. Judy's feet went out from under she and she crashed, butt first onto the hard ice. Brown was at her side immediately. He helped he up, off the ice, and to the picnic table. He fluffed up both blankets so she would have something soft to sit on. She was starting to like how thoughtful he was.

"Are you hungry, Phil?"

"Well, yes, but I thought we should wait for the others. Where are they? I haven't seen them in a while."

"They're across the pond at that picnic table by those three big trees. Over there." Judy pointed toward them. "With Bob leaving for the Army on Monday, they probably have a lot of stuff to talk about."

"Yeah, I imagine so."

The whole time, Phil had been gazing over the pond at Bob and Grace. When Judy cleared her throat, he looked back at her. She was handing him a plate mounded with food. He took it from her and bit into a fried chicken leg.

"My God, Judy. This is amazing. You're a very good cook."

"Thank you. Do you do all the cooking for you and Chris?"

"Yeah, I have to."

"What do you mean?"

"Well, I really like to cook. And Chris is the world's worst cook, so I do it out of self-preservation." Still chewing, Phil reached into the picnic basket and pulled out a bottle of wine. "A little wine to stem off the cold?"

"What cold? So far, the day seems just perfect to me, Phil."

"It is nice, isn't it?"

Chapter Ten

"Chocolate chip cookies, too! My favorite. A man could get fat eating all your good cooking, Judy."

"I wouldn't want to see that, Phil. Why don't you skate for a while, and I'll watch?"

"Are you sure? I would like to see how much rust I've grown since the last time I skated."

"Please, go ahead. Besides, my fanny still hurts a little. I'll just have another glass of wine and watch."

Brown stepped out onto the ice-covered pond. He slowly skated out about twenty feet and stopped. Suddenly he started to spin around in place. Slowly at first, but with ever-increasing speed. Before long he was nothing but a blur, he was spinning so fast. He squatted down and held out his right leg, continuing to spin like a mad man. Holding his arms out from his side, his speed slowed until he stopped facing Judy.

"Well, I sure didn't see any rust fly off," Judy offered as she took a sip of wine.

"We'll see," answered Brown as he took off skating. He was skating near the edge of the pond, all the time gathering speed. Judy watched thinking he had to be going about as fast as a car. Suddenly, Brown cut through the center of the pond, leapt into the air. He did the splits with his legs and touched his toes with his hands as he flew through the air. He landed as softly as a goose feather floating to the ground. He skated off again to pick up more speed, and this time when he cut through the middle of the pond, he jumped up and spun around rapidly. He landed on his left foot, bent over at the waist, with his right leg extended behind him. As he skated backwards, he jumped into the air, spun around several times and landed on his right leg with his left leg extended. Again, while skating backwards, he jumped up, spun around several times in the opposite direction. He landed and skated back toward Judy. He thought he heard someone yelling but didn't give it a second thought. Judy was sitting on the picnic bench, gleefully clapping, as Brown approached. He leaned to his right and dug the sides of his skate blades into the ice. He stopped quickly but sprayed Judy with ice chips.

"Oh, I'm so sorry," Brown apologized as he started brushing the ice off of Judy. They were both laughing when they heard a gruff voice coming from the pond behind them.

"Hey, asshole! You just skated through my game." Brown turned around and saw a burly man dressed in a Detroit Red-Wings jersey, blue jeans, and holding a hockey stick. About eight or ten feet behind the guy were two similarly dressed men.

The man looked Brown up and down. "Jesus Christ. Look at this guy, fellas, I think I got one of those ice skating queers here. "Say there, Sweet Pants, you think you own this place?"

"No. I'm sorry, mister. It won't happen again."

"Fucking A, John, it won't happen again, you queer."

"Leave us alone. He said he was sorry," Judy stated.

"I wasn't talking to you, bitch. Shut up. I was talking to the queer," the big hockey player jeered.

Brown took off his gloves and responded with, "Can you talk with anything besides that big mouth of yours?"

The hockey player dropped his hockey stick, threw down his gloves, and assumed a boxing position. The hockey player threw a huge left-hand roundhouse punch at Brown, who easily ducked under it. The man followed with a huge right-hand roundhouse punch. Again Brown easily ducked under it, but when he came up, he hit the man with two lightning-fast left jabs to the face and bloodied the man's nose. This made the man angry, who again took a huge left-hand swing at Brown. Ducking under it, Brown sent a crushing right hand into the bully's rib cage. The bully let out a loud moan.

"You're going to pay now, Sweet Pants."

"I'm willing to pay you three."

"Three what?" the bully questioned.

"Three punches." As he jabbed the man in the face, he said, "That's one." Another jab to the forehead caused the bully to raise his head. "That was two." Brown then hit the man with a stiff right uppercut. The bully's skates went out from him, and he crashed to the ice, knocked out.

"That was three!" shouted Judy, as she jumped to her feet and started clapping.

The other two men skated slowly over. "We don't want any trouble, mister. We'll just take our hot-headed friend and get out of here." The two men helped the groggy bully to his feet and half-pulled, half-dragged their friend to the far end of the pond.

"That was awesome, Phil. Where did you learn how to fight like that?

Thinking quickly, Brown came up with, "I spent a lot of time in the Police Athletic League when I was a kid in Pittsburgh. You know, that Golden Gloves stuff."

"Do I ever. My brother, Tommy, did the same thing, only now he coaches. He sure would like to talk to you."

"I'd like that, Judy. Now come on, let's teach you how to skate." Brown held his hand out, beckoning Judy to join him on the ice. For the next hour and a half, he patiently showed Judy how to skate. When she started to fall, Brown was right there to catch her. Eventually she caught on and could skate on her own. Brown would skate around her forwards and backwards, all the time offering her words of encouragement. Finally they skated up to where Grace and Bob were sitting.

"Come on back over, you guys. The food is getting cold," advised Judy.

The four of them skated across the pond, Brown holding Judy tightly against his side. They all sat at the picnic table as Grace took food out of the basket for herself and Bob.

"Aw, the chicken got cold," Grace announced.

"That doesn't bother me any. I love cold fried chicken." Bob replied.

"So do I." Judy and Brown said almost as one voice. Judy got them each a chicken breast out of the basket.

While they were eating, Grace started with, "We have something really important to talk to you guys about. Bob and I have been talking, and we want to get married."

"That's wonderful!" exclaimed Judy as she rose up from her seat to give Grace a hug across the table. "When is the happy day?"

"Today." Grace proclaimed.

"Today?" Judy echoed.

"That's what we wanted to talk to you about. Bob knows of a Justice of the Peace in Lansing who'll marry guys going into the service, any time of the day or night. We were wondering if you guys would come to Lansing and be our witnesses."

"You know Lansing is about a three-hour drive each way, and that's if we don't get hit with any bad weather," Judy observed. "That cold wind coming off of Lake St. Clair and those big ugly clouds sure look like it's going to snow."

"Then we'd better leave soon," Brown said as he reached over and put his hand over Judy's, thoughtfully saving her from asking if he would go with them.

***

It took four hours to get to Lansing in the driving snowstorm. Once there, they were told it would be about an hour wait.

"Walk with me to that little market we passed down the street, Phil."

Leaning into the bitter wind and driving snow, Brown asked, "Why are we going to the market, Judy?"

Ding-a-ling went the bell as a gust of wind almost pushed them into the market's door.

"Well, come in and get warm," The old man behind the counter offered.

"I need some rice and flowers," Judy stated.

"Oh, you two getting hitched at the Justice of the Peace?"

Judy felt her face flush, and Brown looked around like he wasn't paying attention.

"Oh, no. It's for my friends. They're getting hitched."

"Here is a bag for the rice. The barrel is right over there," he said, pointing to a big wooden barrel with 'rice' printed on the side. Judy handed the bag to Brown. He took it and shrugged his shoulders as if to ask how much.

"No more than a pound, Phil." Brown smiled and went about his task.

"Come over to the cooler, little lady. I keep small flower arrangements in there. We seem to get a lot of requests for them on the weekends."

***

"You may now kiss the bride," the Justice of the Peace proclaimed.

Bob kissed Grace, taking his time about it. They finally came up for air when Brown said, "Take us home before you start the honeymoon, would you?" Grace kissed Brown and Judy kissed Bob. Of course, Judy and Grace hugged and kissed as well.

"Come on. I'll buy you your wedding dinner at that little Italian place we passed on the way into town," Brown offered.

"Before you leave, all of you have to sign the marriage license," interjected the Justice of the Peace.

***

The four of them sat at a table in the small Italian restaurant, where the checkerboard table cloth reminded Brown that he still had some sewing to do. Grace laid out the marriage license on the table. Judy picked it up and showed it to Phil. He smiled and thought, *I wonder if it will be a good thing for them to have the signature of an SS officer on that license. I guess we will find out once we win the war.*

***

The drive home took even longer, since the snowstorm had kicked up its fury. Grace sat next to Bob and cuddled against him. In the back seat, Judy was cuddled against Phil with her head on his shoulder and his arm around her shoulders. It didn't take long for her to fall asleep. Brown drank in the smells of her hair and perfume. It had been a long time since he had held a woman this way, and he was beginning to like it.

***

Around eleven o'clock, Bob pulled his car into Judy's driveway. Brown shook Judy a little. "Hey, you're home." She woke, looked up at Brown, and smiled. "Everybody has to come in so we can take some pictures." Judy said.

The four of them went inside to find Judy's brother, Tommy, listening to the radio and fighting to stay awake in a big overstuffed chair.

"Where you been, Sis?" he muttered.

"Bob and Grace got married by a Justice of the Peace in Lansing. Phil and I went along to be witnesses. Oh, I'm sorry. Tommy, this is our new neighbor, Phil Brown."

Tommy got up from his chair, walked over and shook Phil's extended hand.

"Nice to meet you, Phil. I've been hearing things about you."

"Well, if they're good things, it's all true." Phil joked.

"Tommy, could you get the camera and take some pictures of us?" Judy asked.

"Sure, Sis."

The four had taken off their heavy coats and piled them on the couch by the time Tommy returned.

"Okay, let's get a few of the bride and groom," Tommy said. He took several pictures of the two, and said, "Now one of you kissing." Grace and Bob kissed when Grace noticed she still had her flowers in her hand.

"I think it's time to toss the bouqet," stated Grace. She turned around and tossed the flowers over her shoulder, directly at Judy. Judy caught the flowers and put them up to her face. She took a deep breath to savor their smell.

"Okay, now the four of you," Tommy said. They all stood together and Tommy took two more pictures and ran out of flash bulbs.

"Sis, why don't you put on some coffee?"

"Oh, none for us. We have a honeymoon to start," Grace said sheepishly.

Judy leaned in and whispered to Phil, "What did you do with the rice?"

"It's in your coat pocket," Brown whispered back.

Judy and Phil helped the newlyweds on with their coats. Phil shook hands with Bob and wished him good luck as Judy and Grace embraced. When they parted, they both had tears in their eyes.

Grace and Bob stood by his car while Phil and Judy pelted them with rice. Phil and Judy stood holding hands as the watched Grace and Bob drive down the street and out of sight. They went back into the house, still holding hands.

Tommy excused himself to go to bed, leaving Judy and Phil standing in the living room. "I should get going, too. It's late." They walked to the front door, still holding hands. Phil let go of Judy's hand and put his arms around her. Pulling her close, he kissed her very deeply on the lips. Judy put up no resistance and began to moan softly as she rubbed the side of Phil's face with her hand.

Phil pulled away a little. He took Judy's hand in his and kissed her fingers.

"It was just a wonderful day, Judy."

"We could start another wonderful day tomorrow at nine o'clock when you come over for breakfast."

"I'll be here with..." Brown couldn't finish what he was saying because Judy put her finger over his lips.

"Leave the bells here, Phil." The two said good night and Brown crunched the few feet though the snow to his house. Judy closed the door, leaning her back on it. She wondered if Mr. Right now lived next door.

Chapter Eleven

At 8:57 on Sunday morning, the front bell of the Nowicki residence rang. Judy went bounding into the living room to answer the door, calling out on the way, "He's here, Tommy!"

Standing outside in the cold, holding the Nowicki's copy of the *Detroit Free Press* under his arm, was Phil Brown, wearing a freshly-ironed white shirt and a black tie. Fresh Brylcreem in his hair, a clean Barbasol shave on his face, a splash of Old Spice in all the right places and today's shine on his shoes. Judy checked the peephole and unlocked the door knob, then the deadbolt above the knob and finally the deadbolt below the knob. It seemed that brother, Tommy, liked having double locks on everything. Judy opened the front door, then unlocked the storm door. When Phil walked in, she said, "Good morning, Phil." She also gave him a little kiss on the cheek.

"Here's your morning newspaper, Judy."

"Hold on to that and bring it into the kitchen. Tommy's there having coffee."

"Hey, good morning, Phil," Tommy offered as he rose to shake Phil's hand with his right and take the paper with his left. "Thanks. Please, have a seat." Tommy pointed to the spot directly across from him at the small kitchen table. Judy brought Phil a cup of coffee and a small plate with little sausages wrapped in dough with a toothpick through each.

"What are these, Judy?" Phil asked, pointing to the little sausages.

"You've never had pigs in a blanket, Phil?"

"They're very good. I really like them, but with the war on, they're hard to get. When she can get them, Judy puts them aside for special occasions. Today you're the special occasion, Phil," Tommy said.

Brown looked at both of them and responded with, "Thanks, guys. It's special for me, too." His words included both of them, but his attention made it clear he was talking only to Judy. Her cheeks turned up, and she sported big dimples from her wide smile.

"How do you want your eggs, Phil?" Judy inquired as she was getting things out of the refrigerator.

"Would poached be too much trouble?" Brown replied.

"No, not at all."

"I'll have mine poached too, Sis." Tommy volunteered.

"Okay, then, poached all around it is. Coming right up, fellas."

***

"These eggs are perfect, Judy. Thank you," Brown offered.

"Thank you, Phil," Judy replied as her foot gave Tommy a little kick under the table. Tommy wiped his mouth with his napkin, took a sip of coffee and said,

"I hear you had a little run-in on Belle Isle yesterday."

"I guess some little bird must have told you that," Brown said, looking directly at Judy.

Judy felt the pressure of his gaze and muttered, "Tweet, tweet." Tommy and Phil broke into laughter.

"What else did this little bird tell you, Tommy?"

"That you're a pretty damn good boxer. Police Athletic League-trained?"

"Yeah, that's right. Back home in Pittsburgh."

"You fought Golden Gloves, right. Did you win?"

"Well, no. In the semi-finals, some big Negro kid turned my ass into a hat for me."

"Ha, ha, ha, that's funny. I have several asshats around here myself."

"What kind of record did you have, Tommy?" Phil inquired.

"I won my Golden Glove Division. Then I just hung around the gym and picked up a few pro fights for a couple of years."

"Really? That's impressive," Phil said.

"Don't be impressed. I've had my ass beaten into a hat more times that I can count. After the last one, I was finally old enough to follow in our dad's footsteps and joined the police department."

"So is your dad retired now?" Phil asked as he reached for his cigarettes in his shirt pocket.

"No," Judy said sadly. "He was killed on duty about ten years ago."

"Oh, I'm sorry. I didn't know. But I bet he was real proud of you guys." Judy and Tommy both took cigarettes when Phil offered. Phil struck a kitchen match ablaze with his thumbnail and lit Judy's and Tommy's cigarettes. When he went to light his from the same match, Judy blew it out.

"Goofy. Don't you know three on a match is bad luck?"

"Yeah, he was my coach and mentor all the way through Golden Gloves. I still have the satin ring robe he gave me the night before the finals," Tommy said.

"You mean this thing?" No one had noticed Judy slipping out of the room and now she'd returned, holding at arm's length Tommy's royal blue satin boxing robe. On the back, embroidered in white, it read 'Terrible Tommy Nowicki.'

"Yep, that was me. Terrible Tommy. What was your ring name, Phil?"

"Oh, I was Fighting Phil Brown." That was the first thing the Olympic boxer could think of to maintain his cover. He then lit another match for his cigarette.

Tommy raised his coffee cup and offered a toast. "Here's to a couple of old pugs."

All three clanked coffee mugs and drank to the toast.

"Why don't you two take your coffee into the living room. I think that Lions and Redskins game is on the radio," Judy said.

"I need to help with the dishes first," Brown stated.

"No, you don't. I've got the dishes. You and Tommy relax and get acquainted." Judy pushed a little and made shooing motions with her hands.

***

Phil sat on the couch as Tommy stood in front of the radio console that was almost as tall as he was. After some playing with the dial, he was able to get pretty good reception of the game. Tommy then sat in his big, overstuffed chair.

"It probably won't be much of a game today, Phil."

"Why do you say that?"

"With the war on, most of the good players are off fighting it. The NFL has had a hard time putting on games. I heard a couple of weeks ago that Detroit fielded a team with only fifteen players."

"That's terrible."

"Once we kick the Nazis' asses, I hope it doesn't take too long for things to get back to normal."

"Yeah! Kick the Nazis' asses," Brown repeated while pumping his fist in the air. About then Judy came in and sat on the couch next to Phil.

"How's the game going, guys?"

"It's going to be another crappy game," Tommy grumbled.

"Then why don't you turn it off? Besides, you wanted to talk to Phil."

Tommy reached up and clicked the radio off.

"Phil, I know our little bird here already told you that I coach the PAL boxing program in my precinct."

"Yes, she did," Phil responded, looking at Judy with a smile.

"I was wondering if you'd be interested in volunteering some of your time to help me coach. I sure could use a guy with your experience."

"That does sound like a lot of fun. When would you need me?"

"We practice Monday and Wednesday night after work for three or four hours. Then on Saturdays we practice and hold bouts."

"My roommate and I only have the one car, though. That might be a problem."

"Nonsense. Get your roommate to drop you off at our gym on the way home from Packard, and you can ride home with me. We aren't that far from Packard. We're just down the street by the railroad yards."

"And Saturdays we can all ride in together." Judy offered.

"You box, too?" Phil looked at Judy, a little surprised.

"Are you kidding? I've spent most of my life at that gym. When I'm not working out, I make a pretty good cut-man. I wrap hands. I referee, and I even judge some of the bouts."

"Okay then, Nowicki family, count me in."

***

Tommy and Phil talked about boxing for the better part of an hour. After picking up on Judy's glares, Tommy finally said "I'm hogging your guest, sis. Why don't you two kids go see a movie or something?"

"That sounds great, Phil. What do you think?"

"Sounds wonderful."

"Here, sis. Take my car," Tommy said as he reached out and handed her the keys to his Nash.

"Oh, Phil, it's so seldom I get to use the car, would you mind if we stopped on the way home and pick up some groceries?"

"Perfect, Judy. I need to pick up a few things as well."

***

"Two tickets for Casablanca," Brown said as he bent down to talk to the person in the ticket booth in front of the theater. He had his gloves off to get at his money, and he blew his breath into his hands to keep them warm. There was a bitter wind blowing off the river. Phil paid the fifty cents and escorted Judy up to the doorman. The doorman ripped the tickets in half, put one half in a large jar and gave Brown the other half.

"Keep your ticket stubs, Mac. We're having a drawing for a twenty-pound turkey at intermission." The nearly frozen doorman recited the message from memory.

Phil bought Judy some popcorn and candy and the two of them went inside to find seats.

The house lights were still on. They picked seats in the middle, toward the back. There was only a handful of other people in the whole place. They took off their heavy coats, and Phil put them on the chair next to him and sat down.

"Not a lot of people here today. One of us just might win a turkey."

"Wouldn't that be nice?" said Judy. "I'm so glad they are rerunning this picture. It's one of my favorites."

"You seen it before, then?"

"Only twice. Have you seen it?"

"No, I'm more of an Errol Flynn, Robin Hood kind of guy."

The house lights dimmed and the projectionist started the newsreel. Most of it was about the Americans fighting the Japanese in the Pacific. Several people booed when the Japanese were on the screen and cheered at anything pro-American. Toward the end, the images on the screen were of Hitler's build-up of the German coastal defenses in France. The narrator referred to it as *"Hitler's Fortress Europe."*

"Hitler's Fortress Europe. I never heard that. What a forbidding name." Phil said, being very careful not to let his Nazi pride show through.

"You don't get out much, do you?" Judy joked.

"No, but I hope to a lot more." Phil put his hand on Judy's knee and rubbed it softly. Judy put her hand on top of his and leaned her head on his shoulder. Phil reached over, took Judy's chin between his thumb and finger. Guiding her mouth to his, he kissed her softly on the lips.

"Mmmm, I like that salty, buttery taste you have," he whispered to her.

"That's the popcorn, Goofy," Judy offered before she took his chin and kissed him back. The movie started to roll. Phil put his left arm around Judy, and she cuddled up to his side.

Chapter Twelve

Phil had his arm around Judy's shoulders as they walked out of the theater. Judy had her arms outstretched, admiring her gift certificate from Ray's Meat Market for one twenty-pound turkey.

"See, I told you one of us would win," Brown remarked as he gave Judy a little tighter hug. "What are you going to with a turkey that big?"

"Every Thanksgiving I cook a big meal for a bunch of Tommy's single friends and some of the kids from the gym. I was hoping this year you and Chris would join us."

"I'll tell Chris. I know I'll be there. Hell, I'll even help you with the cooking."

"That sounds like a lot of fun, Phil."

They continued walking until they reached the Nash in the parking lot behind the theater. Judy started the engine while Phil brushed off the three inches of snow that had fallen while they were inside. Phil then sat on the passenger side of the Nash, and the two waited for the car to heat up.

"Are you still okay with stopping off at the market, Phil?"

"Yes, please. I need to pick up some things to make lunches during this week."

"You don't eat the cafeteria food at work?"

"Oh, God, no. I wouldn't give that crap to a dog."

"That bad, huh?"

"Almost as bad as Chris's cooking."

The two of them laughed at Phil's joke. Judy put the Nash in gear and started to drive. Ten minutes later she pulled into the parking lot of the A&P. Once inside, their first stop was the meat counter. Judy was planning on getting some hamburger and pork chops with her ration card.

"Look, Phil! They have kielbasa." Judy exclaimed.

"Those are the last four I have, ma'am," the butcher responded from behind the display case.

"I'll take them." Phil firmly stated. The butcher took the kielbasa from the case, weighed them, wrapped them in white paper and handed the package to Phil. Judy was disappointed that Phil took all that was left.

"Don't look so disappointed, hon. I was going to make kielbasa and sauerkraut for you and Tommy one night this week."

"Oh, that would be wonderful, Phil. I know Tommy will like that very much." She took his arm in both hands and kissed him on the shoulder.

"How many cans of sauerkraut are you going to need?"

"I don't use that stuff. I make my sauerkraut."

"Please, you must show me how to do that, Phil."

"Sure. Let's get a cabbage. Do you have a large Mason jar?"

"Yes."

"Do you have a smaller jar or glass that will fit into the Mason jar?"

"Yeah, I'm pretty sure I have that."

"How about some kosher salt?"

"I'll have to pick up some of that."

The two finished their shopping and Judy drove home. In Judy's driveway, Phil said, "Let me put my groceries away and I'll come over in a couple of minutes and show you how to make that sauerkraut."

"Great. I'll see you in a few minutes, then."

***

Tommy was putting on his coat when Phil walked into the Nowicki house.

"Where are you headed, Tommy?" Phil asked.

"I'm going down to the gym. The place is a mess, so I thought I'd do some cleaning."

"Do you want some help?"

"Oh, no. Please stay and teach Sis how to make homemade sauerkraut. I'm looking forward to that as much as she is. I'll be back in a couple of hours."

In the kitchen, Judy had everything Phil said she would need for the sauerkraut set out on the counter. Phil took off his jacket and draped it over the back of a chair. He went to the kitchen sink and washed his hands.

"It's important that your hands are clean," he said as he was washing.

Judy put a white apron like the one she was wearing over Phil's head.

"We need a cutting board, a large sharp knife, and a mixing bowl," he said as he tied the apron strings behind his back. Judy brought out what he needed. Phil washed the cabbage, cut out the core, then cut it in half on the cutting board. Setting aside one half, he put the remaining half flat-side-down on the cutting board. With the skill and speed of a master chef, he cut the cabbage into small strips.

"Wow, that's impressive," Judy remarked. Phil scraped the cut cabbage into the mixing bowl and repeated the process on the other half.

"Okay, now it's your turn. Put a tablespoon and a half of your kosher salt in the bowl." Judy did it as instructed.

"Damn. I forgot to tell you to pick up some caraway seeds."

"No problem. I have some in that cupboard behind you."

Phil retrieved the caraway seeds and told Judy to add a tablespoon of them to the mixing bowl.

"Now do I add vinegar or something for the juice?" Judy wondered aloud.

"No, nothing. This stuff ferments in its own juices."

"How does that happen?"

"Put your hands in the bowl and start squeezing and kneading the cabbage. Kind of like squeezing the juice out of a snowball."

"Like this?"

"Sort of," Phil said as he moved behind Judy and reached around her waist, helping with the process. Phil leaned in and softly kissed Judy's neck below her ear. He could see her close her eyes and sensed that she took a deep breath. Phil took his hands out of the bowl as Judy continued.

"Am I doing this right?" she asked.

"No, more like this," he whispered in her ear. He took both of his hands and began to caress and knead Judy's breasts. Judy began to moan as he kissed her neck again.

"Oh, Phil. That feels so good. But, if you keep that up I'll never finish this."

"It can wait," Phil said as he spun Judy around to face him. He took her in his arms and kissed her hard on the lips. She responded by darting her tongue into his mouth. After a couple of minutes, Phil stepped back untied Judy's apron and pulled it off over her head. He did the same to his. He led Judy to the sink and began washing both of their hands together. He caressed and massaged her hands, and she did the same to his. Phil took a towel off of the counter and dried Judy's hands with the same caressing and massaging motions. The two came together again and kissed passionately.

"I think it's time you showed me your room," Phil said.

Judy reached down and took his hand. Without saying a word, she lead him down the hall and up the attic steps. Phil was surprised to see that the attic had been converted into a very elegant bedroom for Judy. They stood at the foot of the bed kissing passionately and removing articles of each other's clothing. Now wearing just her panties, Judy pulled the covers back, lay down and held her arms out, beckoning Phil to join her. Phil got into bed and straddled Judy on his hands and knees. He kissed her deeply before lowering his head to her breasts. He sucked an erect nipple into his mouth and rolled his tongue over it. Judy moaned and softly held his head in place. Phil then licked and kissed down her stomach until he reached her panties. Rising to his knees, he reached down and slowly pulled her panties off. She arched her back to accommodate him. Throwing her panties on the floor, he took her foot and licked and kissed it. He continued up her leg. When he got to her womanhood and began licking slowly, Judy let out a gasp and gently held his head in place as he continued to pleasure her. After a while, Judy placed both hands on his face and guided him up to her. Judy let out another gasp when he entered her. They made long, slow, passionate love together.

***

Lying in bed naked, Phil and Judy were sharing a cigarette. Nothing was said until the cigarette was gone. Judy was the first to speak.

"I've had my kielbasa. Think we should finish that sauerkraut?"

"Didn't I tell you? We have to do this a couple more times first. It's all part of the process."

Judy giggled and reached down and gently squeezed Phil's manhood. "I'd love to. But, Tommy is going to be home soon. I think we should go back downstairs and finish. We can do more of this later."

"As you wish, my dear."

***

Back in the kitchen Phil watched as Judy continued kneading and squeezing the cabbage into a soggy mush.

"That's great. Now you need to put all of that into the Mason jar and pour the juice in too." Phil directed, and Judy complied.

"Now we need something to weigh down the small jar."

"I have a bag of marbles that I use to decorate my potted plants."

"That would be perfect."

Judy disappeared and came back momentarily with a bag of festively-colored marbles.

"Okay, wash the marbles and fill the small jar with them. Then push the little jar down into the Mason jar."

"What does this do, Phil?"

"As the cabbage begins to ferment and break down, the weight of the small jar squeezes out more of the juice. Now cover the jar with a towel and set it aside for about a week and you'll have homemade sauerkraut."

"That's really neat. Kind of a little chemistry experiment right here in my kitchen. You're a pretty good teacher, Mister Brown." Judy said as she wrapped her arms around his neck and passionately kissed him. "Now, when can we do some more of that other thing?" They embraced and began kissing and fondling each other. They stopped when they heard Tommy's car pull into the driveway.

Chapter Thirteen

It was 7:30 Monday morning as Hagen and Brown were driving into work.

"You got in a little late last night. Did you have time to finish the bomb?" Hagen said.

"Yes, sir. In fact, I'm wearing the bandoleer under my coat right now."

"Excellent! If things go according to plan, you should be able to plant it on the boxcar today."

"Yeah. If I can get five minutes alone with the boxcar, I can get the job done."

"How are you and that cute little neighbor girl getting along," Hagen asked.

"Great! She's the reason I got in so late last night."

"Be careful, my friend. It's never good to get involved when you're on a mission."

"I know, but she sure is terrific. Oh, by the way, she and her brother are coming over one night this week. I'm going to make kielbasa and I have a new batch of sauerkraut ready."

"Uh huh."

"Judy has invited us to their Thanksgiving holiday. I told her I'd ask you."

"Sure, sounds great. Hopefully America won't have too much to be thankful for much longer."

"Yep. Heil Hitler, right?"

***

"All clear, Phil," whispered Hagen from his vantage point at the end of the row of lockers in the men's room of Building #10. Brown took off his coat and pulled the deadly bandolier over his head. Brown covered the bomb with his coat and locked his locker. He and Hagen walked out onto the work floor of the Packard plant. They couldn't help notice that there were around fifty new people milling around on the floor. About half of them were women. As he was walking toward his machine, Brown ran into Eddie McKay.

"Eddie. What's with all the new people?"

"Hey, Phil. We're putting on more assembly people. Once they're up to speed, we should be able to crank out over a hundred Merlins a day."

"Wow, that's a big increase. I guess I should crank out a bunch of crankshafts, huh?" Brown said jokingly.

"Good idea. I'll see you in a little while. Bill Shore wants me to give the new people the Cook's tour on what we do here. He thinks it might help the Rosy the Riveters become productive more quickly if they understood the complete process."

"That's some pretty solid thinking. Oh, don't forget to tell all those new folks to load up on the cafeteria food today."

***

A couple of hours later, Phil was working at his machine. Eddie McKay and about twenty of the new people came to Phil's machine. Eddie gave Phil a hand signal to turn it off. Once it had wound down, Eddie began speaking to the group.

"Ladies and gentlemen, this is Phil Brown. Phil is one of the guys that makes crankshafts for us." He proceeded to tell the group how the crankshaft went around inside the engine. The different lobes on it are what makes the pistons go up and down, and also makes the valves open and close. Eddie tried to make his explanation very brief because there were a lot more stops to make. As Eddie spoke, Phil sized up the group. Of the twenty people with Eddie, fifteen were women. Phil guessed that they were in the age range of about twenty to forty-five years old. Most of the women were wearing brand-new coveralls and had their hair tied up with bandannas.

Eddie finished his explanation, and he and the group moved down the aisle to Bob Rice's machine. Phil decided to pour himself a cup of coffee from his Thermos before starting his machine again. He could hear Eddie telling the group that Bob Rice was a tool and die maker. Bob was making the dies that would stamp out of sheet metal a lot of the parts that the new people would be installing. The parts would be stamped out on the 100-ton hydraulic press in the corner.

"I used to run that machine when it was in Building #5, only in those days, I stamped out car hoods, not parts for fighter plane engines," Eddie offered.

***

Phil needed to use the restroom around eleven o'clock. While standing at the urinal, Chris Hagen came into the room and stood at the urinal two down from Phil.

"I have some interesting information we need to talk about," Phil said. When the two of them finished their business, they walked up and down the rows of lockers to make sure they were alone. Keeping his voice down, Phil whispered, "Eddie told me all these new people are assemblers. Eddie thinks that shortly we will be producing over one hundred engines a day."

"Shit! Hagen responded. "We're going to have to rethink this single-boxcar approach to our mission."

"Should I proceed with the plan today?" Brown questioned the mission commander.

"Yes. You're ready to go. Might as well do it. I'll contact Handler tonight for another meeting and see what he wants us to do."

"Alright. I'll see you at the end of the day."

***

At 1:55 pm, the big door of Building #10 opened. A locomotive pushed a boxcar into position for loading the engines that were in front of Bill Shore's office. Two MPs got out of the boxcar and went to the cafeteria next to Building #5. Brown concluded that they went to the Building #5 cafeteria because there were a lot more female employees who worked in that Building. The women assembled the small sub-assemblies that eventually were brought over to Building #10, where everything came together on the final product. Brown was drinking a cup of coffee. He watched as the MPs returned, padlocked and put an official seal on the door of the boxcar. The locomotive pulled the boxcar out of the building and parked it on the spur next to Building #10. The MPs got on the locomotive and rode off. Brown's target was ready for him.

***

Around four o'clock Brown turned off his machine. He told Eddie McKay that he needed to use the bathroom and would be back in a few minutes. Once in the locker room, he went up and down the rows of lockers. Feeling secure that he was alone, he went to his locker. He put on his coat and hid his deadly red and white package under it, cradling it in his left arm. He relocked his locker and turned to walk to the open end of the row. He was startled to see one of the new guys standing there, watching him.

"Hey, how's it going?" the new man said as Brown walked briskly by him.

"Not much. Got to get back to work," the hurried Brown said as he went headed for a small exit door that lead outside. He leaned against the building by a pile of rusted car engines, rejects from before the war. Brown lit a cigarette and waited to see if he was being followed. He finished his cigarette and stuck the butt into some snow on one of the rejected engines. The hot cigarette butt sizzled in the snow as it went out. Brown took a deep breath and tried not to think of the butterflies flying around in his stomach.

Brown walked slowly toward the boxcar. He looked in every direction until he was sure there was nobody around. He got down on his hands and knees and crawled under the boxcar. He made his way to the forward set of wheels. The large wheels of the boxcar hid him from sight as he tied the twenty pounds of explosives to the undercarriage. Once the red and white package was secure, he set the timer for four o'clock.

Brown started to crawl out from under the boxcar when he heard footsteps crunching through the snow. He immediately ducked back behind the large wheel of the boxcar to hide. Two of the new assemblers were taking a cigarette break about ten feet away from where he was hiding.

"Gosh, Alice, I sure am glad they let us girls work these factory jobs while the guys are off to war," one said.

"Oh, yeah! Me, too. Do you know I'm making three times what I did working for the phone company?" the other responded.

"Yeah, the money's great. I hope they let me stay on after the war. What about you?"

"I don't know yet. When my husband gets back from the Pacific, we'll have to sit down and talk about it."

"We shouldn't be out here too long. We don't want to make a bad impression on the first day of work," the first woman said.

From his hiding place, Brown could only see the women from the knees down. He watched as two cigarette butts hit the ground, then he heard them crunching away as they walked through the snow.

Peeking out from his hiding spot until he was sure nobody else was around, he crawled out, ran back to the stack of old car engines against the building wall. He quickly brushed the snow off of himself, lit a cigarette and leaned against the wall while trying to look as inconspicuous as possible.

***

Phil was back at his machine drinking a cup of coffee, wishing it was Vodka or schnapps. He watched as the new guy from the locker room who saw him with the bomb walked toward his machine.

"Can I talk to you a minute?" The new guy said as he showed his US Army identification card.

"Major Gerald Underwood," Brown read the identification card aloud. "What can I do for you, Major?"

"I'm here from the War Department to monitor production. That large object wrapped in a red and white tablecloth that you took out of your locker looked a little unusual to me. Do you mind explaining it?"

"Not at all," the super-cool Nazi saboteur stated. "I think it would be easier to show you rather than tell you. Follow me." Brown related.

Brown led Major Underwood to the 100-ton hydraulic press at the back of the building.

The lights were not on near the giant press. The only light came from a few of the higher up window panes. Most were painted black for air raid procautions.

The two men stood in front of the press.

"I had some placement pins I made for the dies that are going to be used on this machine wrapped up in an old tablecloth. Look over there, you can see a few." Brown stated confidently. Major Underwood looked at the bed of the press machine.

"I don't see anything," The Major said.

"Look closer. They aren't very big."

The Major put his hands on his knees, leaned forward, and squinted trying to see what Brown was talking about. Brown stepped back two steps and charged Major Underwood. He gave him a mighty shove and pushed him onto the bed of the press. When Brown kicked the foot activator, the mighty press crashed down with a floor-shaking thud.

"HELP!, HELP!" Brown shouted as he ran down the center aisle of Building #10, trying to pass off what just happened as a horrible industrial accident.

***

The phone on the Plant Supervisor's desk, Mr. Reed's desk, rang. He was having a production meeting with Bill Shore. Answering the phone, he listened for a moment, then said, "Yes, Mary. Oh, my God!" Hanging up the phone, he turned to Bill Shore. "Bill, there's been a horrible accident in Building #10. You better get down there right away."

Chapter Fourteen

A security guard met Bill Shore in front of the Administration Building and drove him to Building #10 in a Jeep. They pulled into the big door at the front of the building and made a right turn down the center aisle. Bill couldn't see what was going on yet, but he couldn't help noticing the red lights from an ambulance and a fire truck dancing through the building rafters as the red globes spun around on top of the vehicles.

Eddie McKay walked toward the jeep even before it came to a complete stop.

"I've seen this happen once before, Bill. It's not going to be pretty," Eddie commented.

Eddie lead the way through the group of employees that had gathered around the huge press machine. Bill could see a pair of legs from the knees down extending out from between the massive jaws of the machine.

"Oh, fuck," Bill muttered. After a moment of shock, he regained his composure. "Eddie, have the security guards move these people back, especially the ladies. You're right, this isn't going to be pretty."

A young ambulance attendant came up to Bill.

"Sir, can someone open the machine up? We need to check for vital signs."

Shore looked at the young man and said, "Son, you better get yourselves a couple of mops and buckets if you want to check for anything."

Security had the crowd moved back about one hundred feet.

Bill Shore took a deep breath and said, "Okay, Eddie. Open the jaws." Eddie McKay pushed the release button on the big machine's control panel and the bottom plate remained stationary as the top plate raised up. The two partial legs fell to the floor with a thump. The only recognizable thing was Major Underwood's clothing. Everything was covered with a red, gooey, gelatinous mess. Blood and small pieces of Major Underwood dropped off of the top plate to the bottom plate. The goo ran off the machine and started to puddle on the floor. The young ambulance attendant started to gag at the sight. He ran to a trash can a few feet away and vomited into it.

"Eddie, do we know who this was?" Bill Shore questioned.

"Yeah. It's Gerald Underwood," Eddie answered.

"Son-of-a-bitch!" Bill exclaimed. "Step over here for a minute, Eddie."

The two moved out of earshot of everyone else. Bill whispered to Eddie,

"Gerald Underwood was Major Gerald Underwood from the War Department. Shit! Tell security not to let anyone leave the building. I'll call the cops and the Army. I'm sure there are going to be a lot of questions asked about this."

***

Waiting inside Bill Shore's office were Lt. Col. James Harris from the War Department and Detective Sergeant Ed Parker of the Detroit Police Department. Lt. Col. Harris was the younger of the two, a West Point graduate who had quickly risen through the ranks, mostly due to his ability to cut through the bullshit and make quick, accurate decisions. Detective Parker was a grizzled old cop approaching sixty years old; he'd be retiring soon. In his career, he had seen and done just about everything. Now he was only putting in his time and making plans to move to his fishing cabin in the Upper Peninsula.

Phil Brown was the only witness to the accident and the one the investigators wanted to talk to first. Brown knocked on the door of Bill Shore's office and went inside.

"Sit down, Mr. Brown. I'm Lt. Col. Harris, and this is Detective Parker. We need to ask you some questions."

"Sure. Not a problem," the Nazi replied as he sat down on a wooden chair.

"Why don't you just tell us what happened, son?" Detective Parker asked.

"Well, I'd finished running a part on my machine when that Underwood guy came up and introduced himself. He said that he was going to be installing the stampings that came out of the big press. He asked me if I could show him how the press worked. I thought it was a strange request, but the day was almost over, so I said okay. Anyway, we went back over to where the 100-ton press is. It's pretty dark back there with all the lights off. So, I went looking for the light switch. I couldn't find the light switch and went back to the machine. When I got close, I saw Underwood laying in the open jaws of the machine. I yelled at him to get out of there and ran to help him. When he was crawling out, his foot hit the activation lever and the jaws slammed shut, just as I got there." Brown was now pretending to be visibly shaken and reached for his cigarettes.

"What did you do next, Mr. Brown?" Harris questioned.

"I ran back to the front of the building to get some help for the poor bastard."

"Do you have any idea why Underwood crawled into the machine?" asked Detective Parker.

"I wouldn't have any idea why anybody would crawl into an open press."

"Is that Underwood's blood all over your clothing, Mr. Brown?"

"Yeah. Yeah, it is," Brown sighed.

"You can go clean up, Mr. Brown," Detective Parker said. "The officer outside the door will escort you to the locker room." Brown left Bill Shore's office and went to the locker room to wash and change.

***

The accident investigators talked to about twenty other people, including Eddie McKay.

"Mr. McKay, I know you didn't see the accident, but could you answer some questions about the 100-ton press?" Lt. Col. Harris wanted to know.

"Sure. I stamped out a lot of car hoods and doors on that machine." Eddie boasted.

"I guess the first thing I'd like to know is if the machine wasn't being used yet, why wasn't it unplugged?" Lt. Col. Harris asked.

Eddie giggled a little and responded with, "Sir, it takes 440 volts to run that machine. It's not like a toaster that you just unplug. It's hard-wired into a sub-panel."

"Then, my next question is how do you activate the machine?"

"Once the material is in place, you kick the activation lever to close the press."

***

The last of several interviewees left Bill Shore's office.

"Well, Sergeant, what do you think about all of this?" The Lt. Col. asked.

"We only have one witness, and no reason to doubt him. I don't see how we can say this was anything more than an accident." Sergeant Parker concluded.

"I agree, Sergeant. That's how my report is going to read. A stupid but tragic accident."

"Yep, mine too."

***

It was a little before eight o'clock before Hagen and Brown were allowed to go home. Hagen waited until they were in the car and safely away from the factory before he spoke.

"FUCK! Did you have to kill him?"

"Hey, he saw me take the bomb out of my locker. When he identified himself as from the War Department and wanted to know what was wrapped up in the red and white tablecloth, I didn't think I had a lot of choices. Not unless you want to be shot by a firing squad as a spy."

"I guess you're right. Jesus, Brown. Squishing a man to death in a 100-ton press was a little gruesome, even for you."

"I do what I have to for the Fatherland and the Fuehrer."

***

Around four o'clock the following morning, a light dusting of snow was falling on the still-sleeping city of Detroit. The peace and tranquility of the Currier and Ives Christmas Card setting were abruptly disturbed by a loud KABOOM! That came from the railroad yard area.

Special Agent Nick Stark and his wife Debbie ran to look out of their living room window. They had both been abruptly awakened by the sound of the explosion. Standing there in their pajamas, they were trying to figure out what had just happened when their phone rang.

"Agent Stark," Nick answered. "Yes, sir, right away." Stark hung up the phone and turned to speak to his wife. "The explosion was at the railroad yard. The boss wants me to pick up Steve and find out if what happened is anything the FBI should get involved in."

"Do you have time for me to make you something to eat?" Debbie offered.

"No, no time. But, I'll love you forever if you could make me a cup of coffee while I get dressed."

***

The phone rang in the Nowicki house and Tommy Nowicki stumbled down the hall. He knew from experience that a call at this time of the morning could only be from the Police Department. He picked up the candlestick phone and held both pieces in place. After clearing his throat, he said, "Sergeant Nowicki." He listened to the voice on the other end of the line then said, "Aw, shit! Yeah, I'll be right there."

Judy had come downstairs and was standing in the hallway tying the sash of her robe. "What is it, Tommy?"

"That explosion was at the railroad yards. The Watch Commander wants me down there to supervise the men for search and rescue."

***

It was now Tuesday morning and time to most of Detroit to go to work. Hagen was warming up the Ford in the driveway. Brown opened the passenger side door, saying to Hagen, "Just a minute. I'll be right back." He jogged across the snow-covered lawns to Judy's front porch. Phil knocked on the front door. About a minute later Judy opened the door.

"Phil, what is it?"

"Could I talk to Tommy for a minute?"

"He's not here, Phil. He got called into work early this morning."

"Could you tell him I'm sorry about not meeting him at the gym last night? There was an accident at work, and they kept us very late, asking questions."

"Oh, goodness. What happened?"

"A man fell into a machine and got killed."

Judy covered her mouth with her hand to avoid gasping out loud. "That's horrible!" Pausing for a few seconds, she went on to ask, "Did you hear that big explosion last night?"

"I thought I heard something. Do you know what it was?"

"When the watch commander called Tommy this morning, he said something blew up in the railroad yards. They wanted Tommy down there to supervise."

"I hope it's nothing serious," Phil remarked. Just then Hagen blew the car horn, signaling that he wanted to get going. Phil began walking backward down Judy's walkway.

"Tell Tommy that I'll stop by tonight after work. I have got to get to work, so I'll see you later too, okay?"

"Can I get some more kielbasa? And I'm not talking about the kind that comes on a dinner plate."

"Your wish is my command, Princess. I'll be thinking about that all day. Oh! You and Tommy come over tonight about seven for kielbasa and sauerkraut, okay?"

"That sounds great, Phil."

Phil waved and jogged back to the Ford. Judy went inside and closed the door. Walking back to the kitchen for her cup of coffee, she thought to herself, *I'll be thinking about sausages all day too, Phil.*

***

Tommy Nowicki parked his patrol car in front of the PAL gym, unlocked the front door and went inside the old brick building. Once inside, he was amazed to see that the roof and most of the back of the building had been blown off. *That must have been one HELL of an explosion,* Tommy thought as he plodded through the rubble and out the back of the building. Surveying the railyard damages, he couldn't stop from saying aloud, "Son-of-a-bitch!"

FBI agents Nick Stark and Steve Johnson were standing about forty feet from where Tommy was. Nick Stark had been an FBI agent a little less than five years, while Steve Johnson was a three-year man. Neither one had a great deal of experience with investigations. Since the war started, they had mostly been relegated to doing background checks on new people hired to work for the war effort. Right here in the 'arsenal of democracy,' as the President called it.

"Protocol says we're to seal off the area, try to figure out what caused it, gather evidence and issue a cover story if the government is going to be embarrassed," Agent Stark was telling his partner.

"There's a Detroit policeman over there," Johnson said, pointing to Tommy. Stark had his back to Tommy.

"I think we should go with the washing machine story on this one, Nick."

Chapter Fifteen

"Hello, Sergeant. Can I help you?" Nick Stark said to Tommy as he walked up.

"Could you tell me what happened here? I manage the Police Athletic League Gym behind us. When I got here this morning, half of my gym was gone."

"Yeah, a propane tanker blew up next to a boxcar full of washing machines. Made a hell of a mess, didn't it?"

"Washing machines, huh?" Tommy said as he pulled out a pack of cigarettes from his coat pocket. He lit the cigarette from a book of matches and took a long, deep drag. He slid the pack of cigarettes and matches back into his pocket. "I'm sorry, who did you say you were?"

"I'm Nick Stark, with railroad security."

"Well, Nick Stark from railroad security, when your cleanup crew gets here, tell them one of your washing machine engines is still in the crate next to my boxing ring inside the gym. Oh, and there's also a sixteen cylinder manifold in the street by the front door. My guess is that J. Edgar Hoover is using about 1,500 horsepower washing machines to do his laundry."

"How did you know?" Nick Stark asked sheepishly.

"I know most of the railroad security around here. None of them have ever shined their shoes as nicely as yours, much less owned a black suit with matching hat. You also really should cover up that FBI tie pin before you start blowing smoke up people's asses."

"Sorry, Sergeant. You're right, except for the fact that the engines are 1,650 horsepower. There were twenty of them in that boxcar on their way to Texas," Stark related as he pointed to the nearly-destroyed boxcar.

"The explosion wasn't an accident, was it?" Tommy probed.

"No, it wasn't. That's why the public is going to hear that they were washing machines. We don't want to panic the citizens and tell them that Nazi or Jap spies are blowing things up right here in Middle America."

"No kidding. Don't worry, your secret's safe with me," Tommy said.

"Great. Then let's start over." Stark took the glove off his right hand and extended it for Tommy to shake. "Special Agent Nick Stark, FBI."

"Sergeant Tommy Nowicki, Detroit PD," Tommy answered.

"The guy over there taking the photos of the damaged washing machines is my partner, Steve Johnson. Would you mind if I took a look at the engine that's inside your building?"

"Of course not."

Stark walked over to tell Agent Johnson that he was going to look at one of the engines that had landed inside the PAL gym. He then followed Tommy through the rubble and debris to the engine that was on the floor near ringside.

"Damn. That is the first almost-whole one of these engines I've seen. The thing is huge," remarked Stark as he observed the engine laying on its side. The engine looked fairly intact, but the crate was almost completely shattered.

"I don't know how much this engine weighs, but it sure took a lot of force for that thing to fly here without an airplane," Tommy cracked.

Agent Stark knelt down beside the engine to get a closer look. He saw burn and scorch marks on pieces of the wooden crate as well as a faint green residue on the wood and parts of the engine. He pulled off a remaining section of the crate about one foot long and about four inches wide. He held it up to his nose for a better smell.

"That's funny. This thing smells like almonds," he said as he looked at Tommy.

"Almonds? That's funny. It looks like a plain old pine board to me," Tommy responded.

***

Agent Stark thanked Tommy for his cooperation and apologized for trying to give him the story about the washing machines. He walked back through the rubble and joined up with Agent Johnson in the rail yard.

"What's your take on all of this, Steve?" Stark gestured at the explosion damage.

"Well, look at the damages and the disbursement pattern. It looks to me like a bomb went off under that end of the boxcar." Johnson offered as he pointed to the badly damaged wheel assembly. Pointing to the other end of the boxcar, he added, "Notice how that end is hardly damaged and the wheel assembly is still intact." Johnson walked to the damaged end of the boxcar. "So when things went BOOM!, everything went up and out this way." Johnson tried to accent what he was saying with his arm movements.

"Looks pretty accurate to me, partner. Considering the cargo, I'd say we have a clear case of espionage on our hands. I'm going back and see if that cop's phone is still working. We need to call Washington and get an explosives expert out here."

"Yeah, go ahead."

***

"Hello! Sergeant Nowicki!" Agent Stark yelled as he wondered around the empty building.

"In here!" Tommy yelled back. Stark followed Tommy's voice to a small office. Tommy was standing next to a crushed desk, talking on the phone to his superiors about the damages. When Stark walked in Tommy held up a figure to say he'd be off the phone soon. Stark smiled and waited.

When Tommy hung up the phone, Stark asked, "Think I could use your phone? I need to get some more manpower down here. I'm also going to request Washington to send an explosives expert here to look things over."

"Good idea," Tommy said. "I'll put on some coffee, if I can find the damn coffee pot." The two of them started sorting through the debris for the coffee pot and hot plate.

"You stationed here in Detroit, Stark?" Tommy inquired.

"Yeah, sure am," Stark answered.

"Then you must know my neighbor, Michael Kushner," Tommy asked.

"Sure do. Michael is a good man. Hey! I got the hot plate."

***

Stark went back outside when he'd finishd his phone call and handed Johnson a steaming cup of coffee.

"Thanks, Nick. What did Washington say about the explosives expert?"

"They're putting Miles Alexander on a military transport. We have to pick him up at Willow Run Airport about two o'clock."

"Miles Alexander! He's the best. He taught at the Academy when I went through. They say he's so good that not only can he tell everything about a bomb, he can tell you what color socks the guy had on when he made the bomb."

"Did he teach you that arm gesture and the finger wiggling thing to show the debris falling?"

"Why, yes, he did," Johnson smirked as he took a sip of his coffee.

***

Miles Alexander walked down the steps from the airplane and into the terminal at Willow Run Airport. Alexander was accompanied by the FBI Special Investigations Team, six agents who each had a different area of expertise. Washington wanted this case of espionage solved quickly, so they'd sent the best of the best.

Johnson and Stark were waiting inside the terminal. Johnson recognized Alexander and called him over. Alexander was an average-sized man in his forties. He looked much larger than he really was because of the heavy top-coat he wore over his suit. His wire-framed glasses had fogged over when he entered the warm building. He carried a black bag like a doctor's. He looked every bit the part of a doctor ready to make some house calls. He was a doctor, but not a medical doctor. Miles Alexander had received his Ph.D. in chemistry from Stanford University; he was the head of the chemical analysis division for the FBI in Washington D.C. and the leading explosives expert in the country.

"Hi, Doc!" exclaimed Johnson as the two men embraced. "It's good to see you."

"Hello, Steve. How's my favorite student?" Alexander returned.

"Hello, Agent Stark. Nice to meet you." Alexander stated as they were shaking hands.

"Steve, here, has told me all about you, Doc, so the pleasure's all mine."

"Let's get to work, gentlemen. I hope you brought two cars." Anderson stated.

"We've got two station wagons parked out there. Have your team meet us out those doors after they get their luggage," Johnson replied.

"We don't have any luggage, just what we're carrying."

"Brought all your scientific equipment in one bag?" Johnson probed.

"Yep. A slide rule, a clean shirt, a change of underwear and two peanut butter and jelly sandwiches. I'm ready for anything."

The group had a small laugh at what Alexander had said as they headed for the door. They split up between the two station wagons, putting the hand-held bags in the back of Stark's station wagon to leave more room in Johnson's wagon.

***

At the railyard, the team went right to work. Alexander confirmed Johnson's opinion that the bomb had been set under the wheel assembly at the end of the boxcar. The team broke up. One pair measured the distance of the large debris pieces back to the origin of the explosion. Another group marked and logged the location of the debris. The third group piled up the debris pieces that they could move.

"Agent Stark, do you have trucks coming to pick up all of this?" Alexander inquired.

"Yes, sir. I have four trucks and a forklift on the way. They should be here shortly."

"Excellent. Where are they taking all of this?"

"The Army is going to let us use one of their hangers at Willow Run Airport."

"Good work, Agent," Alexander said just before he crawled under the damaged end of the boxcar. Alexander emerged about five minutes later. He had with him a small piece of wood and some red and white fabric fibers. He sat down on a pile of railroad ties. Looking at the wood sample with a magnifying glass, he took out a notebook and made some notes. He then smelled and tasted the piece of wood. He took out a small manila envelope from his bag, put the red and white fibers into it, wrote on the front of the envelope and put it into his bag along with the piece of wood.

"Come up with anything, Doc?" Johnson asked from a short distance away.

"I need one more piece of the puzzle." He then called out to the group that was measuring the debris fall. "Hey, Bob! Can I see some of these figures?" The other agent showed him the pad he was recording on. Alexander took out his slide rule. It almost looked like he was playing a musical instrument as he worked the slide figuring out some complicated equation. Johnson and Stark looked at each other, a little bewildered.

"Okay, gentlemen. I can't tell you who did this, but I can tell you what they used."

"What do you have, Doc?" Stark questioned.

"The explosive was about twenty pounds of Plastique, wrapped in a red and white checkerboard cloth and set off by a simple clock mechanism."

"I have never heard of Plastique, Doc. What is it?" Stark asked.

"Plastique was invented by The Nobel Company in England before the war. British saboteurs use the stuff to blow things up all the time. It's pretty neat stuff. You can cut it into small pieces, wrap it around stuff like putty, and it'll only blow with the use of a detonator."

"Okay, now I'm wondering how a British explosive winds up blowing up a boxcar full of airplane engines here in Detroit," Stark said.

"I heard that the British left several hundred pounds of the stuff, along with lots of other equipment, behind when they bailed out of France at Dunkirk. Besides, any third-year chemistry student could reproduce the formula for you."

"Can you tell what color socks the bomb maker had on, Doc?" Johnson asked.

"Yes, they were black," Doc Alexander replied.

Agent Stark looked around at all the men. His eyes darted from one face to another. Everyone kept a straight face. Finally Johnson started to giggle, then the whole group began laughing.

"Good one. I almost believed you assholes," Stark remarked as he started walking away.

Chapter Sixteen

Chris Hagen got up from his chair to answer the knock at the front door. When he opened it, he found Judy and Tommy Nowicki standing there. Judy was holding a cake she had made.

"Hey, neighbors, welcome, welcome," he said as he held the door open for them to enter.

"Sure smells good in here," Tommy observed.

"That would be Phil working his magic in the kitchen. Here, let me take your coats." Chris held Judy's cake in one hand and helped her with her coat with the other hand. "This sure looks delicious," he said as he handed it back.

"I'll just put this in the kitchen and see if Phil needs any help," she said.

Phil was washing vegetables in the kitchen sink in preparation for a big salad.

"Here, sweets for the sweet," Judy said as she held up her cake and gave Phil a little kiss on the cheek.

"How nice of you. German chocolate is my favorite," Phil responded while giving Judy a little peck on the lips.

"Let me help you. I'll finish washing, and you do the cutting. I just love watching you cut things up." Phil took out a cutting board and a knife and entertained Judy with his ability to cut and chop with all the skill of a master chef.

In the living room, Chris had turned the radio to some music.

"Tommy, would you like a beer?"

"Yeah, sure that sounds great."

"All I have is Pabst, is that okay?"

"Just happens to be my favorite, thanks."

Chris went into the kitchen and took down two beer mugs from the cabinet.

"Tommy and I are going to have a beer. You kids want one too?"

"Yes, please," Judy replied.

"Sure thing," was Phil's answer.

Chris took down two more beer mugs from the cupboard, then retrieved four bottles of beer from the refrigerator. Searching in a drawer awhile he finally found the bottle opener and popped the caps off of the beer bottles. He put two mugs and two beers on the counter next to Phil and took the other two into the living room.

Phil poured a beer into a mug and handed it to Judy. He poured the second one for himself and held his mug at chest height.

"Toast. Here's to a wonderful night."

Judy gave him a quick kiss on the lips. The two clinked glasses and took a drink of their beers.

***

"Dinner is served!" Phil yelled from the kitchen. Judy and Phil met Tommy and Chris in the dining room. Phil assisted Judy with her chair while the others took their seats.

"Looks great, Phil," Tommy said as he unfolded his napkin.

"You are going to swear that grandma made this, Tommy," Judy said excitedly.

"Then we should offer thanks for it," Tommy said as he crossed his hands and bowed his head. The rest of the table did the same, but nobody said anything.

"Go ahead, Phil," Judy said.

Brown felt a pang of nerves shoot through his body. He had never said Grace, and he was pretty sure Heil Hitler would not be appropriate. In a flash, a funny line popped into his head, so he said,

"Here's the bread, here's the meat, come on, people, let's eat."

"Sounds good to me," Chris said as he picked up a large bowl of potato soup and held it for Judy while she ladled some into her soup bowl.

"This smells so good, Phil. Did you make it yourself?" Judy inquired.

"Of course he did. He's going to make someone a real good wife someday," added Chris.

"I almost forgot," Phil announced as he disappeared into the kitchen. He returned shortly with a loaf of French bread and a loaf of pumpernickel bread. "I didn't have time to make these, so I picked them up at the market on the way home."

"See what I mean?" joked Chris.

"Delicious soup, Phil. Could you pass me the salad?" said Judy.

"You have to try some of my dressing on your salad. I came up with the recipe myself," Phil shared.

"What's in it?" Judy questioned.

"It's a vinaigrette, but I add some blackberry schnapps, a touch of sugar, and some finely chopped walnuts."

"My God, that is delightful," commented Judy after tasting it.

"You should hide that. I'm going to want to drink whatever's left; it's that good," quipped Tommy.

"Then we'll have some blackberry schnapps after dinner," Chris offered.

The main course of kielbasa and sauerkraut was dished up. Tommy took a bite and said, "Mmmm, that is really good, Phil."

"Just like grandma's, huh, Tommy?"

"Phil, if you cook like this every night, I'll marry you," Tommy joked, and the rest of the table laughed.

"Say, Tommy, Judy told me this morning that the Police Athletic gym got blown up in that explosion this morning. What happened?"

"A boxcar full of washing machines blew up right behind the gym. The blast took off the whole back half of the building," Tommy answered.

"Who the hell would blow up a boxcar full of washing machines?" Phil asked.

"I never said somebody did it. A propane car on the next set of tracks over had a leak and exploded." Tommy was a little surprised by Phil's question. Who'd think that the explosion of washing machines would be deliberately set?

"Do you still want me to stop by tomorrow after work, Tommy?"

"No, there's too much damage to the building. I'm going to have to find some temporary quarters for us to work out in. I'll let you know when we start up again. Oh, that reminds me, Sis, I met a couple of guys at the rail yard that work with our neighbor Michael," Tommy remarked, pointing toward the Kushner house.

"They're FBI agents, too?"

"Michael, the neighbor, is an FBI agent?" Hagen asked.

"Yeah. I thought you knew," Tommy responded.

"Phil, we're surrounded by cops. We better behave ourselves," Hagen joked.

"Why was the FBI checking into a boxcar of washing machines that blew up?" Phil asked.

"Well, there's a war on, and those boys get involved any time there is a problem with interstate transportation of goods."

"What did they say?" Chris asked.

"Not much. They had a cup of coffee and nosed around a little. I guess they were satisfied that it was an accident, because they left."

Hagen and Brown knew at this point that Tommy was lying.

Tommy's suspicions of their interest in the explosion was starting to strengthen.

"Who's ready for cake and coffee?" Judy asked.

***

After dinner, the group went into the living room. Chris poured everyone a small glass of blackberry schnapps and left the bottle on the coffee table. Tommy drank his right down and poured himself another glass.

"This is like the best soda pop I have ever had," Tommy exclaimed.

"Careful, Tommy. That stuff can sneak up on you in a big hurry. Hey, does anybody mind if I put the Abbott and Costello Show on the radio?" Hagen asked.

"That would be great, Chris. Tommy and I listen to them all the time," said Judy.

Abbott and Costello did their famous "Who's on first" baseball routine. Judy and Tommy laughed loud and freely at the routine. Tommy poured himself another blackberry schnapps. Resting back in his chair, Tommy couldn't help but notice that Phil and Chris weren't laughing much. Tommy wondered how could that be. It was a very funny routine, unless you didn't understand baseball. Tommy stopped wondering about anything after another five or six glasses of schnapps. He just quietly passed out in his chair.

***

"Tommy! Tommy! Time to go home," Judy said as she shook Tommy to wake him. Tommy opened his eyes, moaned, shifted himself in the chair and went back to sleep.

"Sorry, you guys. He's had a long day, and it looks like that schnapps has kicked his ass."

"Don't worry, Judy. I'll help you get him home." With that, Phil helped Tommy to his feet. Judy draped his coat over his shoulders, and Phil put Tommy's arm behind his head and his arm around Tommy's waist. Judy thanked Chris for a delightful evening. Tommy, Phil, and Judy stumbled through the snow to the Nowicki house. Inside, they steered Tommy to his bed. After laying him down, Judy took off Tommy's shoes and covered him with blankets. They turned out the light and closed Tommy's door.

In the living room, Phil turned to give Judy a goodnight kiss. Judy pushed him backward, and he wound up sitting on the couch. She knelt down in front of him and began stroking his crotch. When she undid his pants and began licking and sucking him, Phil realized that he wouldn't be going home any time soon.

Chapter Seventeen

The first light of day peeked into the Nowicki living room window. Phil woke up laying on his back. He was on the couch, and Judy was lying on top of him. They were both naked but covered with a heavy quilt. Phil kissed Judy on the forehead several times, and she began to stir. When her eyes opened, he kissed her on the tip of the nose.

"Good morning," he said.

Judy arched back a little and brought a hand to her face. After rubbing it for a while, she said, "Good morning."

"As much as I like this, I have to go home and get ready for work."

"Are you sure?"

"Yeah. Packard would be lost if I missed a day of work."

"After work tonight, would you like to go bowling with Tommy and me and a couple of his friends from work?"

"I love to ball you anytime I can. But I'm not interested in balling Tommy or any of his friends."

Judy broke into laughter. She playfully bit Phil on the nose and said, "Goofy, I said bowling, not balling."

"That sounds like fun. But right now I have to get going." Judy rolled off of Phil toward the back of the couch. She held out her arm to hold the quilt up as Phil slid out. She wrapped herself up tightly in the quilt and watched Phil get dressed.

"Do you work today?" Phil asked as he pulled his undershirt over his head.

"Yeah, but just a few hours this afternoon. I think I'm going to go back to sleep for a while."

By the time Phil finished dressing, Judy had already fallen back to sleep. He bent down and gave her a kiss on the forehead. He let himself out, went home and got into a hot shower. He was concerned that he was developing very strong feelings for Judy.

***

Chris Hagen backed the Ford out of the driveway and started the drive to work at the Packard Plant.

"After you went next door last night, I radioed Mr. Handler. He wants a meeting with us tonight," Hagen advised Brown.

"When and where?"

"Eight o'clock at a bar in Windsor."

"I'll have to tell Judy that I can't go bowling with her."

"Bowling! What the fuck is bowling? You need to get your head back on our mission and out of that girl's skirt!' Hagen barked.

"Yes, you're right," Brown returned. "The problem is I think I'm falling in love with her."

***

Downtown at the FBI office, Nick Stark gave the morning briefing. All the field agents assigned to the Detroit office were present.

"Gentlemen, yesterday we had Dr. Miles Alexander and the Special Investigations Team down at the rail yard working on the boxcar bombing. The good doctor says there is no doubt that someone placed a bomb under a boxcar full of Merlin aircraft engines. The cover story is that a boxcar of washing machines got blown up because of a defective propane tanker parked next to it. The bomb was made of plastique and wrapped in a red and white material. The blast was detonated by a simple clock-type device. For those of you like me who are not familiar with plastique, it was invented by the British before the war. It's moldable like kids' clay, has a green tinge to it and smells like almonds."

"How did this stuff wind up here in Detroit blowing up airplane motors?" one of the agents wanted to know.

"I asked the same question, Bob. The doc says the Brits probably left a bunch of the shit behind when they evacuated France at Dunkirk. I contacted the Brits to ask them how much of the stuff they left behind, and I expect to get an answer to that later today."

"Anything to go on with the detonator?" Michael Kushner asked.

"The timer was a common Westclox alarm clock. Made in the U.S.A and for sale by the millions in every drugstore and five-and-dime in the country," Stark replied.

"Anything to go on with the red and white fabric?" an agent in the back wanted to know.

"Doc Alexander said we should have something to go on this afternoon. Hopefully he can narrow them to a specific manufacturer, and we can start beating the bushes and get a make on some buyers," Stark said hopefully. "Anybody got anything they want to add?'

"Yeah, last night I was listening to my radio about 9:15. I picked up so much static; I thought it was coming from next door. It wasn't voiced, more like Morse code, but it wasn't because I know Morse code. I talked to the boys on the top floor and checked the log book. They picked it up, too, coming from my part of town." Michael Kushner shared.

"Too bad it comes so infrequently. We could try setting up a triangulation team and see if we could catch them," Stark offered. "Oh, Michael, I met one of your neighbors yesterday."

"Yeah, who?"

"Tommy Nowicki, a sergeant in the Police Department."

"Tommy is aces, and his sister Judy is a real sweetheart. Good people, those two."

***

At the Packard Plant, Hagen and Brown noticed some changes when they got to work. The loaded Boxcar on the side rail next to Building 10 was no longer left unattended. Stationed at each corner was an Army MP armed with a Thompson submachine gun. Inside the building, another boxcar was being loaded with Merlin engines. That boxcar was also guarded by four heavily-armed Military Policemen.

Bill Shore ordered Eddie McKay and the other area supervisors to assemble all the workers in the middle of Building #10. Once done, Shore climbed and stood on a workbench to address the workers.

"Ladies and gentlemen. You have probably noticed the increased military presence in the shop today. Yesterday, saboteurs blew up a box car at the rail yard that contained some of our engines. The FBI has strong reasons to believe that it was the work of spies." A strong murmur went through the crowd of workers. Shore held up his hands to quiet things down.

"These guards are here for our protection as well as the engines. We don't want any assholes thinking they can come around here and blow stuff up. Leave the guards alone and let them do their job. It's our job to put the engines together; it's their job to see that they arrive in Texas safe and sound. The Army tells me that the more of these engines we can produce, the quicker this damn war will end. So let's get back to work and make that happen."

A round of applause went up, and the workers filed to their workstations and began work.

***

That evening, Phil told Judy that he had to accompany Chris to Canada to see his sick aunt.

"If you have any of that soup from last night, you should take it to her," Judy suggested.

"I'm way ahead of you. I thought a nice slice of that German chocolate cake might help her spirits, too."

"You're a nice man, Phil." Judy and Phil were standing on the Nowicki porch. Judy moved in close to Phil and put her hands into Phil's jacket pockets. She pulled him close and they kissed.

"Will I see you tomorrow, Phil?"

"Of course."

"Good, tomorrow I want to discuss a little ice fishing trip I'm thinking about."

"Ice fishing? I've never done that."

"Then it should be fun."

***

A little before eight o'clock, Hagen parked the Ford in front of the Solo Club in the Waterfront area of Windsor. Hagen and Brown went inside and sat at the bar. The place was rather seedy and rundown. A man and a hooker, the only other patrons, were at a booth in the darkly-lit back of the room. The bartender was a burly man who looked like he was of German descent.

"What'll ya have, gents?" the bartender asked.

"I'll have a boxcar, and my friend will have a Merlin," Hagen replied.

"Through that door," the bartender said as he pointed to a wooden door at the end of the bar. Hagen turned the doorknob, but it was locked. The bartender pressed a button under the bar. An electronic buzz sounded, and the door unlocked. Hagen and Brown descended a dimly-lit flight of stairs to the cellar. It was a small room, with the walls lined with shelves holding beer, bottles of booze, and bar supplies. The only light was a bare bulb hanging from a cord over a small table in the center of the room. Seated at the table were Mr. Handler and an older man. Hagen recognized the older man and snapped to attention, clicking his heels and raised his right arm in a Nazi salute.

"General Arensdorf, a pleasure to see you again." Hagen had worked for the general in the early days of the war on spy missions to England.

"Captain Smoltz, nice to see you again as well. This must be Lieutenant Richter?"

Brown snapped to attention and also gave the general the Nazi salute.

"Pleasure to meet you, General Arensdorf." Brown offered.

"Sit down, gentlemen. We will be very informal at this meeting, and please, let's keep it in English. I wouldn't want to see you get accustomed to speaking German until this mission is over. Now tell me, Mr. Hagen, what kind of progress have you made?"

"Well, General," Hagen began, "We have been successful at becoming trusted Packard employees. The lieutenant was able to smuggle twenty pounds of explosives into the plant and place a bomb under one of the boxcars before it left the Packard yard. The bomb went off as scheduled in the railyard several hours later. We drove past the railyard and discovered that twenty pounds of explosives had only destroyed about half of a boxcar."

"Well then, use more explosives!" The general snapped.

"Sorry, sir. It's not going to be that easy anymore," Brown inserted.

"What do you mean, lieutenant?" the general asked.

"Sir, since the first explosion, the Americans are heavily guarding the loaded boxcars. The plant has also ramped production up to one hundred Merlin engines a day. There is no way I can even get close to the boxcars, much less plant enough explosives to take out five boxcars at a time."

"Do you two have any suggestions?" the general wanted to know.

"We need to destroy the plant and prevent it from making the engines instead of concentrating on the finished engines. We could fill our lockers with several hundred pounds of explosives, but that will take some time." Hagen stated.

"Excuse me, sir. I have given this some thought. Detonating several hundred pounds of explosives in our lockers is not our answer," Brown said.

"What do you mean, lieutenant?" Hagen asked.

"Sir, an explosion like that would certainly make a big mess, but it wouldn't solve our problem. All we would do is blow up the locker room, the bathroom, and some offices. We wouldn't do any damage to the production capacity of the plant."

"You are the expert, lieutenant. Can you come up with a way to destroy the manufacturing capacity of the plant?" General Arensdorf asked.

"I will try, General."

"Don't *try*, lieutenant. *Do* it!" the general commanded. "We will meet back here in one week to discuss your plan. Do either of you have anything else?"

"Yes, sir, I do." Brown began. "What idiot rented us a safe house that has a cop on one side and an FBI agent on the other side?"

"For your information, lieutenant, that idiot was me," The general growled. "That house belongs to someone who is very loyal to the Party. Let me ask you something, lieutenant," the general went on, stressing the word *lieutenant*. "If you were the Americans trying to find us, would you start looking at the broad picture of things, or would you start looking right under your nose?"

"The broad picture, sir."

"Absolutely! And that is exactly why you are where we put you. Your job is to follow orders, lieutenant, not question things! Am I clear on that!"

Yes, sir! Sorry, sir."

"Then we meet back here one week from tonight," the general said as he motioned them away with his hand.

***

Hagen and Brown went back upstairs, left the bar, and drove back to Detroit. During the drive home, Hagen said, "HOLY SHIT, lieutenant. General Arensdorf is the last person in the world you want to piss off. You might as well have just shit in Hitler's hat. General Arensdorf does not take well to criticism. He is also a very vindictive and cruel man."

"He'll forget all about it once our mission is successful," Brown boastfully stated.

"You better damn well hope so."

Chapter Eighteen

Thursday morning around nine o'clock, the telephone rang on Nick Stark's desk. "Hello, Agent Stark."

"Stark, this is Doctor Alexander from Washington."

"Yes, Doctor. Do you have anything more definitive on the color of my bomber's socks?"

Chuckling, Doctor Alexander replied, "No, I can't be of any more help there. But, I do have an analysis on the red and white fabric strips I found at the explosion scene. Based on the fabric and chemical composition of the dyes used, I've narrowed it down to two manufacturers."

"That's great Doc. Go ahead and give me the names."

"The first one is Custom Fabrics, of Cleveland, Ohio. The second is Lansing Linen, and they're in Lansing, Michigan. The material is the kind of stuff you would use to make a tablecloth or napkins out of."

"Or a carrier for a bomb," Stark commented back.

"Yeah, I'm afraid so. Anyway, I'm sending you a teletype in a few minutes with the addresses of these companies and a complete description of my findings. I just called to give you a heads-up."

"Thanks, Doc."

"No problem, keep me posted on what you find out."

"I sure will, Doc."

Nick Stark got up from his desk and walked toward the Special Agent In Charge's office. Steve Johnson came out of the bathroom right in front of Stark, folding a newspaper back to its original shape.

"Come on, partner, if you're done with your business, we got business with the boss."

Stark and Johnson walked into the office of Ron Steele, the Agent In Charge of the Detroit FBI office.

"Ron, I just got off the phone with Doc. Alexander in Washington. He narrowed down the manufacturers of the type of fabric used in the railyard explosion. One's in Lansing, the other's in Cleveland. I should be getting a teletype with all the details in a few minutes."

Ron Steele had been with the FBI since the Prohibition Days. During his rookie year, he had been shot in the throat while part of a bootlegging raid on the infamous Purple Gang. He survived, but he was left with a rough and gravelly voice. As Agent Stark was speaking, Steele bit off the end of a huge cigar and spat it in the trash can. He struck a kitchen match with his thumbnail and lit the cigar. Before he answered Stark, he was engulfed in clouds of gray-white smoke.

"Okay. You two guys split up. One of you go to Lansing, and the other to Cleveland. Find out who they distribute to within, say, a fifty-mile radius of Detroit. Then report back to me."

"Couldn't our Cleveland office check out the company in Cleveland?" Stark asked.

"Of course they could. But this is our case, and I don't want those Cleveland boys to get any credit when we solve it. This is our chance to show Washington that we aren't just a bunch of fucking records clerks here."

"We'll do you proud on this one, boss," Johnson said as he and Stark left Steele's office.

***

Five minutes later, the teletype machine began to clatter. Stark stood in front of the machine, reading the printout as fast as the machine could spit it out. He tore off the printout when the machine stopped. Stark returned to his desk. He took a pair of scissors and cut out the parts of the teletype that had the company names and address information. He walked over to Johnson's desk.

"Okay, partner. Do you want to go to Cleveland or Lansing?" Stark asked.

"Well, hell, if you're giving me a choice, I'll drive to Lansing," Johnson quickly replied.

"Okay, then. You have a ninety-mile drive to Lansing one way, and I have about a one hundred and seventy-mile drive to Cleveland one way. We'd better get started. We'll get together with Steele and exchange our information in the morning," Stark said.

"You should stop by your house and get Debbie to make you a Thermos of coffee and some sandwiches, Nick."

"Good idea."

Stark and Johnson took the elevator down to the ground floor of the Penobscot Building. The outside temperature was about 20° in the parking lot, but it was otherwise a clear day. They said goodbye and left in their cars. Johnson was on his way to Lansing, thinking that he got the better part of the split. Stark was on his way to Willow Run Airport, thinking that he was glad he'd listened to the weather report on the radio that morning.

***

At five o'clock that afternoon, the workday at Packard was over for Hagen and Brown. They were in the Ford driving home.

"Any new ideas on where we could put bombs in the plant?" Hagen asked.

"No, none. I looked real carefully today, too. People are going to notice anything new and large that suddenly appears in their work area. Besides, remember how well that guard went through my tool box when I brought it into the plant? I just can't think of how we get hundreds of pounds of explosives into the plant and hide it until we are ready to set it off."

"The general isn't going to be very happy," Hagen warned.

"Fuck the general! If it can't be done, it can't be done."

"You tell him that, but I'd leave out that 'Fuck the general' part if you want to continue breathing."

"I know. I just don't like it when a stupid man comes up with a stupid plan and expects us to pull it off."

"Yeah, you're right, Phil. Anyway, we're home. Let's have a couple of drinks and relax."

Hagen and Brown got out of their car and walked up the walkway to the front door of their safe house. Taped to the front door was a piece of paper folded in half with "Phil" written on the exposed part in a woman's handwriting. Hagen took the note down and got a whiff of a perfume from it. He put it under his nose and took a deep breath. "Smells like our cute little neighbor." Hagen then handed the note to Brown. The note read: 'Phil, please stop by after work. I want to talk to you about this weekend. Judy.'

"She wants to see me. Here," Brown said as he gave Hagen his lunch pail to take inside. He walked across the yards to Judy's front door.

"Hi, honey! Come in. Do you want some coffee?"

"Sure," Brown said. They walked into the kitchen. Brown put his coat on the back of a chair and sat down. Judy poured two cups of fresh coffee and got the cream out of the refrigerator, then sat down opposite of Brown.

"What did you want to discuss about the weekend?" Brown asked.

"My dad built a cabin on Squaw Lake, about fifty miles outside of town. It's in the middle of the woods and a perfect place to get away from your problems for a couple of days. Besides, we could be completely alone for the entire weekend. Oh, and I could teach you how to ice fish."

"Ice fish? Is that what you want to do when we're completely alone?"

"For a few hours. Then we could find other things to do," Judy reached across the small table and stroked Phil's cheek.

"Well, count me in then, at least for the other things."

"Great! Tommy's going to let us use his Nash. I'll pack all the food and other stuff, and we can be ready to go tomorrow when you get off work."

"Say, where is Tommy?"

"He's working late today. He won't be home until about eleven o'clock. Would you like to take our coffee upstairs?"

"You know I would."

***

Chris Hagen is looking out the attic window of the safe house. He has no light on in the room to give himself away. He watches the silhouettes on the blinds of Judy's bedroom. He sees Judy and Phil undress each other, and then the light went out. He thinks, *The lieutenant won't be home for a couple of hours. Now would be a good time to send in my report about him.*

Hagen gets the radio from its hiding place and sits against the wall and by candlelight, coding this message:

Lieutenant Richter is impulsive, lacks self-discipline, and has no respect for superiors. He has been unable to come up with solutions to problems that face the mission. Richter's shortcomings and failure to stay on task will certainly cause this mission to fail.

After he'd transmitted the message, Hagen leaned back against the wall and lit a cigarette. He sat quietly, blowing smoke rings, and waited for a return message. Aiming the smoke rings at his toes, he watched as each ring slowly rolled and boiled through the air until it burst apart against his boot. Hagen stubbed out his nearly-finished cigarette on the bare floorboards of the attic. Gulping down half of a bottle of beer, he lost himself in thought.

I wonder if the message I just sent will be the lieutenant's death warrant, or will the general simply send him to the Russian front? Either way, it would seem that Richter's days are about to become very limited. Too bad. I really like the kid. Hell, we could be friends if it wasn't for this fucking war. The neighbor girl is going to be broken-hearted no matter what the general decides. I know I'll be sent to Russia if this mission fails. I sure hope I can spend some time with my family before they send me there.

The crackling of the radio brought Hagen out of his thoughts. Busily he wrote down the coded message. Once the message ended, he sent back an acknowledgement. Pulling the candle closer, Hagen decoded the message. It was from General Arensdorf. *We meet again at the Solo Club on Wednesday night. If there are no valid ideas to satisfactorily complete this mission, be prepared to kill Mr. Brown and make it look like an accident. I will advise you at the meeting.*

Hagen lit another cigarette and re-read the message. "*Fuck!*"

Chapter Nineteen

Friday morning Hagen and Brown were driving to work.

"Chris, I'm going to spend the weekend with Judy. They have a cabin outside of town on Squaw Lake. We're leaving tonight after work."

Hagen paused for a few moments before saying anything. He thought about how he'd hardly slept the night before. He'd wrestled all night over his allegiance to the Third Reich and how he had betrayed his friend.

"Why do you spend so much time with her, Phil?"

"I love her, Chris."

"How does she feel about you?"

"I'm sure she loves me, too."

"Then ask yourself this, my friend. Judy loves Phil Brown, the machinist that works at Packard. Don't you think her feelings would change very quickly if she knew who you really were? Especially if she finds out some of the things you have done?"

"Shit, Chris. How do I tell someone that I love that I'm really an SS officer?"

"I don't know, Phil. All I know is that you've gotten yourself into one very complicated mess."

"I can't help but think about her. When the mission is over and they pull us out, it'll break her heart. If I tell her who I really am, it'll break her heart. I can't see any way that this will turn out good for her."

"You're right. There is no way this isn't going to hurt her. But right now, we have to think about us," Hagen said.

"What do you mean, Chris?"

"We have to come up with something good to tell the general on Wednesday, or we're both fucked."

"Yeah, yeah. I'll come up with something."

"You'd better. I'm deadly serious here, my friend."

***

Nick Stark sat at his desk waiting for Johnson to come in. Yesterday, Nick had flown to Cleveland and spoken with the president of Custom Fabrics. He got a list of the businesses that they sold to in the Detroit area. His flights to Cleveland and back had been on a military transport, and his entire assignment that day took a little over five and a half hours. He'd been home for an early dinner with his family and to help his children with their homework.

Around 9:20, Steve Johnson came into the office. He had on the same suit he wore yesterday, and it looked like he'd slept in it. He hadn't shaved, and his hair was not combed.

"Holy shit, partner! It's a good thing J. Edgar can't see you. You look like someone beat the shit out of you," Stark commented.

"I feel like it, too. Just about the time I arrived in Lansing yesterday, a freak storm blew in off of Lake Michigan. I've never seen it snow so much in my life. So much snow came down that all the highways were closed until six o'clock this morning."

"Where'd you sleep?"

"The Michigan State Police escorted everyone off of the highway and took us to Lansing High School. I spent the night on a wrestling mat in the school gym."

"Did you get to meet the school principal?" Stark asked.

"Well, yeah, I did. Why do you ask?"

"I bet he had on black socks, didn't he?" Stark asked, trying to restrain his laughter.

"How the fuck would I . . .wait a minute! You asshole, you knew there was a storm coming into Lansing, didn't you?"

"Well, they did mention something about it on the radio yesterday."

"Motherfucker," Johnson muttered under his breath. "Okay, partner. We're even for that Doc Alexander joke. For now."

Ron Steele walked up to Stark's desk and said, "Damn, Johnson. You look like shit."

"Thanks, boss."

"What did you two boys find out yesterday?"

"I'll go first," Johnson said. "Lansing Linen no longer sells to the public. They only sell to institutions like the military, prisons, jails, and places like that. They also haven't made anything other than plain old white fabric since 1935. So we can scratch them off of our list for red and white tablecloths."

"What did you find out, Nick?" Steele asked.

"Custom Fabrics is a big outfit. They sell to Sears, Montgomery Wards, and I also have a list of seven fabric stores in and around Detroit that they sell to."

"You boys know what to do next. Start pounding the pavement and asking questions. Let's hope our assholes bought their tablecloth close to home," offered Steele.

"Yeah, and that somebody remembers them," Johnson added.

"Johnson, the Bureau's got standards. Get yourself cleaned up before you go out there and talk to anyone."

"Yes, sir."

***

There was a knock on the door of the safe house around six o'clock that evening.

"Hi, Judy. Phil's in back, getting ready for your fishing trip. Go on back," Hagen said as he opened the door for her. Phil heard Judy walking down the hallway on the hardwood floor. He hurriedly hid the .45 under some clothing in his suitcase.

"Hi, sweetie. You about ready?" Judy asked, standing in the doorway of Phil's room.

"Sure am. I just need to get my razor and stuff from the bathroom. Why don't you start the car and I'll be with you in two shakes."

"Two shakes of what, lover?"

Phil walked to the doorway and kissed Judy, then he grabbed her shoulders and spun her around. After he had slapped her on the ass, he said, "Go on, you nasty little girl, I'll be right there."

Judy squealed in delight and went out to start the car. Phil went to the bathroom and got his toilet articles, then threw them in his suitcase. He then reached into the nightstand drawer and took out the silencer for his .45 and hid it in the bottom of his suitcase. Chris walked into the room and said, "You're playing with fire, Phil, and you know what happens when you do that."

"Yes, I do. But I'm like a moth drawn to the flame, my friend," Phil said as he walked out of the house and toward Judy waiting in the Nash.

***

"You're awfully quiet tonight, Phil. You haven't said anything in the past twenty minutes."

"Yeah, I know. I guess I'm just tired. It's been a hard week at work. Why don't you tell me about this ice fishing thing? Do we sit out on the lake and freeze our asses off?" Phil said as he lit two cigarettes and handed Judy one.

"No, silly. My dad built an ice fishing shanty. We tow it onto the lake, cut a hole in the ice and fish."

"You drive the car onto the lake? Is that safe?"

"Goofy, this time of year the ice is about a foot and a half thick. I bet you could drive a tank on the ice."

"This Nash is about as heavy as a tank. Are you sure about this?"

"Don't worry. This old tank has been out on the ice plenty of times."

"If you say so. Would you mind if I took a little nap? I think I'm going to need my strength tonight, lover."

"Please do, sweetheart."

Phil nestled down in the seat and just looked at Judy for a few minutes until he fell asleep.

***

"Wake up, sleepy-head, we're here."

Phil sat up and rubbed his eyes. Out the window, he could see in the moonlight that they were parked next to a log cabin in the middle of the woods.

"Wow! Haven't I seen this on a postcard somewhere?"

"I told you it was beautiful. Come on, let's unpack and get a fire going."

Judy unlocked the door and went inside. She knew right where to go to find a kerosene lamp and some matches. She lit the lamp and two others. Phil came in, loaded down with their gear. He put it down on a table and looked around.

"My God, Judy. This place is amazing."

"Yeah, daddy was quite the craftsman. All the comforts of home except electricity and hot water. Our bedroom is through that door, and the bathroom is through that door."

"You mean we don't have to go outside to use the bathroom?"

"Of course not. But I'll have to prime the toilet before it can be flushed."

"What do you cook on?"

"That big old wood-burning stove in the kitchen. Why don't you get a fire going while I unpack and get things set up? The wood pile is around the back of the cabin."

Phil brought in a couple of armloads of firewood and set about building a fire in the fireplace. After he had warmed his hands, he took off his coat and started to look closer at things.

"Were all these mounted fish on the wall caught here?"

"Of course. I caught that twelve-pound bass that's over the front door." Judy turned to look at the fish. "I caught that the last year daddy was with us. Hey, do you want a drink?"

"Okay."

Judy poured Phil a glass of bourbon and handed it to him.

"Do you want ice in that?"

"Ah, okay, but how...?" Phil stopped talking as Judy walked by him and went out of the door. She snapped an icicle off the eve of the cabin and dropped it into Phil's glass as she walked back inside.

"You must have been a real tomboy, Judy."

"Take a look at that picture of me on the end table."

Phil retrieved the picture and brought it closer to the light of the kerosene lamp.

"Pigtails, flannel shirt, bib overalls, and barefoot. This is cute. Do you still have that outfit? I think I'm finding it a bit arousing." Phil joked.

"Here, fill this with snow and cool off a little," Judy said as she handed him a large pot.

Phil went outside and filled the pot with snow, not having the slightest idea why he was doing it. He brought it back inside and gave it to Judy, who set it on the bricks in front of the fire.

"There. Now I'll have some warm water to get the well primed."

"Well primed?"

"You really are a city slicker, aren't you?"

"Yeah, I guess so. I'll just keep my mouth shut and watch you." Phil sat in an overstuffed chair that faced the kitchen, with Judy's picture in his lap. He watched as she went through her routine. When the snow in the pot was melted, she poured a little down the throat of the cast iron pump next to the kitchen sink. After pumping the handle several times, the pump began to spew up a yellow fluid.

"What the hell is that?" Phil asked.

"About two quarts of vegetable oil," Judy replied. "Come here, city boy. Pump this handle until you have pumped about five gallons out. That should clean out all the oil."

Judy took the remaining warm water and poured it into the toilet tank. She returned to the kitchen, got two flashlights out of a drawer and said, "Okay, finish your drink. I want to show you the shanty."

Judy and Phil walked about fifty yards to the edge of the lake. A small version of the cabin was resting on logs close to the shore.

"My dad took his ice fishing very seriously. You are about to step into the Packard of ice fishing shanties. This one is the best on the lake," Judy remarked as her words seemed to come out in billows of steam in the cold air.

"How so?" asked Phil.

"Behold," Judy exclaimed as she unlocked and opened the door and stepped inside. "Notice the solid wood floor. It's elevated four inches away from the ice, and insulated from below, so your feet don't get cold. Pull on the recessed handle on the floor."

Phil pulled the handle to find an opening about two feet square.

"That's where we chop a hole through the ice to fish in."

"Nice. Are those Birchwood planks on the wall? They are beautiful."

"Sure are. Daddy milled them himself from some of the trees that were on the property. There's insulation behind them as well under those Birchwood ceiling boards."

"What's under this?" Phil asked as he pulled away a dusty tarp to discover an old couch that was still in good shape.

"If it gets too cold, there's a kerosene heater under that other tarp."

"Wow, this place is terrific. You could almost live in here," Phil said.

"When I was a little girl, this would be my play house in the warmer months."

"It must have been delightful."

"Oh, it was. I'd play in here all day. There are a lot of good memories in this place for me, not the least of which were the times I spent ice fishing with my dad. It didn't matter if the fish weren't biting. We would just sit and talk about everything." Judy's eyes started to well with tears as a flood of memories rushed over her.

"Hey, don't do that," Phil said as he hugged Judy. "Let's see if we can make more memories tomorrow when we take this lovely little house out on the ice."

Judy smiled and said, "We should get back to the cabin. I'm getting cold."

Chapter Twenty

Friday night was spent in the cabin with some torrid love making taking place. The first time was on the couch in front of a roaring fire. The second and third time took place in the bed under a down comforter. After the third session, Phil lite two cigarettes and gave Judy one.

"I sure am glad you took that nap."

"Yeah, me too," Phil said as he smoked his cigarette and stared at the ceiling. A mood of somberness came over him. Then he said, "Judy, how do you feel about me?"

Judy rolled over and hunched up on her elbows. Looking Phil straight in the eye she said, "I love you, Phil."

"That sure makes me happy, because I love you too, Judy."

Judy was happy to hear Phil say that; it put her in a playful mood.

"Oh, I bet you say that to all the girls."

"No, I've never said that to anyone in my life who wasn't part of my family. What about you? I bet you've had a lot of boyfriends in your day."

"No, just one."

"What happened to him?"

"He drowned when his car fell through the ice out on the lake."

Phil sat up in bed as quickly as he could. "What!"

She laughed. "You should see the look on your face! I'm joking, you silly boy."

Phil lay back down in bed. "I'm going to get you for that," he said as he reached over and softly pinched her nipple.

"I hope so, but no more tonight. We need to get some sleep." Judy positioned herself against Phil spoon-style and promptly fell asleep. Phil lay there for the better part of an hour, watching over her shoulder as her perfect breasts rose and fell with her breathing. He caressed her smooth skin and smelled her hair. Looking at her face, he kept thinking to himself, *How the hell am I going to get out of this without breaking her heart?* A tear rolled out of the corner of his eye and dropped onto the bed.

***

Phil rolled over and threw his arm onto the bed, expecting to find Judy, but the bed was empty. He opened his eyes and saw it was daylight. Taking a deep breath, the wonderful smell of cooking bacon forced him to get up and get dressed.

"Good morning, sweetie. The coffee's done."

"That coffee smells almost as good as you look, cutie," he said as he got his coffee and sat at the table watching Judy cook in her flannel pajamas. The longer he watched her, the more he thought about his situation. *Those bastards in Germany would probably tell me to shoot her and drop her body in the lake. Nobody would find her until the spring thaw, and the problem would be over. How can I do that? This beautiful, innocent creature's only mistake in life has been to fall in love with an asshole like me.*

"Why do you look so glum, Phil?" Judy asked as she put a plate of pancakes and bacon in front of him.

"Oh, I guess I'm still a little scared that the car is going to fall through the ice."

"Well, don't be. That old Nash has been out on that ice plenty of times. Besides, I wouldn't do anything that would put you in danger."

Phil put the first bite of pancakes in his mouth and thought, *Oh, God. How I wish, I could say the same thing to you.*

***

Judy drove the Nash up to the front of the shanty. She leaned out the driver's window and yelled,

"Okay, Phil. Hook that chain to the back bumper." Once Phil did what she said, she shouted, "Okay, get in the car." "You're sure about this, right? I mean, absolutely sure," Phil nervously asked.

"Absolutely. Oh, you better roll your window down, just in case we have to get out in a hurry." Phil turned and fumbled for the window handle. He rolled the window down as fast as he could. If he had been watching Judy, he would have seen her shoulders bounce up and down as she tried to suppress her laughter.

"Okay, here we go," Judy said as she inched the Nash forward. The chain became tight, and the shanty started to roll off of the logs it rested on. The Nash was now on the ice-covered lake, with the shanty in tow.

"How, how far out are we going?" Phil asked.

"Oh, just a couple of hundred feet. There's a good spot there I want to try."

Shortly Judy stopped the Nash and turned off the motor.

"Here we are. You can get out now. I'll get the tools out of the shanty."

Phil got out of the car, and while Judy was getting the tools, he jumped up and down to test the ice. Judy came back with two axes and a long metal bar. One end of the bar had been sharpened to a point, and the other end had a net attached to it.

"Son-of-a-bitch, it's cold out here," Phil said as he pulled up his collar around his ears.

"The thermometer on the porch read 10°, but it feels colder than that with the wind blowing. Here, take this axe and start chopping. That should help warm you up."

Phil started chopping with the axe and Judy chipped away with the sharp end of the metal pole. Every so often she turned the pole around and used the net to clear out the ice chips. Before too long they had a hole through the ice about two feet in diameter.

"The ice is almost two feet thick this year. That's the thickest I've seen it in a while," Judy said. She started the Nash and pulled forward a few feet, positioning the shanty over the top of their freshly dug hole.

"Come on, Phil. Let's go inside and light the heater. I'm freezing my ass off."

***

"Damn, that feels good," Phil said as he held his hands in the heat waves emanating from the kerosene heater.

"It sure does," Judy replied as she faced the other direction, rubbing her butt for extra warmth.

"I have to ask you this. If we heat up this space, will it melt the ice under us?" Phil said.

She chuckled. "You're paranoid, Phil, but that's cute. The answer is no. The same insulation under the floor that keeps the cold from the ice away from us also keeps our warmth away from the ice. You ready to start fishing?"

"Yeah, but I've never fished before."

"No problem, city-slicker. Open the floor hatch and sit down on the couch."

Judy got a fishing pole from the corner of the shanty. She sat down on the couch next to Phil and tied a hook and a sinker to the line.

"Open that can of sardines, would ya?"

"Yum, I love sardines."

"Yeah, well, don't start eating all of our bait. Hand me a sardine and I'll bait your hook. Okay, here you go. Let your line out until you hit the bottom," Judy said as she handed the pole to Phil.

"How do I know when I have a fish?" Phil asked.

"The tip of your pole will start to jiggle. That means you're getting a nibble. Pull back on the pole to set the hook, and reel in your fish."

"Sounds easy enough."

***

Thirty minutes passed by, without a bite on their lines.

"This fishing stuff is boring," Phil said.

"Oh, really? Maybe I can help you with your boredom," Judy said as she got on her knees between Phil's legs. She undid his pants and pulled them down to around his ankles. With Phil's manhood in her mouth, she began sucking.

"Oh, my God, that feels good," Phil said as he sat back on the couch.

Three or four minutes later Phil was fully aroused. He looked down at Judy and moaned, "I think I'm getting a nibble."

Judy thought he was referring to what she was doing. Rather than stop, she giggled with Phil still in her mouth.

"No, really. I think I'm getting a nibble."

Judy looked over to see the end of Phil's fishing pole bounce up and down like crazy.

"You have a fish, Phil! Looks like it might be a big one! Quick, reel him in!"

Phil stood up to reel in his fish. Forgetting that his pants were around his ankles, he took a step forward, and fell feet first into the hole in the ice.

"FUCK! That's cold!" he yelled.

"Grab my arm so I can help you out," Judy yelled back and helped Phil out of the hole.

Standing by the hole in the ice, soaking wet from head to toe and half-naked, he began to shiver violently. Judy threw a blanket around his shoulders.

"Are you okay, honey?" Judy asked.

"Look! I still have the fish!" Phil exclaimed as he pointed to the still bouncing up and down end of his fishing pole.

"Reel him in!"

Phil reeled the fish up to just below the surface of the water. "Okay, now what?"

"Give him a big yank and pull him out of the water," Judy advised.

Phil gave the line a mighty tug, and the fish came flying out of the hole and smacked Phil in the chest. Not expecting that to happen, Phil tried to take a step backward. His feet got tangled in his pants again and he lost his balance once more. Phil knocked the door open and wound up laying flat on his back in the snow with a six-pound catfish flopping all over his half-naked body.

"Don't move!" Judy laughed. She started taking pictures with a camera that she kept in the shanty for special occasions.

"Smile," was all she could say through her laughter. She walked outside onto the ice. "That was the funniest thing I ever saw!" she said as she bent over at the waist and continued to laugh hysterically.

"Think you could help me up? I think my ass is stuck to the ice."

Still laughing, Judy helped Phil to his feet. He waddled back into the shanty with his pants still around his ankles.

"You need to get out of those wet things. I'll turn up the heater," Judy advised.

"What about my fish?"

"Leave him out there. He isn't going anywhere."

Judy got Phil a second blanket and helped him out of his wet things. As Judy was hugging him, trying to give him some of her body heat, he looked down. "This must be how that old boyfriend died," he said with a smirk.

"You got me back, you big jerk," Judy laughed and pinched Phil's nipple. "You stay in here where it's warm and I'll tow you back to the cabin."

***

Phil stood in front of the dwindling fire in the fireplace, trying to warm himself.

"I'll get some more wood," Judy offered as she went around to the back of the cabin.

She threw several logs into the fireplace and lit a fire in the big pot-belly stove. She then filled several large pans with water and put them on the stove. "There you go. You'll have some nice hot water for a bath soon."

When the water was hot enough, Judy poured it into the claw-foot bathtub.

"The bath is ready, Phil. Come on."

"Why don't you get in with me?" Phil said as he tested the water with his toes.

"Okay," Judy said and got undressed. The two sat facing each other and washed. Judy moved around and sat between Phil's legs with her back to his chest. They lay back and enjoyed soaking in the water. Phil enjoyed the warmth while Judy explored Phil's hands.

"I bet there's a story behind each one of these scars," she said as she pointed them out.

"Not really. They're just from working with sharp metal."

"The calluses must mean you're a hardworking man, Mr. Brown."

"I guess."

"Look how much bigger your hands are than mine," she said as she held her hand out flat against his.

***

"The water is getting cold. I think we should get out," Judy offered.

"Why don't you heat up some more? I could stay here forever."

"No, no. Get out and show me how a master cook is going to cook that catfish. You do know how to clean one, don't you?"

"Yes, my dear. I may have only caught one fish, but I've cooked lots of them. Fish is one of my favorite dishes."

Judy and Phil dried off, got dressed, and went into the kitchen.

"This catfish is big enough to fillet. Do you have a really sharp knife?"

"Sure," and she handed him a butcher knife. Phil tried to cut the fish, but the knife wasn't very sharp.

"Is this the sharpest knife you have?" Phil asked.

"Yeah, it is."

Phil reached into his pocket and took out his switchblade. When he clicked it open, it startled Judy a little. "Why the hell do you have that?"

"I grew up in a tough neighborhood. I guess it's force of habit. Besides, it was made in Germany. Those Germans make some very good steel that really holds an edge."

Phil finished filleting the fish and laid the knife down on the counter. Judy picked it up.

"Phil, why does the handle have an eagle holding a swastika on it?"

"Oh, ah, my dad picked it up in Germany for me before the war."

***

Their meal consisted of broiled catfish in a lemon-butter sauce, baked potatoes, and a salad.

"That was delicious, Phil. Bring your wine and sit on the couch with me."

They sat and watched the fire burn in the fireplace. One thing led to another, and they spent the next few hours in the bedroom. They explored every aspect of each other's bodies for a few hours before falling asleep from sheer exhaustion.

Chapter Twenty-One

Sunday afternoon, Judy and Phil left the cabin and drove back toward Detroit. Phil was looking out the window at the things he'd missed seeing on the trip to the cabin Friday night. He noticed that there was a railroad track that ran parallel the highway for quite a distance. A fast-moving freight train approached and whizzed by in the opposite direction.

"Wow, Judy. Look at all those tanks," Phil commented as about thirty flatcars with two tanks on them each flew by.

"Yeah, looks like those boys at Chrysler have been busy."

"This track must run out of Detroit, huh? I bet some of my stuff is on that train."

"Oh, yeah. That's one of the main rail arteries in and out of Detroit."

"They sure are going fast."

"We have a war to win, Phil. Everybody wants that to happen quickly."

Farther down the road Phil noticed that the highway and the railroad tracks had to cross bridges that were about five hundred feet long. The bridges allowed both to cross a canyon that was about one hundred feet deep. He peered over the window ledge and saw there was a large river at the bottom of the canyon.

Perfect, he thought to himself.

***

Judy parked the Nash in her driveway. Phil carried Judy's things into her house.

"Want some coffee or something to drink, Phil?"

"No, thank you, sweetheart. I should get home. I have a lot of things to get done before Monday comes around. Thank you, my darling, for an unforgettable weekend."

"You made it unforgettable for me too. Especially when you fell into the lake," Judy said giggling.

"I'll never live that down, will I?"

They hugged and kissed in the kitchen.

"Will I see you tomorrow, Phil?"

"Of course you will."

***

Phil dropped his things off and went directly to Chris's room, where Chris was lying on his bed reading the newspaper.

"Chris, come into the kitchen. I think I have something that will make Handler and the General happy."

Chris sat at the kitchen table and watched Phil rifle through all of the drawers until he found some paper and a pencil. He sat down next to Chris and started to draw on the paper.

"This is the highway that leads toward Judy's cabin. Right alongside the highway is a railroad track that Judy says is the main rail artery in and out of Detroit. Right here, about thirty minutes out of town, is a bridge that goes over a deep ravine. If we could blow the bridge, we could send a hell of a lot of boxcars to the bottom of that ravine."

"Did you see a train running on that track?" Chris asked.

"I sure did. As we were coming back to Detroit, it was headed in the opposite direction."

"How fast was it going?"

"I would say at least fifty miles per hour, maybe even sixty."

"Excellent. Could you tell if there was any military stuff on the train? I'd hate to think we might blow up a trainload of corn flakes and baby rattles."

"Oh yeah. I couldn't tell what was in the boxcars, but there must have been at least fifty Sherman tanks on flat cars coming from the Chrysler plant. I would think the odds are high that there would be some Merlins transported, too."

"You make a good point. Get your coat. I want to look at this bridge," Hagen said.

***

Darkness was rapidly approaching as Hagen and Brown pulled to the side of the highway and parked near the end of the bridge behind some bushes. They got out of the car and walked to the edge of the canyon.

"Good, it's not too steep up here. Let's go under the bridge and have a look," Brown said.

"Typical old railroad bridge. Rails above supported by concrete pylons and cross-members connecting the pylons for added support. I want to see the other end of the bridge."

Hagen and Brown went back to the car and moved it to the other end of the bridge. They got out of the car and crawled under the bridge.

'Okay, this is the far side of the bridge to a train coming out of Detroit," Hagen said.

"You mean like this one coming?"

A southbound freight train went flying by overhead. The vacuum created by the fast-moving train sucked up loose snow, dirt, leaves, and any debris on the ground. The two Nazis pulled their coats over their heads to protect themselves from the material swirling around them. They were laying in the snow about three feet under the tracks. The noise of the heavy train speeding overhead was overwhelming. It seemed to take forever for the train to pass, but eventually the last car went by.

"Son-of-a-bitch," Brown said, half talking and half coughing.

"Yeah, shit. Let's get out of here." Hagen also coughed.

* * *

Hagen and Brown headed back toward Detroit. About halfway back, Hagen pulled into the parking lot of a small diner. They went inside and sat in a booth as far away from the few other patrons as they could. Each ordered a cup of coffee and a piece of cherry pie. After the waitress had delivered their order, Hagen started diagramming his plan on a paper napkin.

"We need to start at the far end of the bridge. We will have to crawl out on the superstructure about one hundred feet. You go down one side and I'll go down the other. We need to put charges on the tracks where they rest on the pylons, here, here, here and here," Hagen said as he pointed to his drawing and put X's where the charges needed to be placed.

"You are going to have to make a couple of bandoliers so our hands will be free for climbing."

"How much Plastique do you think we will need, Chris?"

"We have to blow reinforced concrete, so I'm thinking twenty pounds at each spot."

"That's forty pounds per man. I think knapsacks would be a better way to go."

"Yeah, you're right, Phil. We can pick up a couple of cheap ones at Sears on our way home from work tomorrow. Do we have one of those twist detonators and about three-hundred feet of wire?"

"No, we don't."

"I'll radio Handler tonight and tell him what we need."

"You better tell him we need five-hundred feet of wire. I don't want to be too damn close when it all goes off. Answer me a question, will you?" Brown said.

"Sure."

"Why are we only blowing two pylons, not the whole damn bridge?"

"No need to. The laws of physics come into play here. All we need to do is start the train on a nose-dive to the bottom of that canyon. With the speed those trains are going, momentum will cause the rest of the train cars to follow."

"This should be fun to watch," Brown offered.

"I wish we had a train schedule. I hate to think we might freeze our asses off to blow up that trainload of corn flakes. We only have one shot at this, so we need to get it right," Hagen remarked.

"Remember that contact list you made me memorize when we were on the U-Boat?"

"What about it?" Hagen asked

"We have a man in the rail yards. See if Handler can set up a meeting with him. He may be able to supply us with the information we need."

"Great idea! A toast. To Mission Detroit," Hagen said as he held out his coffee cup for Brown to clink.

"To Mission Detroit," Brown echoed.

***

"Shit. It's cold in here," Brown announced as the two Nazis walked into the safe house. "I'll put some more coal in the furnace while you radio Handler."

The two split up. Hagen went up to the attic to use the radio, and Brown went downstairs to tend to the furnace. When Hagen came back downstairs, Brown was sitting at the kitchen table, drinking a beer.

"Handler said that the man from the railyard will be at the meeting with the general on Wednesday," Hagen related.

"Great. I have a lot of questions for him. I have a question for you, too. I'm thinking of asking Judy to see a movie with me tomorrow after work. Think I could use the car?"

"You know I don't approve of you spending so much time with her. I'm afraid you're getting too close to her, and that never works out well in our business. But I won't stop you. Go ahead, just be careful," Hagen advised.

***

Tommy Nowicki answered a knock at the front door of his house.

"Phil, how's it going? Judy's upstairs. Hold on and I'll get her." Tommy went into the hallway and yelled up the staircase, "Hey Sis, Phil's here to see you."

"I'll be right down," Judy yelled back.

"Phil, what is it? Is everything okay?" Judy asked as she walked toward Phil standing by the front door.

"Everything's great, cutie. I just wanted to know if you'd like to go to a movie tomorrow after work?"

"Of course I would. I love going to the movies."

"Great. I can use the car tomorrow, so we can get some dinner out, too. I'll pick you up around six o'clock."

"Do you want to sit down and have a drink or something, Phil?"

"No thanks. All that ice fishing wore me out this weekend. I'm going home and get some rest," Phil said as he winked at Judy. Judy smiled and gave Phil a quick kiss on the lips.

"I'll see you tomorrow night."

Chapter Twenty-Two

Monday morning and the sleepy city of Detroit started to awaken. Nick Stark arrived at the Penobscot Building little before seven o'clock. He was the first to arrive, so he put on a pot of coffee. While the coffee was brewing, he picked up the direct phone line to the top floor.

"Top floor, Army Air Corps, Sergeant Miller speaking."

"Yeah, Miller, Agent Stark. Did you guys pick up any radio traffic in the last twenty-four hours?"

"Brother, did we! Last night the group we've been following were yakking back and forth for about twenty minutes."

"Could you get a fix on them?"

"The best we could tell is that one of them is broadcasting from across the river in Canada. We think it's coming from somewhere in about a three-mile stretch of the waterfront, near the end of the bridge."

"What about from our side?" Stark asked.

"Well, we're still looking at the West side, say somewhere between Six Mile and Ten Mile Roads, and Woodward Avenue and Mack Avenue."

"Shit man, that's about a third of the city."

"I know, but next time we'll know where to start searching and maybe we can narrow that down."

"Miller, do you think you can write this up and bring it down? I need to have something to show my boss. Maybe he can light a fire under somebody and get us some triangulation equipment to find these pricks."

"You bet. I'll drop it off in about a half an hour."

***

Hagen and Brown reported for work at the Packard plant. Walking into Building #10, they noticed five boxcars on the rails next to the plant. Several MP's armed with Thompsons were standing guard. Inside the building, another boxcar was being loaded. The security guards were advising everyone to get together in the center of the building, as Bill Shore had some announcements to make.

Ten minutes later, Bill Shore and Mr. Reed, the plant manager, came out of Shore's office. Bill Shore got on top of a work table while Reed stood next to it.

"Good morning, everyone," Shore said. Several people returned it, but mostly just a dull murmur came up from the crowd.

"The first thing I want to say is thank you to the assembly crew for working this weekend. You guys and gals put together a hell of a lot of engines over the weekend. In fact, I just spoke to Mr. Reed," pointing to Reed standing next to the bench, "He said that if we can keep production high for the next three days, you people will get a four-day weekend for the Thanksgiving holiday." Cheers, whistles and applause erupted from the workers. A couple of the workers shook Mr. Reed's hand. When the noise subsided, Bill Shore went on to say, "Get lots of rest, because when we come back, we'll be working six- and seven-day weeks and as many double shifts as you can handle. The past couple of months, we've worked on getting the right people in the right spots and ironing out the bugs in our production. Our contract calls for us to make seventy-five thousand Merlin engines. We've just scratched the surface, but if we all pull our weight, we can kick some real Nazi ass. What do you say!" exclaimed Shore as he pumped his fist in the air. A loud and thunderous cheer erupted from the workers.

***

Ron Steele and Steve Johnson walked in the door of the FBI office at the same time.

"Hey, Nick. Steve was telling me in the elevator on the way up that you didn't have any luck with the fabric stores this weekend," Steele said.

"Yeah I'm afraid so, boss. Nothing with the small shops, but we were told at Sears and Montgomery Wards to come back this evening when the late crew is on."

"Good."

Michael Kushner came into the office a few seconds later.

"Michael, did you get a lot of radio interference last night?" Stark asked.

"Sorry, I can't tell you. We were at the in-laws last night," Michael answered.

"Boss, Army Air Corp picked up a lot of radio traffic last night. In fact, here's Sergeant Miller with his report."

"If you guys can get some triangulation trucks on this, we can nail these bastards," Miller stated.

"I think we need to have a meeting on this, boss," Stark said as he handed Steele the sergeant's report. Steele glanced at the report and said, "Thank you very much, Sergeant. The rest of you guys in my office, now," Steele uttered.

**

Ron Steele sat at his desk and studied the Army Air Corp report before passing it around for the others to read. As the report went around the room, Steele bit off the end of one of his big cigars, struck a match and held it to the cigar. He puffed away, sending big billows of grey-blue smoke into the room. Kushner was the last agent to read the report. When he finished, he passed it back to Steele.

"I'm going to contact Washington on this one, fellas. We need to get the cooperation of the Canadians on this.

Somebody higher up than me needs to authorize the use of those radio triangulation trucks. Maybe I'll call J. Edgar," Steele said with a grin on his face.

"Hey, it couldn't hurt," commented Stark.

"How the hell do those triangulation trucks work?" Kushner asked.

"We need three trucks equipped to pick up radio signals. Each one is at a different location. When they pick up a signal, all three trucks plot the direction it came to them from. Where the signals of the three trucks cross is where the signal originated. That's why it's called triangulation," Johnson said.

"You know much about these trucks, Steve?" Steele asked.

"We studied it in the Academy when I went through."

"Good. If we get some of these fucking trucks, you'll be in charge of the detail. Right now I have some phone calls to make. You go catch some bad guys," said Steele.

***

"Did you hear what Shore said this morning? Seventy-five thousand of those engines. Fuck me! No wonder the general was so determined to destroy the plant," Brown said as the two Nazis were driving home from work Monday night.

"Yeah, I had no idea they were going to make that many, either. It makes sense now why they sent us here," Hagen returned.

"No shit!" Brown replied as the two Nazis pulled into the Sears parking lot.

***

FBI agents Stark and Johnson arrived at the Sears parking lot at the same time. They entered the building from the east entrance, headed to the linen and fabric department. Hagen and Brown had entered the building and taken the down escalator to the sporting goods department. The two groups of men passed each other near the center of the store. They exchanged glances, not knowing how intertwined their lives would become in the next few days.

Stark and Johnson didn't have any luck interviewing the sales staff about the red and white fabric strips.

"I guess we're off to Montgomery Wards, partner," Johnson remarked.

"Yep, that we are," Stark returned.

Hagen and Brown purchased two backpacks in the sporting goods department, which they threw in the back seat of the Ford before driving home. Brown had to get cleaned up for his date with Judy.

"I wish there was a way we could tell the boxcars from Packard from the rest of all those boxcars."

"Yeah, that would be nice. I'd hate to fill up that river with cornflakes," Brown joked.

***

"I'm sorry, Gladys doesn't start her shift until six o'clock," said the clerk at Montgomery Ward's fabric counter.

"That gives us about a half-hour to kill, partner," Stark said to Johnson.

"What do you want to do?"

"I could do a little early Christmas shopping," Stark replied.

"In that case, I'm going next door to Woolworth's and get some dinner at the counter. Want to join me?" Johnson said.

"No thanks. Debbie will have dinner waiting for me when I get home."

"You married guys got it made."

"Try it sometime, you might like it," Stark responded.

"Yeah maybe. I'll see you in a half-hour," Johnson muttered over his shoulder as he headed to get himself dinner.

***

Thirty minutes later Stark and Johnson rendezvoused at the fabric counter to talk to Gladys Whitney. Stark set the large Teddy Bear that he'd just bought for one of his daughters on the counter. Johnson took the toothpick out of his mouth and put it in his coat pocket.

"Are you going to give that bear to Ron Steele?"

"Hell no, I bought it for J. Edgar."

"How can I help you, gentlemen?" Gladys Whitney asked.

"Agents Stark and Johnson of the FBI. We would like to ask you some questions about a sale you might have made," Stark said as he produced his badge and credentials.

"Sure, how can I help?"

Johnson reached into his coat pocket and took out a small manila envelope. He removed the fabric strips and showed them to Gladys.

"Have you sold this type of fabric to anyone lately?" Johnson asked.

"Why yes, I have. It's table cloth material, I have the bolt right here. Do you want some?"

"No ma'am, do you remember anything about who you sold it to?" Stark questioned.

"Boy, do I. Two of the cutest guys I've seen in a long time. That taller one, he was a real dreamboat. I wish I could turn the clock back about thirty years for him, if you know what I mean?"

"Yes, ma'am, could you describe them," Johnson said.

"Well, they were about your age. The shorter one was about his height." Gladys pointed to Stark, who was six feet tall. "The other was about two inches taller."

"What about hair color, eye color, did they have any facial hair."

"Both were clean-shaven. They both had blonde hair and blue eyes. I thought they might be brothers. The shorter one had a scar in his left eyebrow."

"How were they dressed? Did they do anything out of the ordinary?"

"I could see that the taller one had on a dress shirt and tie under his coat. The other man dressed like a factory worker. Oh! And yes! The factory worker paid me with a twenty dollar bill."

"How long ago did you make this sale?" Stark asked.

"About a week or so ago."

"Do you think you remember them well enough to describe them to a sketch artist?" questioned Johnson."

"Oh, sure, especially the tall one."

"Give Agent Johnson your address and phone number. I have to find a pay phone and make arrangements to get an artist here from Washington," Stark said.

"There's a pay phone by the restrooms, right over there," Gladys said as she pointed in the direction of the restrooms.

***

"Hi, Phil," Judy said as she greeted him at her front door. "I'm all ready to go, just let me grab my purse."

"What movie are we going to see?" Phil inquired as he helped Judy on with her coat.

"It's called 'The Lady Takes a Chance' with John Wayne and Jean Arthur."

"Great. I like John Wayne. Do you want to eat now and go to a later movie, or do you want to see the movie and have a later dinner?"

"Let's see the movie first, okay?"

"As you wish, my dear."

***

Phil paid for the movie tickets, and they went inside. They were a few minutes early, so they stopped at the snack bar.

"That'll be one dollar, mister," the kid behind the counter said when he completed their order.

"A dollar! For two Cokes and a bag of buttered popcorn? Jesus, going to the movies is starting to get expensive."

Judy and Phil took seats in the middle of the theater, which wasn't very crowded. They sat eating popcorn and waited for the start of the movie.

"Did you ever pick up that big turkey you won the last time we were here?"

"Tommy picked it up for me a couple of days ago. It's a beauty. Do you think you can come over Wednesday night and help me with some cooking?"

"I'm sorry, Judy. Chris's aunt invited us to dinner. She wants to pay us back for helping her when she was sick."

"Oh, that's so nice. If you can't come Wednesday night, can I have you early Thursday morning?"

"You can have me anytime you want me," Phil said as he put his hand on Judy's knee.

Judy gave him a quick kiss on the cheek just as the theater lights started to dim. First came the previews of coming attractions. The newsreel ran next. It was almost exclusively about the war.

"Look how those guys write stuff on the bombs they're going to drop on Germany. I like the one that said 'This one's for you, Adolph.' That's cute," Judy said.

"Say, that gives me an idea. We should write stuff on the boxcars that leave the Packard plant. I think it would help keep spirits up, and show the rest of the country that the Arsenal of Democracy is kicking ass to win the war."

"That's a great idea, sweetheart."

"Do you mind if we stop at Woolworth's? I'd like to buy some chalk."

"No, darling, I think that's a great idea."

Brown thought to himself, *Yeah, it is a great idea. That would make it easier to tell which boxcars had the Merlin engines in them.*

Chapter Twenty-Three

Hagen and Brown arrived for work at the Packard plant Tuesday morning. Brown was setting up his machine when he noticed Bill Shore walking by.

"Hey, Bill. Do you have a minute?" he asked.

"Sure, Phil. What do you need?"

"Well, my girl and I were at the movies last night. The newsreel showed a bunch of our bomber guys chalking messages on the bombs they were going to drop on Germany."

"Yeah, I've seen that."

"Well, I was wondering if it would be okay if we wrote some messages to Hitler on the sides of the boxcars that go out of here."

"Great idea, Phil. I'll check with Mr. Reed and the Army to see if it's okay with them. I'll let you know."

***

Later that afternoon, Bill Shore walked up to Phil Brown's machine and signaled Brown to turn his machine off so they could talk.

"Phil, when I pitched your idea to Mr. Reed, he went crazy, he liked it so much. He thought it would be great for morale, and even though there's a war on, it never hurts to keep the company name in the minds of the public. He's going to send some guys down from the Art Department to help out. Tomorrow morning, he's coming down to present you with a twenty-five dollar War Bond. The only restriction he wants is that nobody uses any swear words. You know, stuff like 'Hey Hitler, go fuck yourself,' wouldn't be too good for the Packard image as it makes its way across the country."

"Oh, yeah, that's understandable. What did the Army have to say?"

"They don't want anyone to know what's actually inside the boxcars."

"I was hoping it would be okay. I even brought in some chalk."

"That's great, Phil, but Mr. Reed said the guys from the art department are going to bring everything to help you guys do it up right. Great idea. You're a good man, Phil," Bill said as he extended his hand.

Brown went back to operating his machine, and his thoughts started to wander, *Glad they liked the idea. I wonder what I'm going to do with a fucking American War Bond? Maybe I'll frame it. That Bill Shore sure is a nice guy. I kind of hope he isn't in the building when I blow this fucking place up.*

***

That evening, Phil was sitting in Judy's kitchen, having coffee with Judy and Tommy.

"Judy, remember that idea I had about putting messages to Hitler on the side of the boxcars that leave the plant?"

"Sure, Phil, what about it?"

"Well, I told the boss about it, and he liked it, so he took it to the plant manager, who liked it a lot, too. In fact, he's going to give me a twenty-five dollar war bond tomorrow morning for it."

"That's wonderful, Phil!" Judy exclaimed.

"What are you going to do with the money, old man?" Tommy asked.

"I thought I'd frame it," Phil responded with a shrug.

Tommy thought to himself that it might be nice to hang over a week's pay on the wall. What the hell, it wasn't his money.

"Phil, are you still interested in helping me with the Police Athletic League boxers?" Tommy went on to say.

"Oh, hell, yeah, Tommy. When do we start?"

"A friend of mine is going to let us use his gym downtown. You'll meet him on Thursday when you come over for Thanksgiving. I thought we could start on Monday."

"I'm looking forward to it. Judy, you do remember that I have to go to Chris's aunt's house tomorrow night? What time do you want me here to help with the cooking on Thursday morning?"

"Do you think you could come over around five o'clock? We're going to have close to thirty people here."

"Thirty! Wow, that's a lot of people to feed."

"Yeah. Most of them are either Tommy's cop friends or his boxers, so you know they're going to eat like an army," Judy joked.

"We could use my kitchen, too, since I'm right next door."

"Thanks, Phil, that would be very helpful."

"Do you think you could make some more of that salad dressing like you made the other night?" Tommy asked.

"Sure, Tommy, if you promise not to drink it."

***

The first thing Wednesday morning, Bill Shore had the crew assemble in the middle of Building #10. As usual, Bill stood on top of a workbench so he could be seen and heard.

"Ladies and gentlemen, Mr. Reed has come down here this morning to make a presentation to one of your co-workers. Mr. Reed, why don't you come up here and make your presentation?"

Mr. Reed looked at Bill, very puzzled, as if to say, 'How is a man in his 60's in a three-piece suit going to get on that bench?' His question got answered when three men scooped him up and set him on the bench. Feeling a little disheveled, he adjusted his suit and tie before speaking.

"Thank you, Bill, and thank you guys up front here for the lift up. I want to start by introducing Ralph and Sarah, from the art department," Reed said as he pointed out the two standing near the bench. "They're here today to help you guys with a special project. This project is based on an idea from one of your very own co-workers, Phil Brown. Where are you, Phil? Come on up here."

Brown worked his way through the assembly and jumped up onto the bench.

"We have all seen in the newsreels how our G.I.'s are writing messages to Hitler on bombs, artillery shells, tanks, and all kinds of things. You know what I'm talking about here. Stuff like, 'Here, Adolph, have one on me,' that kind of thing. We can't do that on our engines, but Phil here thought it would be a good idea to send Hitler some messages on the sides of the boxcars that we send out of here. I think it's a good idea, too. That boxcar at the front of the building is going to be the first one in our next shipment to Texas, and I've instructed Ralph and Sarah to paint this on the sides." Reed reached in his pocket and held something up.

"Those of you who don't know what this is, it's one of the Packard hood ornaments from the early 1930's. It represents Nike, the Greek Goddess of strength, speed, and victory. Now I can't think of a better message to send to those German bastards other than that American strength is going to speed this war to victory. Can any of you?"

A huge cheer and a round of applause went through the crowd. When the noise subsided, Reed went on to say,

"Phil, thanks for the great idea. On behalf of the Packard Motor Car Company, I would like to present you with this twenty-five dollar war bond." Reed shook Brown's hand as he presented him the bond. They held a pose briefly as the company photographer popped a couple of flash bulbs. Brown waved the bond over his head and jumped down as the crowd applauded him. Brown wanted to get out of the limelight as quickly as he could.

"Thank you, Phil. Now, folks, you will find poster paint, chalk, and crayons at the front of the building. Feel free to write something on the boxcars before they leave. There are two restrictions on what you can write. First, no swear words. I don't want to hear about some kid asking his mommy what 'fuck Hitler' means as he sees the passing train. Second, there can be no mention of what's inside the boxcar. Any questions? Okay, great. Let's go to work." When Reed was finished, the same three men helped him off of the bench. He shook hands with Bill Shore and the two men headed toward the front of the building.

***

"Hello, Gladys Whitney?" Stark spoke into the telephone.

"Yes," the lady responded.

"This is Agent Nick Stark of the FBI. Remember we spoke the other night at Montgomery Ward?"

"Of course, Agent Stark. How can I help you?"

"We have a sketch artist coming in today. Could you be here at ten o'clock and help him by giving descriptions of the two men you saw?"

"Oh, gosh, getting downtown to the Penobscot Building is going to be tough, with all the changes and transfers I'll have to make. Not to mention all those people on the bus doing their Thanksgiving shopping."

Stark wanted Gladys Whitney relaxed for her meeting with the artist. Sensing a long bus ride downtown wasn't going to help matters, so he said, "How about if I pick you up in my government car?"

"Wow, I'm going to get to ride in a real G-man car! Does it have a siren?"

"Yes, it does."

"Can I blow the siren, please? I've always wanted to do that."

"Oh course, you can, Gladys. But I can't let you play with the shotgun or the Tommy gun in the trunk," joked Stark.

"Oh, Heavens, no. I wouldn't want to do that."

***

A little before ten o'clock, Agent Start pulled up in front of Gladys Whitney's house. He went to the front door and rang the doorbell. Gladys answered the door.

"I'm all ready to go, Agent."

Stark escorted her down the walkway and held the car door open.

"It's nice to see a young man with manners these days, Agent Stark."

"Yes, ma'am, it's also nice to see citizens willing to get involved. It sure makes our job easier."

The drive downtown only took a few minutes. Most of the conversation consisted of Gladys asking a lot of questions about how the work with the sketch artist was going to go. Nick didn't mind answering the questions. Gladys was a sweet little old lady who could have been anyone's grandmother. Looking at her as he spoke, he couldn't help but think how impeccably she was dressed. Lovely flower print dress, with nylons and heels. Her hair and makeup were perfect. She had on a fur stole and a little hat, complete with veil. She had clearly gone to special pains to look her absolute best. He put things in perspective for himself when he thought that a trip to the FBI office was nothing more than routine for him. To a law-abiding citizen, it was probably the outing of a lifetime. He hoped he would never forget that.

"Okay, Gladys, we are going to travel the last couple of blocks to the office with the siren. Let me just flip this switch. There. Now reach over here and push the horn ring down."

Gladys did what she was told to do. The siren began as a low growl at first and increased in loudness and pitch the longer she held the horn ring down. When she let up pressure on the horn ring, the siren wound down and quit within a few seconds.

"Oh, boy! Can I do that again?" Gladys said with all the excitement of a little girl.

"Absolutely," Stark replied.

Gladys depressed the horn ring again and the siren started off once more as a low rumble and worked its way to a high-pitched wail. As Stark turned into the parking lot, Gladys let up on the horn ring and the siren worked down and turned itself off.

"How was that, ma'am?" Stark asked.

"Oh my goodness! I feel just like a G-man."

***

Agent Stark introduced Gladys to Ed Parker, the FBI sketch artist. The two of them went into a small interview room where they wouldn't be disturbed. About five minutes into the interview, Ron Steele walked into the room. He introduced himself and with his rough and gravelly voice, said, "On behalf of the rest of the department, I want to thank you for taking this time and helping us with our case."

"You are so very welcome," Gladys said. She was proud to be there and offer whatever help she could give. She was also a little giddy at all the attention she was getting.

***

Building #10 had almost a party atmosphere as the day wore down toward quitting time. The company artists had done a wonderful job of painting the Nike logo on the boxcar. Completed, it was nearly ten feet long. Almost the entire crew had written their sayings on the side of the boxcar. At the very least, people signed their names. The boxcar was so festive looking and brightly decorated that Bill Shore called the company photographer over to take pictures.

***

At five-thirty that afternoon, Ed Parker walked into Ron Steele's office. "Ron, I'm afraid we are going to have to continue the sketching on Friday."

"That's right, tomorrow is Thanksgiving, isn't it? What's the problem?" Steele asked.

"It would seem that our little old lady has a crush on the taller perpetrator. She says that I'm just not making him handsome enough."

Ron Steele leaned back in his chair and struck a match to light the cigar in his mouth. "Well, make the motherfucker pretty for her."

"I'll do what I can. I'll see you on Friday," Parker said as he was walking out of Steele's office.

"Stark!" Steele yelled out his door, "Come in here."

"Yeah, boss?" Stark said as he walked into Steele's office.

"You need to take Gladys home for the day. Make arrangements with her to pick her up and bring her back Friday morning," Steele said.

"Sure thing, boss."

***

Hagen and Brown stopped at the small diner on Eight Mile Road to have dinner on their way home from work. After dinner, they went home to clean up, have a couple of beers and waste about an hour before they headed to the bridge. Driving over the bridge to Windsor, Canada, they made their way to the waterfront district. They parked the Ford behind the Solo Club and entered the back door. The bartender recognized them from before and buzzed them through the door that led to the basement. They went down the dimly lighted stairs to the storeroom. Seated at a card table were General Arensdorf and another man they would be introduced to shortly.

"Heil Hitler," Hagen and Brown said in unison as they gave the general the Nazi salute.

"Sit, gentlemen. Say hello to Gruber, our man who works in the rail yard. His family are long and trusted members of the party. Tell them what you do at the rail yard, lieutenant."

"I'm the night dispatcher at the rail yard. What that means is that I'm the guy who puts trains together. Every train comes with routing slips. I make sure that all the cars that are leaving get attached to the correct engine and in the right sequence."

"So you know exactly when each train is leaving, where it is going?" Brown inquired.

"That's right," the dispatcher responded.

"What do you have in mind, Lieutenant Richter?" The General asked.

"Sir, we have discovered a railroad bridge about a half an hour out of town. I have been informed that almost all of the rail traffic leaving Detroit must cross this bridge. Is that right, Gruber?"

"Yes, that is correct," Gruber responded.

"The captain and I want to take the explosives, wire and detonator we requested and blow up that bridge as a train crosses it. We should be able to send a shipment of five or six boxcars to the bottom of the canyon and into the river below."

"How are you going to tell when the boxcars from Packard are on the bridge?" Gruber asked.

"This is the beautiful part. Today all of the workers in Building #10 decorated the sides of the boxcar that will be the first one ready to go Monday. If Gruber can make sure it's the lead boxcar, we can blow the tracks when we see it on the bridge. The lead boxcar should drag several of the cars behind it into the canyon."

"What kind of decorations are on this boxcar?" the general asked.

"The Packard art department has painted a large picture of the Goddess Nike on both sides of the boxcar.

The employees have written various sayings and signed their names to it in several different and bright colors," Hagen answered.

"Sayings? What kind of sayings?" questioned the general.

"Our favorite reads 'Happy Hanukkah Hitler, from the Jews of Detroit,'" Brown quoted.

The general bellowed in loud laughter. Hans Gruber laughed loudly as well. Gruber was very careful to keep his laughter from sounding fake. Gruber had been smuggled into the country in January of 1942, part of the early planning of Mission Detroit. His position at the railyard enabled him to keep track of wartime production, and he was now highly valuable to the sabotaging of the Arsenal of Democracy. However, the other Nazis in the room were not aware of a problem they had. A little over a year ago Gruber had been caught red-handed by the FBI. Gruber was given a choice of being hung as a spy or becoming a double agent for the Americans. Gruber chose to be a double agent.

"Your plan is very plausible, lieutenant, but what about the destruction of the manufacturing facilities?" General Arensdorf wanted to know.

"Yes, sir. The second part of my plan is this. It will take a while for them to repair the bridge. In the meantime, the plant will continue to make the engines and store them on the rail spurs next to Building #10. If Lieutenant Gruber can get me a boxcar in some remote corner of the rail yard, I can put a few thousand pounds of explosives in the undercarriage and set the timer to go off when that car is the one inside Building #10. Boom! We destroy all of the production and the means of producing more engines."

"Excellent, lieutenant, excellent. Do we know if a train will be heading to Texas on Monday?" The general looked at Gruber for a definitive answer.

Gruber took a pad out of his pocket to be certain of his answer. "Yes, sir. There is a pickup scheduled at Packard at six o'clock Monday evening. The routing slips say that train will be delivering five boxcars to the aircraft plant in Texas."

"What time does that train leave?" asked Brown.

"She pulls out of the rail yard at eleven o'clock that night."

"Perfect! Then it sounds like you know what to do. Here, Gruber, take my car keys and help Richter with the supplies they requested. Captain Smoltz and I have something to talk about," General Arensdorf said as he handed Gruber his keys. The general and Smoltz waited quietly as they listened for Richter and Gruber to climb the stairs. When he heard the door at the top of the stairs close, the general said, "I have changed my mind about Richter for now. I'm not saying I like him, but he seems to want to get the job done. Right now that's all I care about. Make sure he stays alive, at least until the mission is over. Then we will talk about him again."

"As you wish, general," Smoltz said. He stood up and gave the general the Nazi salute with a 'Heil Hitler.' He then left the building and joined Richter and Brown in the parking lot.

"Looks like the general likes your plans. I'm glad for you," Hagen offered.

"Yeah, me, too. I hate to think about getting sent to the Russian Front."

"No shit, pal, no shit." Hagen replied. He went on to think, *Or worse!*

Chapter Twenty-Four

Phil Brown softly knocked on Judy's front door at five o'clock on Thanksgiving morning.

"Good morning, sweetie," Judy said as she answered the door and kissed Phil on the cheek. "Are you ready to start cooking?"

"Anything for you, cutie," Phil replied as he hugged her close.

"Come on into the kitchen. Coffee's on, and we need to talk about what we are going to do."

Phil sat at the kitchen table as Judy poured two cups of coffee and got the cream from the refrigerator. She sat at the table next to Phil.

"I noticed that your car's gone. Where's Tommy?" Phil asked.

"He's downtown, working the Thanksgiving Parade. He volunteers for it every year. He enjoys doing it, and a little overtime never hurts."

"When will he be home?"

"He should be here about two o'clock. He and a couple of his buddies will be bringing some folding tables and chairs from the department."

"Yeah, I was wondering where you were going to seat thirty people," Brown said as he sipped his coffee.

"Tommy and his friends will move all the living room furniture into the extra bedroom and set up the tables and chairs."

"Sounds like you've done this before."

"Ever since I was a little girl. Only then it was Daddy's single friends and boxers. If we get time later, I'll show you some pictures."

"So, when do your guests arrive?"

"They should start showing up around four o'clock. Dinner's at five."

"What do want me to do?"

"Well, last night I went ahead and baked two hams. I'm going to need you to heat one of them up in your oven a little later. Right now I need you to put one of the turkeys into your oven."

"Looks like you have them ready to go. Did you stuff them both?" Brown said, looking at the counter.

"Of course."

"Did you use the gizzards? I hate gizzards."

"I know some people like them and some don't, so I put the gizzards in one but not the other."

"Say, which one is the bird you won at the theater?"

"The larger one, on the right. That's the one I'd like you to take."

"Well, I guess I'd better get started," Brown said as he finished his coffee and went to the counter. He picked up the roasting pan with the big turkey and headed for the door. Judy followed to open the door for him. After opening the door, she rubbed his shoulders and said,

"Thank you so much, Phil."

Brown leaned over and kissed her on the forehead and said, "I'd cook your bird anytime, cutie. I'll see you in a few minutes."

Judy slapped him on the ass as he went out the door.

***

Phil returned to Judy's house a few minutes later. While he was pouring himself another cup of coffee, he asked, "What's next?"

"Well, there are some potatoes on the landing by the back door. I could use having them peeled."

The back door landing was right off the kitchen. Phil went down the three steps and discovered four ten-pound bags of potatoes. He shouted up to Judy, "How many of these bags do you want peeled?"

"All of them," Judy called back.

Shit! Brown thought. He brought the bags up to the kitchen and sat at the table with them. He took a drink of coffee and clicked open his switchblade. He held the potatoes over a paper grocery bag that was on the floor. He let the peels fall into the bag as he whittled away at each potato. After Phil had finished the second bag of potatoes, he sat up straight and stretched. He lit a cigarette and drank his coffee.

"Taking a break?" Judy asked. "Good idea, I think I'll join you." Judy sat down at the table and took a cigarette from Phil's pack. Phil was a little surprised when she lit a kitchen match with a flick of her thumbnail.

"You never stop surprising me," Phil said.

"I told you I was a tomboy. Guess I never outgrew it."

"What comes after the potatoes, tomboy?"

"About twenty pounds of carrots need cleaning and have to be cut up. Oh, then there's twenty pounds of green beans that need to have the ends taken off and cut. Don't forget to baste your turkey from time to time."

"You're feeding an army."

"I told you these guys eat like an army, and I bet there won't be a lot of leftover's by the time they leave."

"Guess I'd better get back to work," Phil said as he reached down and opened the third bag of potatoes. Judy went to the kitchen counter and began making pies. Phil watched her for a while. He thought, *What a good woman and kind person to feed so many friends. It must be nice to have that many friends. Too bad their Thanksgiving celebrations will be coming to an end when Germany wins the war.*

***

"Okay, Judy, I've finished the fourth bag of potatoes. I'm going to go next door and baste the turkey."

"Great, Phil. Have you already made your salad dressing?"

"Yep, I made a gallon of it a couple of days ago."

"Could you bring it with you when you come back?"

"Sure."

***

Phil returned about ten minutes later. He brought two half-gallon milk bottles of his salad dressing, two steaming plates of kielbasa and sauerkraut, and a large leather pouch.

"Phil! You made me lunch?" Judy asked.

"Sure did. Sit down, can I get you a beer?"

"I'd better stay with coffee for now."

The two sat at the crowded kitchen table to eat.

"What's in the leather pouch, Phil?"

"My cooking knives. A man has to have the proper tools to create greatness," Phil joked.

"I don't know about greatness. All this crowd cares about is does it taste good and is there enough," Judy cracked.

Phil cleared the lunch plates and washed them. He sat back down with a fresh cup of coffee and started to clean the carrots into a paper grocery bag. He took the clean carrots up to the counter and began to chop them. Judy stood and watched in amazement at how fast his hands and fingers moved. When he finished the carrots, Phil cut the stems and ends off of the green beans.

"Wow! French cut, that's fancy," Judy said.

"Yeah, just a little greatness. What's next?"

Judy opened a drawer and handed Phil a potato masher.

"No lumps please."

Phil spent the next hour or so mashing potatoes in ten-pound batches as they came off of the stove.

"Tommy just pulled into the driveway. It must be about two o'clock," Judy remarked.

Two minutes later, Tommy and two of his friends came into the house, all in uniform from the parade detail. Tommy stepped into the kitchen.

"Hi, Phil. Damn, Sis, it sure smells good in here. Phil, come meet my friends, Jerry and Bob."

Phil followed Tommy into the living room, where Tommy introduced the three men and they shook hands.

"How did the parade go, fellas?" Phil asked.

"Seen one parade, you've seen them all. But everything went pretty smooth," Bob reported.

"Yeah, but this year was the coldest it's been in a while," Jerry added.

"I think I might have something that might take the chill off." With that, Phil went to the grocery bag he had left on the couch.

"Blackberry schnapps! Fellas, you have *got* to try this. I'll get some glasses," Tommy said. Tommy came back into the living room with the glasses and Judy followed him. Phil poured everyone a glass, and they clinked all around.

"Happy Thanksgiving," Tommy said, and everyone echoed it.

"You behave yourself with the schnapps, Tommy. I don't want you drunk before the guests arrive," Judy said.

"Yes, Sis. I'll behave myself. Come on, guys, let's get the furniture moved out and set up the tables and chairs."

Detroit's finest began to move the furniture while Judy and Phil went back to the cooking.

***

The food table was set up along the wall of the living room where the sofa usually was. The cops set the tables in two long rows down the middle of the room. When Tommy and his friends finished putting down tablecloths, centerpieces, and place settings, the room looked like it was meant to be a dining room that could sit forty or so people. Judy and Phil brought out the food and placed it on the food table. Judy went upstairs to clean up and change while Phil went home to do the same. Entering the house, he found Chris listening to the radio.

"Did you pick up the flowers last night?" Phil asked.

"Yes, I did. A corsage and a dozen roses."

"Great! I'm going to shower and put on my suit. What are you going to wear?"

"I don't have a uniform here, so I guess I'll wear a suit, too," Chris said.

"Funny, wise guy. No Heil Hitlers today, huh?" Phil joked back.

***

"Thank you so much for the roses, Chris. That was sweet of you," Judy cooed as Chris handed her the roses. Judy kissed him on the cheek. Chris felt like he had made Judy's day, but he had no idea how he was going to make Tommy's day.

"Holy shit! Four bottles of Crown Royal. We're going to have us a cop party," Tommy said when he looked into the bag that Chris handed him. Tommy shook Chris's hand and patted him on the back so hard it threw Chris a little off balance.

"Hey fellas, meet our good neighbor, Chris," Tommy announced to his buddies as he held a bottle of Crown Royal over his head like a prized trophy. Jerry and Bob followed Tommy and Chris into the kitchen to open one of the bottles and share in the holiday spirits.

"You look nice, Phil. What's that you have behind your back?" Judy asked as they were still standing by the front door.

"Oh, just a little something for the cutest little tomboy in town," Phil said as he brought his hand in front of himself and presented Judy with the corsage.

"Phil! What a wonderful surprise." Judy said as she opened the package and handed the flowers back to Phil. "Here, pin it on me."

Phil dutifully pinned the flowers onto Judy's dark blue polka-dot dress and the two shared a passionate kiss until Tommy came in the room.

"Hey, knock that shit off. We're getting hungry," Tommy joked.

Still hugging Phil, Judy said, "You'll just have to wait until everyone gets here, big brother."

"Okay, I guess I'll just have to go back to the kitchen and help share some more holiday spirits."

***

The guests arrived and the eating began. Tommy sat at the head of one long table, while Judy sat at the opposite end of the other table. The guests were mostly Tommy's friends from work. Some were married and brought their wives, but most were single, some of them with dates. Six of Tommy's fighters came, too, and Tommy warned them not to eat themselves out of their weight class. He was only kidding, but they knew that.

Chris sat at Tommy's table, where he continued to drink and joke and laugh with the cops. Phil sat at Judy's left side. He was soon engaged in an in-depth conversation with some of the boxers over the Joe Louis and Max Schmeling fights of 1936 and 1938. Judy was pleased that everyone was having a good time. She watched her brother for a while. She couldn't help thinking of how he reminded her of their dad sitting there. Tommy was the same fun-loving, gregarious person Tom Sr. had been. Her mind started to wander, and she began thinking of her childhood.

***

"Daddy, you got me a BB gun for my birthday! Thank you so much," Judy said as she ran to give her dad a big hug and a kiss on the cheek.

"Well, you're ten years old now, princess. I think you've outgrown that slingshot, don't you?"

"When can I shoot my new gun, Daddy?"

"We can go up to the cabin tomorrow, if you want to."

"You're the best daddy in the whole world."

"Yeah, I know. Just don't you forget it," joked Tom Sr. as he gave her a big hug.

Judy never did forget it. Thomas Sr. had been a kind, loving, single parent. Judy's mother passed away when Judy was two years old. Thomas didn't know how to raise a girl, so he raised her just like he raised Tommy. The result was a tomboy extraordinaire. By the time she was a teenager, she could shoot tin cans off a fence post at fifty yards with any pistol. She could hit practically anything she could see with a rifle.

Judy remembered the time Thomas got called to her school because she got into a fight with a boy.

"You have to control your daughter, Mr. Nowicki. We don't condone fighting at this school," the principal said.

"I'm sure it was justified. Tell me what happened, princess," Thomas told his daughter as they sat in the principal's office.

"This bully in the class kept bothering me all day. He tripped me once. At recess, he pushed me. When I pushed back, he socked me in the stomach."

"What did you do honey?" Thomas asked.

"I did just what you taught me, daddy. I set him up with two quick jabs, and then let him have it with a right cross."

"She knocked him down and bloodied the boy's nose, Mr. Nowicki," the principal said as if to admonish Thomas.

"Sounds to me like the little shit got what he deserved. Come on, princess, let's get some ice cream. I don't think the principal has anything more to say about a clear case of self-defense, do you?" Thomas said, looking at the principal as he stood up and reached for his daughter's hand.

"Well, ah no. Just next time, tell a teacher or someone before things build up to fighting."

"Yes, sir," Thomas and Judy said in unison as they left the principal's office.

Thomas Nowicki was his daughter's idol. Thomas would share how his day had gone at dinner time. Judy and Tommy thought the stories of their dad's day were the thrilling and exciting. When she grew up, Judy wanted to be just like Thomas. Many of their conversations were about why she couldn't be a police officer like him.

"I could get you a job at the police department, Princess."

"I know, Daddy, but it would be as a secretary or a records clerk job. I wouldn't find that very satisfying."

"I know it's unfair, princess. No police departments will hire a woman for a sworn officer position. That's just the way it is now. Maybe it'll change someday."

Chapter Twenty-Five

The Thanksgiving meal went very well. Everyone got their fill. Judy's prediction about having very little food left over came true. Phil helped Judy serve pie and coffee, and about half the people left shortly after that. Two of the ladies volunteered to help with the dishes. Judy put things away as soon as Ann had them dried. The three of them took on the task of the dishes with assembly-line precision. Phil continued to chat with the boxers, and Chris drank with the cops.

"I think your roommate is about half in the bag," Judy said to Phil when she rejoined him at the table.

"That's good. He's under a lot of stress at work. We all are. Letting off a little steam will do him some good," Phil stated. He figured it would be good to keep an eye on Chris, though.

Tommy walked up to Phil. Standing next to the seated Phil, Tommy said with his arm around Phil's shoulders,

"Hey pal, we're going to start a little poker game over at the other table. Care to join us?"

"No thanks. I'm not much of a gambler," said the steel-hearted Nazi. He would have enjoyed playing cards, but he'd rather spend time with Judy.

"Judy, would this be a good time to look at that scrapbook? I find this big gathering so interesting," Phil asked.

"Sure, I'll get it."

Judy sat down with the scrapbook and Phil sat right next to her, his arm around her shoulders. Judy pointed out various people in the pictures and updated Phil on what they were doing now.

"This picture was taken about twenty years ago. See that fuzzy-faced officer in the background? He's now our Chief of Police. This real serious-looking guy is now the District Attorney. Oh, and this guy shaking hands with my dad is Bill Donovan. He was my dad's commanding officer during World War I."

"Didn't I see his picture in your cabin?"

"Very observant, Phil. Yeah, he and my dad would go fishing there a couple of times a year, whenever they could work it into their schedules. Oh, and this big guy is...."

"Joe Louis! the heavyweight champion," Phil blurted out before Judy could finish what she was saying.

"Yeah. He was a big supporter of my dad's PAL boxing program."

Everyone at the party left before midnight, except for Tommy, Chris, and three of Tommy's friends who were still playing poker. Judy and Phil were exhausted, so they kissed for a short time on the front porch before Phil went home.

"I take it none of you guys have day shift tomorrow," Judy said to the poker players as she stood next to Tommy. "Glad to see you drinking coffee now, Chris."

"I had to. The protectors of Detroit are some pretty good card players. I had to start protecting my paycheck from them"

"I'm going to bed," Judy said as she bent down to kiss Tommy on the cheek.

"Good night, sis. Great meal."

The rest of the table offered goodnight wishes and thanked her for the Thanksgiving feast. Judy went upstairs to bed.

"Chris, I think your roommate is getting pretty serious over my sister," Tommy said.

"I think you're right. I also think that seems to be a two-way street. What do you think about that?" Chris asked.

"He seems like a nice guy. She could do a lot worse."

***

Friday morning, Nick Stark pulled into the parking lot of the Penobscot Building at eight o'clock. It was a cloudless, bright, sunshiny day. The forecast on the radio called for a high of 23° today. Nick joked with himself that today must be the start of a heat wave.

"Hey, Nick, have a good holiday?" Ron Steele said. Ron was standing with a cup of coffee looking at the radio log book.

"I sure did, boss. How about you?"

"Great time. My kids are both home from college this week. The coffee is on. Get yourself a cup, Nick."

"That sounds great." Nick got a cup of coffee and sat at his desk. Ron Steele sat on top of Johnson's desk, dangled his feet, and drank his coffee.

"What's going on with our sketch artist?" Steele asked.

"Steve is picking up Ed Parker at nine o'clock at the airport. Then they're picking up Gladys Whitney on their way in," answered Nick.

"Great. We'll have to get copies circulated, and J. Edgar wants to put these guys on the Ten Most Wanted list."

"Hopefully, that will get us some leads, Boss."

"That's the way we bagged Dillinger," Ron said, a little boastfully.

***

Phil and Chris were sitting in their living room when there was a knock on the front door.

"Tommy, come in. What brings you here?" Phil asked as he held the door open.

"Come looking to get some of your money back, Tommy?" Chris joked from his chair.

"No, but I want a rematch someday. Phil, do you remember me introducing you to my friend, Jimmy Duncan?" Tommy asked.

"Sure, he's the guy that owns the gym downtown we're going to practice at."

"Well, between having too much to drink and losing my ass to Chris, I forgot that he gave me four ringside seats to the fights at the Civic Auditorium tonight. Jimmy has a couple of fighters on the card. Would you guys be interested in going?"

"Hell, yes!" Phil responded.

"Count me in. With my thirty-five dollars in new-found wealth, I'll buy the beer." Chris said.

"Great. Come on over around seven o'clock. We can all go in the Nash."

***

"Good morning, Agent Stark," Gladys Whitney said as she walked into the FBI office.

"Good morning, and thank you for coming back," Nick replied.

"Can we use the same room?" Ed Parker asked.

Nick nodded yes, and Parker and Gladys went to work.

"You know that old lady wanted to sound my siren?" Johnson whispered to Stark.

"How strange. You didn't let her, did you?"

"Of course not, but I said maybe on the trip home."

"Why, Steve, you old softy."

"Hey, come on. She's like everybody's grandmother."

"Yeah, I know."

***

At two o'clock, the door to the conference room opened. Ed Parker was thanking Gladys for her cooperation.

"We're finished, Agent," Parker said to Stark. Nick got to his feet and shook Gladys' hand, thanking her for all she had done. Steve Johnson helped her on with her coat.

"Can I blow the siren this time?" Gladys wanted to know.

"You certainly can, ma'am. Right this way," Johnson said with a big smile on his face.

"How did it go in there, Ed?" asked Nick.

"The proof is in the pudding, as they say. I'll let you be the judge. Come on," Parker said as he led Nick into the room he'd been using. Parker's drawings were face down on the table.

"Sit down. This is the drawing of the taller of the two suspects," Parker said as he handed Nick a twelve by eighteen-inch drawing.

"No fucking way! This is a drawing of Clark Gable with blonde hair!" exclaimed Nick.

"Here's the other guy," Parker said as he handed over the second picture.

"Oh, Jesus Christ! This is just great. You mean that our suspects in the rail yard bombing are Clark Gable and Cary Grant? Fuck me, the boss is going to shit."

"Well, keep in mind that Gladys is an old lady. She keyed into her mind that the suspects were two very handsome men. When she tried to recall them, she recalled two handsome men. These are what she came up with. This kind of stuff happens, especially when you're dealing with someone's memory," Parker advised.

"If this weren't so sad, it'd be funny. No, wait, it *is* funny," Stark said as he burst into loud laughter. Parker joined in laughing loudly as well.

"What's so damn funny?" Ron Steele asked as he walked into the room.

"Here, boss. Put out an APB on these two guys," Nick said, still laughing as he handed over the two drawings to Steele.

"Aw, fuck. Hoover's going to chew my ass," said Steele.

"Just tell him that the witness's memory was too fuzzy to come up with anything useable," Parker offered.

"I like that idea, Ed, I will. At least I have some good news. Washington is giving up three radio trucks to use next week. When you see Johnson, tell him I need to talk to him."

"Will do, Boss. Ed, can we keep these drawings?" Nick said.

"Of course."

"Nick, take Ed to the airport so he can catch a flight back to Washington. Thanks for everything, Ed," Steele said as he shook Parker's hand.

"You're welcome, Ron. Sorry it didn't work out."

***

Agents Stark and Johnson arrived back at the office at the same time. In the elevator on their way up, Stark said, "We got some great drawings from Gladys. The boss wants you to send out an All-Points Bulletin on our suspects before you do anything else. This is top priority."

"Hell, yes! I can't wait."

The two arrived at the FBI office and hung up their coats and hats. Stark handed Johnson the drawings.

"What the fuck! Is this a joke?"

"Unfortunately, it isn't. That's what Gladys provided us. Ron wants to see you. We got an okay on some radio trucks."

"Now *that's* good news," Johnson said as he walked toward Ron Steele's office.

Nick Stark just stood by his desk looking at the suspect drawings and chuckled.

"You wanted to see me, boss?" Steve Johnson asked as he walked into Ron Steele's office.

"Yeah, sit down, Steve. We got approved for three of those radio directional trucks. They arrive here on Monday, along with four extra agents. I'm putting you in charge of the detail. Check the log book and with the Army guys on the top floor. Figure out the best places to set the trucks up, and the best times to catch these guys transmitting. I want your proposal on my desk first thing Monday morning."

"Sure thing, boss."

***

"I guess you two lovebirds want to sit together," Chris said as he held the door and pushed the seat back forward so Phil and Judy could get in the back seat of the Nash.

"Thank you, Chris," Judy said as she got in the car. Once Phil sat down, she snuggled up against his side and he put his arm around her shoulders. Twenty minutes later, they were walking down the ramp toward their seats in the Civic Auditorium. Jimmy Duncan was coming up the ramp, and they met at the half-way point.

"Hi, Jimmy," Judy said as she gave him a hug.

"Hey everybody, glad you could make it," said Jimmy as he shook hands with all the men. "I'm headed back to check on my first fighter. He's going to be a good one, Tommy. You guys want to meet him?" Jimmy said.

"Sure," Tommy said.

"Yeah, let's go," added Phil.

"Judy, how about helping me with some hotdogs and beers?" Chris asked.

"Okay, Chris," Judy said. She turned to the rest of the group and said, "We'll meet you guys at the seats, okay?"

Sitting on a table in the locker room was Mike Maloney. Mike was a heavyweight and the best prospect to come out of Jimmy's gym in a long time. The trainer, Ed Scarpelli, was busy taping Mike's hands. Doc Booth, a jovial black man, was going through his bag, making sure he had what he needed to treat any cuts that might happen. Jimmy introduced everyone and they all shook hands.

"Okay, Jimmy. I got my bucket full of water and a brand-new sponge," said the man who just walked into the room.

"Tommy and Phil, meet Patrick MacDonald, our bucket man. Patrick fought in the 1936 Olympics in Germany. He lost in the bronze medal bout. Around the gym, we call him Paddy Mac."

Paddy shook hands with Chris. When he stood in front of Phil, the two looked at each other like they had just seen a ghost. Paddy pumped Phil's hand for at least fifteen seconds without saying a word.

Phil contained his alarmed reaction. *Holy shit! This is the guy that kicked my ass in the elimination bout. Fuck! His reaction tells me he recognized me, too.*

"Five minutes until fight time. You guys should head to your seats," Jimmy said.

Phil and Tommy walked down the ramp to the seats. The whole time, Phil's mind was whirling a thousand miles an hour.

"What's wrong, Phil? You don't look so good," Judy said as he sat next to her.

"Nothing a beer and a hotdog won't cure," said Phil as he took them from Judy and took a long pull from his bottle of beer.

Back in the locker room, Paddy said to Jimmy, "I know that guy, boss. I fought him in Germany. I'm the one that put that scar in his eyebrow. Only then he was a Nazi."

"Sure, Paddy, sure."

Chapter Twenty-Six

Tommy left the aisle seat open for Jimmy; Judy sat between Tommy and Phil, and Chris was on the end. Jimmy came down the ramp, sat down and leaned in to talk to Phil.

"Phil, Paddy is convinced he fought you in the Olympics, only then you were a Nazi."

Phil felt a shockwave go up his spine and for the first time in a long time, he could taste his fear. He looked at Judy and Tommy and couldn't understand why they were laughing.

"What's so damn funny?" he asked Judy.

"You tell him, Jimmy."

"Paddy Mac did fight in the Olympics and lost in the bronze match. He turned professional when he got back. He had over twenty professional fights, but in the process he managed to get his brains scrambled. I don't know what the doctors call it, but around here we call it punch-drunk. You're about the tenth guy this year he swore was the Nazi he fought in Germany. He also thinks he's a personal friend of The Lone Ranger."

"The actor on the radio?" Phil asked.

"No, the actual Lone Ranger."

"Okay, I get it now," Phil said with a genuine smile on his face. He spent the next two minutes breathing in very slowly and exhaling slowly. The thought of getting caught had triggered an adrenaline surge, and he had to calm himself down.

***

Mike Maloney was in the first match of the night. Maloney was a large man who didn't have a lot of movement in the ring. His opponent danced around Mike like he was standing still, which he practically was.

"He doesn't move a lot, does he? Tommy asked Jimmy, who shook his head.

In the third round, the other fighter danced right where Mike wanted him to. Mike let go a face-smashing right hand. The other fighter stood up straight, then fell over backward to the canvas. The referee counted him out and raised Mike's hand in victory. The group at ringside stood and applauded. Judy put two fingers in her mouth and let out an incredibly loud, shrill whistle.

Phil hugged her around the waist and whispered in her ear, "My cute little tomboy."

***

The sixth and last fight on the card tonight was also one of Jimmy's fighters, Mario Pena from some Central American country. He would be fighting one of his countrymen in a ten-round, non-title middleweight match. The first two rounds were very exciting as the fighters mixed it up a lot. It was very apparent that they were matched evenly. Between the second and third round, Chris knelt down in front of Tommy.

"Tommy, I got twenty bucks that says the kid in the blue trunks is going to win. Are you interested?" Chris enquired.

"Hell, yes, I'd like to get back some of my money from last night. You're on," Tommy said as he patted Chris on the shoulder.

The rest of the fight was filled with action. Both fighters put on a good show of their talents. Judy got a kick out of watching Tommy and Phil as they bobbed and weaved in their seats and pretended to throw punches as if they were in the bout themselves.

The fight went the distance and had to be decided by the judges. When the ring announcer said that Mario Pena won on a split decision, Tommy jumped up clapping. He then pointed to Chris and said, "Yeah, baby! Slip me my twenty bones."

Chris begrudgingly took twenty dollars from his pocket and handed it to Tommy.

***

Tommy pulled the Nash into the parking lot of the Fraternal Order of Police Lodge. It was a Friday night and the bar was open. Tommy and Judy were instantly recognized when they went inside. Bob from last night was sitting at the bar. Tommy had to run over to him and show off the twenty-dollar bill he'd just won from Chris. The group took a booth near the dance floor. Phil put some money in the jukebox and returned to the table. Standing next to Judy, he extended his hand and said, "Madame, would you care to join me in our first dance?"

"That would be delightful, kind sir," Judy replied as she slid out and took Phil's hand.

Judy was not surprised that Phil was an excellent dancer. He took control of the dance floor the way he had taken control of the ice skating rink at Belle Isle. After four dances, they returned to their table. A young redhead in a yellow blouse and a skin-tight black skirt came over to ask Chris to dance. Chris put his elbows on the table and rested his chin in his hands.

"My God, not only are you beautiful, but you read minds, too," Chris laid it on pretty thick.

"Whatever do you mean?" she said coyly.

"I mean that when I first saw you over there, I wished that you would come over and ask me to dance, and here you are. You must have read my mind."

"No, not really," she replied.

"Then it must be fate, or karma, or something out of our control that says we should be together tonight."

"Do you think so?" the girl asked.

"I certainly do," Chris said as he was leading her to the dance floor.

"Who's the girl?" Phil asked.

"That's Sally. She works in records," Judy said.

"The guys in the precinct call her 'Inkwell Sally,'" Tommy offered.

"What the Hell does that mean?" Phil asked.

"You never heard that before?" Tommy asked.

"No."

"In polite terms, it means that almost every guy in the precinct has dipped his pen into Sally's inkwell."

"That's funny. You mean that my stiff-ass roommate just might get himself a little action tonight?"

"He'd have to work very hard not to be a part of Sally's action tonight," Judy said, laughing.

Another round of drinks came to the table. They watched Chris and Sally paw and grope each other through five dances. Then Chris and Sally took seats at the bar. Through several drinks, the kissing and groping continued. Chris returned to the table but did not sit down. He leaned in and said to Phil, "I'm going to go home with this little angel. Don't wait up."

"Why, you old dog. Be careful, and I guess I'll see you tomorrow," Phil said.

"Let me shake your hand, Tommy, and thank you for a good time tonight," Chris said. "Judy, it's always wonderful to spend time in your presence," Chris said before kissing the back of Judy's hand.

"Chris! When did you become so smooth?" Judy asked.

"Oh, I've had it bottled up. I guess it's okay to let loose a little when you're with friends." With that, he held his hand out to Sally and they left the Lodge arm-in-arm.

No sooner had they left when Phil leaned back and said, "Wow, I never saw that one coming."

"Oh, I did the moment I saw Sally come in the door," Judy offered.

"How so?" Tommy questioned.

"Hey, Chris is a good-looking guy and a lot of man. I knew she'd head for the prime cut before she started on Bob or some of the other slobs around here," said Judy.

"I'll have to tell Bob you think so highly of him," Tommy jabbed.

"Bob is a sweetheart. I love him to death, but he isn't exactly my idea of someone to go home with. You know what I mean, Tommy. Hasn't Sally come sniffing your way?"

"Oh, sure, lots of times."

"How was she?" Judy jabbed.

Tommy was in the middle of taking a drink from his beer bottle. He slammed the bottle down as he started to cough to prevent from choking. With half a voice and gasping between words he replied, "Not me...no, no, no, not me."

Judy slapped Tommy on the back several times to help him with his coughing.

"When you catch your breath, big brother, you might like to know that your on-again off-again girlfriend Linda is sitting in the booth in the back of the room," Judy offered.

"Don't make me look. Is she sitting with anyone?" Tommy asked.

"Nope. I've been watching for about twenty minutes. She has already turned away two guys."

"No shit! Well, I think I'll try for three. Excuse me," Tommy said as he slid out of the booth and walked back toward Linda. He stood beside the table for a few moments and then sat down.

"She's smiling. Things are looking up for Tommy. So what's the deal with the two of them?" Phil said.

"Linda's a dispatcher at Tommy's precinct. They started dating about two years ago. They're great together for a few months, and then they break up over something stupid. They stay apart for a month or so, then get back together and then the whole cycle starts all over again. They split over something stupid. This time, they've been apart for about three months. I thought he might be done with her by now."

"What do you think the problem is?" Phil asked.

"Honestly? I think they're afraid to commit to each other."

"Looks like they've committed to dance. Here they come," Phil said.

"Hi, Judy!" Linda chirped as they stopped at the table.

"Linda! So nice to see you again," Judy said as she got up and gave Linda a hug. She introduced Linda and Phil, then sat back down when Tommy and Linda left for the dance floor.

"Wow, she's really pretty," Phil offered.

"Hey, you, watch it!" Judy pretended to be mad.

"I prefer the cute tomboy type, myself," Phil said as he slid closer to Judy and put his hand on her thigh. Judy put her hand on his cheek and kissed him on the mouth. She then cuddled into the side of his neck and whispered,

"I sure hope we get some time alone tonight."

"Me, too, cutie, me, too."

***

On the dance floor, Tommy and Linda danced the first two dances at arm's length, engaged in conversation. The third dance found them much closer together. They kissed and barely moved throughout the entire fourth dance. When the dance was over, they sat down with Judy and Phil.

"I have to give Linda a ride home. She came here with Sally, of all people. You guys don't mind if I drop you off first, do you? Linda and I have a lot to talk about," Tommy said as he turned and he and Linda smiled at each other.

"Of course, that's all right. If everyone is ready, let's go," said Judy.

***

Tommy pulled the Nash into his driveway. Judy and Phil got out of the back seat.

"Good night, Linda. It was nice to see you again," Judy offered.

"Good night, Judy. Yeah, me too."

"Nice to meet you," Phil added.

Judy and Phil stood in the snow and watched Tommy back the Nash out of the driveway and drive down the street.

"Did you leave your furnace on?" asked Judy.

"Yeah, why?"

"Then tonight we go to your house."

Inside Phil's house, they threw their coats on the couch and went down the hall to Phil's bedroom. Phil scrambled to throw his dirty laundry into the corner and make the bed presentable before he sat on the edge of the bed. When Judy approached, he grabbed her around the waist and pulled her down on top of himself. They kissed passionately and wrestled to get each other's clothing off. The next hour was devoted to them sexually pleasing each other.

Chapter Twenty-Seven

Phil threw back the covers. After announcing he had to use the bathroom, he left the room. Judy rolled onto her stomach and reached for the pack of cigarettes on the nightstand. There weren't any matches with the pack of smokes, so she pulled open the drawer and blindly searched with her hand for some. Her hand landed on an object she was familiar with. When she pulled the object out, she was shocked to see that she was holding a German Luger.

"What the fuck is this?" Judy demanded when Phil came back in the room.

"It's a German Luger," Phil replied calmly.

"I know that," Judy said as she sat up in bed. "What the hell are you doing with it, and where the hell did you get it?"

"I bought it off of a Merchant Marine in Pittsburgh. He said he got it in England on one of his convoy runs."

"Okay, but why do you want it?"

"Aside from the fact that it's a gun, and I might need it to protect myself, I think it might be worth a lot of money someday."

"You mean like a collector's item?"

"Exactly. Look, I've done some research on this. Do you know that there are two very special Lugers that gun collectors would spend what you could buy a very expensive house for?"

"Is this one of them?"

"No, but I still think it will go up in value."

"What makes those two you talked about so valuable?"

"They are very, very rare. Back in 1910 or 1911, the U.S. Army put out an open competition to gun makers for a new sidearm. The specifications said that they had to be chambered in .45 caliber. The Luger Company entered two .45 caliber Lugers into the competition. They lost the competition to Colt, so those guns were the only two ever chambered in .45 caliber. That makes them very rare and worth a hell of a lot of money."

"Sounds like you've done your homework," Judy said as she pulled the toggle on the gun up partway to discover it was unloaded. "Jesus, Phil. If you want this thing to gain in value, you might clean it once in a while. It's filthy."

"I don't know how."

"Really! Tommy and I are going to the police range on Sunday. Why don't you bring this along and we'll see how it shoots."

"Wonderful idea," Phil said as he took the gun from Judy and replaced it the drawer. He embraced Judy and lowered her back on the bed. Kissing her passionately, he said, "Now, where were we?" All the time he was thinking, *Shit! I'm glad I rehearsed that story. I hope she doesn't ever find those Thompsons in the basement.*

***

"Phil. Phil. Wake up," Judy said, was shaking Phil's shoulder. Phil woke up to see her standing next to the bed.

"Huh? What's wrong?"

"Nothing's wrong, sweetheart. I'm going home to shower and change. If you come over in a half-hour, there might be some breakfast in it for you."

Phil sat up and put his legs over the side of the bed. Judy straddled his legs and hugged his head to her torso. Phil reached around her and rubbed her ass with both hands.

"Okay. Now I know you're awake," she said as she stepped away.

"I guess I'll get in the shower too. See you in a bit," he said.

Judy let herself out and crunched through the snow on Phil's front yard. She got to her driveway and noticed that the Nash wasn't there.

Tommy must have had an interesting night. Good thing he has today off, she thought. Judy took a shower, got dressed, and went downstairs to start breakfast. Making a pot of coffee was the first order of events. She started some bacon cooking in a frying pan but decided to add some more in case Tommy came home. The doorbell rang, and she went to let in Phil.

As she was letting Phil in the house, they both noticed a taxi cab pull up in front of Phil's house. Chris got out of the cab and walked toward his front door. Judy stepped out on her porch and called out, "Hey, Romeo! Want some breakfast?"

"No thanks," he called back. "I just need to get some sleep."

"Have a good time, did ya?" Judy teased. Chris just flashed her an ear-to-ear grin and continued walking to his door. Judy went back to her house.

"Okay, lover. A couple of poached eggs, bacon, and some toast sound good?" she said to Phil.

"Oh, hell, yes," Phil said as he took off his coat and threw it on the couch. "Is the coffee on, cutie?"

"Yep. Pour me one too, would you?"

***

"Do you want some more coffee, cutie?" Phil said as he was getting up to put his plate in the sink.

"Yes, please."

Phil poured himself another cup of coffee and warmed up Judy's cup. He put the coffee pot back on the stove and sat back down at the table.

"You've been in Detroit for what, about three weeks now? How do you like it here, Phil?"

"I love it! Honestly, I never knew life could be this good."

"Why is that, Phil?" Judy asked.

"I have a good job here. The people at the plant are really nice to me. I've worked for people in the past that held a gun to your head, and God forbid you should have an idea. Here, I got a reward for my idea. Then there's the very friendly neighbor."

Judy punched Phil on the upper arm. "You asshole."

"Sorry, bad joke. I should have said that I've never met anyone like you. I've never loved anyone before. I just want to be with you all the time. Do you know what I mean?"

"Oh, Phil," Judy said as she reached out for Phil's hands. They intertwined their fingers as she went on to say, "Phil, I love you with all my heart. No matter what happens, I want you to remember that."

"What's going to happen?" he asked.

"Nothing. It's just that you never know what the future might bring."

"Hello!" Tommy shouted as he closed the front door behind himself.

"We're in the kitchen," Judy called back.

"Hi, sis. Hi, Phil," Tommy said as he came into the kitchen.

"Late night, there, lover boy," Judy joked.

"It wasn't like that. We spent all night talking and working out our problems. I think if it works out, I'm going to ask her to marry me."

"That's wonderful, Tommy!" Judy squealed as she rushed to give Tommy a big hug and a kiss on his cheek. Phil stood up and shook Tommy's hand.

"Sit down, brother. I'll make you something to eat."

"Want some coffee? I'll get it for you," Phil offered.

"Sure. I have some PAL matches today at one o'clock today down at Jimmy's Gym. Can you be my corner man today, Phil?"

"I'd love to help."

"I'll be your cut man," Judy said raising her hand like a school kid.

***

Tommy parked the Nash in the lot behind Jimmy's Gym, and they went in the back door.

"You guys wait here while I look for Jimmy," Tommy said. Judy and Phil stood watching the boxers work out.

"Hey, isn't that Mike Maloney working on the heavy bag over there?" Phil asked.

"I think you're right. We saw him fight Friday night, didn't we?"

"Yeah, he was the winner of the first match. Boy, that guy has a hell of a right hand. That's Patty Mac coming up on my right side, isn't it?"

"Yeah, I'm afraid you're right," Judy said.

"I know you, I know you," Patty said to Phil as Patty was standing in front of Phil with a towel around his neck and holding a bucket in his right hand.

"Sorry, friend. I'm not whoever you think I am," Phil said calmly.

Tommy and Jimmy walked up about then, and Jimmy said, "Patty, leave these people alone. It's time you gave Bobby C. his rubdown."

"Okay, boss," Patty said, and he walked away, looking over his shoulder at Phil.

"That's creepy," Judy offered.

"Don't worry about him. He's harmless," said Jimmy.

"Phil, we need to go to the locker room and get my boys ready for their matches," Tommy said.

***

The first bout was between two ten-year-olds that were new to the PAL. Tommy helped one boy get ready. Phil took Tommy's lead and helped the other.

"What's your name, son?" Phil asked of the boy sitting on the edge of a padded trainer's table.

"My name is Kenny," the boy said.

"Kenny, my name is Phil. I'm going to be your corner man today."

"Hi."

"You been a fighter long, Kenny?"

"Just a couple of weeks. My dad's off to the war, so my mom thought it would be a good idea for me to learn how to take care of myself."

"Sounds like your mom's a pretty smart woman. Hold out your right hand so I can start taping you."

"Why do you do that?"

"Because fighters in my corner hit so hard they might break a bone in their hand on the other guy's face," Phil said, smiling. Then he nudged Kenny's chin with his right fist.

Phil started to tape Kenny's hand quickly and expertly as Kenny watched his every move.

Tommy was also watching from across the room. Tommy thought, *Wow, he's good with that tape, and he's a natural at dealing with the boys.*

"Okay, champ. Let's see what you got," Phil said as he finished taping Kenny's right hand. Phil held up his open hand. "Punch my hand."

Kenny punched Phil's hand but not very hard.

"No, Kenny. I mean punch my hand with all you got," he said. Kenny reared back and gave it everything he had.

"Ouch!" Phil exclaimed, shaking his hand and pretending Kenny hurt him. Kenny smiled, and Phil reached out and ruffled the boy's hair. "Nice shot, Champ. Now let's tape that monster left of yours."

Taping completed, Phil helped Kenny put on his boxing gloves. Lacing the gloves up, he thought the sixteen-ounce gloves looked like pillows on the end of the boy's arms. Next came the padded head gear. Lacing it up, he asked, "You nervous?"

"Yeah, a little," the boy replied.

"I've been in a lot of fights, and I got nervous before every one. Don't worry, it goes away as soon as the first bell rings," Phil reassured the boy.

***

Phil led Kenny out of the locker room and to the ring in the center of the room.

"You guys are in the white corner," Jimmy said as he pointed where to go. Phil held the ropes open so Kenny could enter the ring. Kenny started dancing around and shadow boxing as they waited for the other fighter. Tommy led the other boy out of the locker room. Judy was sitting on some makeshift bleachers.

Tommy stopped and whispered to her, "Your boyfriend is good, and he's great with the kids." A huge smile across Judy's face as she waved to Phil.

The referee introduced Kenny to the small group of spectators. Kenny's mom stood up and clapped wildly. Tears filled her eyes as she turned and said to Judy, "I'm so proud of him. I know his dad would be, too."

"I know the feeling," Judy said back to her.

The referee called the fighters and their cornermen to the center of the ring and gave them their instructions.

"Any questions?" the referee asked. When nobody said anything, the referee said, "Okay, return to your corners and when the bell rings, come out fighting." Phil put in Kenny's mouthpiece as they walked to the white corner. The referee looked at the judges' table where Jimmy, Mike Maloney and another boxer were sitting.

"Judges, are you ready?" the referee asked. Jimmy waved his hand. "Timekeeper, are you ready?" he asked another fighter at the table holding a stopwatch. The referee pointed at the timekeeper, who then rung the bell.

The two boys met in the center of the ring. It was obvious that their boxing skills were not developed yet. For three minutes they stood toe-to-toe, flailing away at each other with big, sweeping roundhouse blows. The bell rang to end the round. The referee stepped between the boys and directed them to their corners. Kenny sat on the stool that Phil brought into the ring. Judy walked over and stood outside the ring by the white corner so she could hear what Phil was saying.

"You're doing great, Kenny. Here, rinse out your mouth and slip it in the bucket."

"Can I have a drink?" the boy asked.

"Just a sip. You don't want a lot of water on your stomach, in case you get hit there."

"Okay," Kenny said as he took just a sip from the water bottle that Phil held to his mouth.

"How do you feel? Has he hurt you?"

"Nah, he can't hurt me," Kenny replied.

"That's why you're going to be champ someday, Kenny. You got heart, son."

Judy held her hand to her face as she felt a shiver run through her. She thought, *That's the same kind of thing dad used to say to Tommy as he was coming up through the ranks.*

The ten-second buzzer sounded, signaling the corner men to leave the ring. Kenny stood up, and Phil leaned over the ropes and said, "Get him, Kenny. You can do this."

The bell rang and once again the two boys stood toe-to-toe in the center of the ring. Each one was swinging wildly, trying to get the best of the other. Phil saw Judy standing a few feet away. He turned to her and said, "This kid really has heart." She smiled at Phil because she knew exactly what he meant.

The bell rang, ending round two. Kenny sat down on the stool.

"You're starting to get winded, huh?" said Phil. Kenny nodded yes. "Long deep breaths through your nose, and blow it out your mouth." Kenny did what he was told and was surprised that he was breathing normally in no time.

"Okay, this is the last round. Don't leave anything in the tank. Give it everything you got, okay?" Phil told the boy. Kenny nodded yes as Phil put the boy's mouthpiece back in his mouth.

The buzzer sounded, then the bell rung. The referee made the two young combatants touch gloves before they started fighting. Toe-to-toe they stood. Very little evidence of the sweet science, just pure guts and determination. Three more minutes of flailing away at each other with neither one backing down. The bell rang and the fight was over. The twenty or so people watching the match all stood up and applauded. Phil put a towel on Kenny's shoulders. He stood behind the boy, rubbing the young man's shoulders while they waited for the judges' decision. Jimmy entered the ring, went to the center, and motioned to the fighters to join him.

"Ladies and gentlemen. It has been a long time since we have seen such guts and determination in two fighters this young. So, our decision is that they are both winners," Jimmy announced, and he held both boys' hands in the air.

Kenny ran back to his corner where Phil picked him up, spun around, and held the boy's hand high in the air. "Way to go, champ. Way to go!"

Phil held the ropes apart so Kenny could get out of the ring. Kenny ran to his mother and hugged her around the waist. "Mom, this is Phil, my corner man," Kenny said.

"Hello. Thank you for helping my son."

"It was my pleasure, ma'am. Your boy has a lot of heart. Come on, Kenny. Let's get that gear off of you. He'll be out in a few minutes, ma'am," Phil said. Phil and Kenny walked back toward the locker room. Judy was standing by the door. "Come on back, cutie. Everybody is dressed by now." Phil said. Phil picked up Kenny and sat him on the trainer's table. Judy stood in the background. "Good fight, champ. I'm proud of you," he told the boy.

"Phil, can you be my corner man all the time?" the boy asked.

"I'd be proud to, Kenny. In fact, I'm going to ask Tommy if I can help train you," Phil said as he was taking off the boy's headgear. "Now give me that right so I can take the glove off."

"Phil, can I keep my hands taped until I get home? I want to show my friends."

"We'll even go one better that that. I'll even sign it for you like they do in the pros."

"Gee, that would be great," Kenny said. Phil turned and was going to ask Judy for a pen, but she was already holding one out for him. She had a huge grin on her face. Once both gloves were off, Phil signed the tape on the back of Kenny's hands. "There you go, champ. Now go to your mom, and I'll see you at practice."

Kenny ran out of the room. Phil turned and looked at Judy.

"You were really good out there," Judy said.

"Oh, I just did what I was supposed to do," said Phil.

"Oh, no. There's a difference between someone who does what they're supposed to do and someone who loves what they do. You love it, don't you?"

"Yeah. Yeah, I do."

Chapter Twenty-Eight

"The second match is canceled. One of the boys is sick today," Tommy said as he walked into the room. "You'll be getting a seventeen-year-old middleweight to get ready."

"Great," Phil replied.

"Great job with Kenny. His mom just told me she was impressed, too."

"Thanks, Tommy."

The next fighter walked into the room. He was wearing a gray sweatsuit.

"Hi, Miss Judy," the young man said.

"Hi, Mario. How are you?"

"I feel real good today, Miss."

"Mario, my name is Phil. I'll be in your corner today," Phil said as he shook the young man's hand. "Hop up on the table and let's get you taped."

Mario got on the table, and Phil started to tape his right hand.

"How long have you been fighting in the PAL, Mario?" Phil asked as he continued to tape.

"Since I was nine," Mario answered.

"I bet you looked a lot like Kenny when you first started. Have you gotten any better?" Phil joked.

Laughing, Mario responded, "Yeah, a little."

"Okay, that's done, now give me your left hand," said Phil.

"Mario is entering the Golden Gloves competition in January," Judy said from behind Phil.

"Is that right? Good luck with that. Okay, I'm done taping, see what you think," Phil offered. Mario punched his right fist into his open left hand. He then switched and hit his right with his left hand.

"Wow, this is a real good tape job, Phil."

"Okay, get that sweatshirt off and let's get the gloves and headgear on."

***

Phil put a towel on Mario's shoulders to keep him warm and led him to ringside.

"You're in the blue corner this bout, Phil," Jimmy informed them. Phil held the ropes open for Mario as he entered the ring, and Judy took a seat in the bleachers behind the blue corner. The referee, judges, and timekeeper were the same as they were from Kenny's bout.

The referee gave his instructions at the center of the ring, then the fighters returned to their corners. Putting Mario's mouthpiece in, Phil said, "Okay, Mario. Let's see what you got."

The bell rang and the fighters met in the middle of the ring. Phil was pleasantly surprised to see what a polished fighter Mario was. He was most impressed with the young man's footwork. Phil turned toward Judy and gave her a thumbs up.

There was less than a minute left in the first round. The two fighters were clenched on the ropes. The referee stepped between the boys to separate them. As they broke up, Mario got accidently elbowed. The blow caused a large gash above his left eye.

"Time! Time!" the referee announced as he directed Mario back to his corner. Phil looked at the cut and motioned for Judy. She handed Phil the stool and got into the ring. Mario sat on the stool. Judy went into her purse and retrieved a small bag.

"How does it look, Miss Judy?" Mario asked.

"Your girlfriend is going to love it. It gives you character. Look at Phil. He has scars, and he's really a character," she joked. Mario laughed as Judy put a cotton swab in the wound and pinched it closed.

"How is it?" the referee leaned in to ask.

"He'll be fine," Judy returned.

"Okay, I'll let it continue. If it gets any worse, I'll stop the fight."

"Understood," Phil said as he stood back and watched Judy work. Judy had gotten the bleeding stopped. She put a large gob of Vaseline over the wound. Phil held the ropes open for her and said, "Nice job, tomboy!"

Judy looked back and smiled. Mario stood up, and Phil said to him, "Your opponent's going to try to open that cut, looking for the referee to stop the match. There's less than a minute left, so protect that eye." Phil instructed.

The referee called the fighters to center ring. The boys shook hands and began boxing again. Mario did exactly what Phil had told him. He used his footwork to stay out of the other boy's reach and covered his face when he had to. The bell rang, and the boys returned to their corners. Mario sat on the stool, and as Judy was tending to his cut, Mario asked, "What do I do? I can't just cover up for the rest of the fight!"

"Here is what you do. Keep dancing to your left. Throw a couple of jabs, and when he starts to turn to meet you, give him a big right uppercut to the stomach. Keep that up until you can back him into the ropes. When you have him on the ropes, throw nothing but body shots. Go for the stomach and the ribs. Do that as many times as you can during this round, okay?"

"Okay," Mario said.

The bell rang, and the fighters returned to the center of the ring. Once again, Mario did exactly what Phil told him to do. He danced to his left, throwing left jabs. He followed the jabs with a big uppercut to his opponent's stomach. He backed his opponent into the ropes several times, and Mario threw a flurry of lefts and rights to the ribs and stomach. The bell ended round two and the fighters returned to their corners.

"You're doing great, Mario," Judy said as she tended to his cut.

"Same thing this round, Phil?" Mario asked.

"Take a look at your opponent. See how hard he's breathing? Take away his air and he'll fall soon. This round, I want you to get him on the ropes once and nail him with as many body shots as you can. The second time you get him on the ropes, give him a left to the body. He's going to expect you to throw another flurry of body shots. When he drops his hands to protect his body, give him an overhand right to the head with everything you got, understood?"

"Understood," Mario mumbled as Phil was putting the mouthpiece in the boy's mouth.

The bell for the third and final round. The fighters shook hands and began boxing. Mario continued to apply Phil's strategy. The second time he backed the opponent onto the ropes, Mario threw a hard left uppercut to the stomach. Mario could hear the boy moan and saw him drop his hands. Mario let go with a crushing right to the boy's jaw. The boy slumped down and fell unconscious to the canvas.

"Neutral corner! Neutral corner!" Phil yelled and motioned to Mario.

The referee knelt down by the young man, looked at the boy, then motioned for Tommy and Judy to come into the ring. The referee stood up and announced to the crowd,

"This fight is over."

"Welcome back," Judy said to the boy as he began to respond to the smelling salts she was holding under his nose. "How do you feel?"

"I'm okay. Can you help me up?" he asked Tommy. Tommy helped the boy to his feet and directed him to sit on the stool in the white corner. Mario went over and shook the boy's hand.

"Winner by knockout, Mario!" the referee announced to the crowd as he held the boy's hand in the air. Mario put his hand down and ran to Phil. He jumped on Phil, wrapping his legs around Phil's body and his arms around his neck.

"Thanks, coach, thanks," Mario said in Phil's ear, his voice muffled because he still had his mouthpiece in.

***

In the locker room, Judy looked at Mario's cut again. "Your mom should take you to see a doctor. You might need a couple of stitches on that cut. I'll get the insurance papers from Tommy and tell her," Judy said before she left the room.

"That was great, coach. Can you coach me from now on?" Mario asked, still excited from his victory.

"We'll see. I'll talk to Tommy, but if I'm still around, I'll be glad to coach you."

"Are you going somewhere?" Mario asked.

"I'm not sure yet."

"Great fight, Mario!" Tommy proclaimed as he entered the room.

"Can Phil be my coach from now on, coach?" the boy asked.

"Mario, Phil and I are going to talk about that real soon. Obviously, you think it's a good idea," Tommy said. "Now get dressed, and no practice until you see a doctor about that eye, understood?"

"Yes, sir, I understand," Mario said as he gathered up his things. Walking toward the door, he stopped and turned to say to Phil, "Thanks again, coach."

Judy walked into the room. She walked up to Phil and kissed him on the cheek.

"Great fight, coach," she said.

"Hey, I'm starving. Let's get some lunch. I'm buying."
Tommy offered.

***

Tommy pulled the Nash into the parking lot and turned off the engine.

"White Castle? Tommy, you cheap bastard," Judy said.

"Oh, come on, Sis, you know you like them," Tommy returned.

"Yeah, once in a while, it's okay."

"What's White Castle?" Phil asked. "We didn't have them back home."

"Your new addiction," Tommy replied.

***

Inside the restaurant, Judy and Phil sat next to each other in a booth. Tommy went to the counter to place an order.

"Damn, this whole room is covered in sparkling clean white tile. It looks like an operating room in here," Phil observed.

"Yeah, they do keep it clean. So tell me, did you enjoy yourself today?" Judy asked.

"Boy, I sure did. That was a lot of fun. Do you know that today's the first time anyone called me coach? I liked that a lot," Phil confessed.

"I knew you'd be right in your element," Judy said.

"Speaking of being in your element, you're a damn good cut man. Where did you learn how to do that?" Phil wanted to know.

"I told you. I've been hanging around a boxing gym since I was a little girl. I also took a lot of first aid classes at the Red Cross, and ah, another place in Canada," Judy said.

Tommy came to the table with a tray. He had a box of twenty mini-burgers, a bucket of French fries and three Cokes.

"Here ya go guys, dig in," Tommy said.

"Why are they so small?" Phil asked as he held up one of the burgers that was about two inches square.

"They're called mini-burgers. Eat as many as you want. If this isn't enough, I'll get more," Tommy stated.

"Not bad," Phil said as he was chewing his first bite. "I see what you mean, Judy. I wouldn't want a steady diet of these things, but it is a treat. Thanks, Tommy."

"You're welcome," Tommy said. "I have to confess that I was watching you very closely today, Phil. You're absolutely wonderful with the kids, and that strategy you gave Mario today was brilliant, absolutely brilliant."

"I agree," Judy added.

"We'd consider ourselves very lucky if you could help me coach the PAL kids," said Tommy. "We have practice at Jimmy's Gym Monday and Wednesday nights."

"Thanks for the vote of confidence, guys. But I'm afraid next week is out. Everybody at the plant is pulling double shifts next week to make up for this long weekend," Phil related.

"I totally understand if you're busy with other things to do. Maybe next Saturday?" Tommy said.

"Yeah, sure. That sounds good," Phil said. Continuing to eat, Phil thought about the other things he had to do. *Let's see. Monday night I have to blow up that railroad bridge. Then Wednesday or Thursday I'll be blowing up the Packard Plant. By Saturday, I'll either be at the extraction point in Mexico or I'll be dead. Ha, ha. Whatever happens, I guess you could say I'll be busy.*

Chapter Twenty-Nine

Sunday morning, the doorbell rang at the Nazi safe house. Phil answered the door.

"Good morning, sweetheart. It's ten o'clock. Are you ready to go to the range?" Judy asked.

"Hey! Yeah sure, come on in. I'll just be a second," Phil said. He then went to his room and retrieved his Luger from the nightstand drawer. "Okay, I'm ready to go," he said as he walked back into the living room with the Luger in his hand.

"You better take the clip out of that thing and make sure it's empty before Tommy has a cow," Judy said.

***

Tommy was waiting behind the wheel of the Nash with the motor running. Phil and Judy got into the car. The three of them all sat on the front seat.

"Phil, can I have a look at the Luger I've heard so much about?" Tommy said. Phil handed over the pistol butt first. Tommy held the Luger up to admire it. "You have to give it to the Germans. They sure make some nice weapons."

"Could we stop somewhere so I can pick up some shells for it? I only have the eight in the clip," Phil asked.

"Sure. We'll stop at Frank's Sporting Goods. If he doesn't have what you need, then nobody does," Tommy replied.

***

"How can I help you, mister?" Frank said from behind the counter of his sporting goods store.

"I need a box of bullets for this," Phil said as he took the Luger out of his coat pocket and laid it on the counter.

"Wow! Don't see many of these around here. I'll give you one-hundred dollars for it right now. No questions asked, and I don't even care if it shoots," Frank said.

"Oh, no, thank you, I just want a box of shells for it," Phil responded.

"Okay, one-fifty, but that's as high as I can go," Frank returned.

"No, just a box of shells, please," Phil stated.

"Okay, mister. Have it your way. If you ever want to sell it, bring it back in here, would you?"

Phil paid for his shells and went back to the Nash to join Tommy and Judy.

"Frank just offered me a hundred and fifty dollars for my Luger," he said as he got back into the Nash.

Tommy whistled, and Judy said, "Geez, Phil. That's about six weeks' pay, isn't it?"

"Yeah, that's a hell of a lot more than I paid for it. See, I told you it was going to go up in value," Phil said confidently.

***

The police department's indoor shooting range is in the basement of the headquarters building in downtown Detroit. The range is over twenty-five yards long and fifteen yards wide. The side walls are lined from floor to ceiling with sand bags. The receiving end of the range is equipped with a heavy steel plate that deflects the shots into a deep bed of sand. The range is safe for any caliber handgun or shotgun. The shooter's end is divided into several bays, each with its own overhead cable and pulley system that allows the shooter to send his target downrange without walking into the line of fire.

Tommy, Judy and Phil walked into the headquarters building. Tommy signed everyone in with the desk sergeant and got a key for the range. Judy and Phil followed Tommy down a flight of stairs. Tommy unlocked the steel soundproof door and pushed it inward.

"It's always so spooky how dark it is in there when the lights are off," Judy said, still standing in the hall and waiting for Tommy to turn the lights on.

"Okay, come on in," Tommy yelled. "Phil, could you close that door behind you, please?"

"Are you qualifying today, Tommy?" Judy asked.

"Yeah, I have to. That's why we're here on a Sunday. If I don't do it today, the boss'll chew my ass tomorrow," Tommy said.

"What do you have to do to qualify?" Phil questioned.

Tommy went to a table at the back of the room and took a silhouette target off of the stack. Holding it out at chest level, he said over the top of it, "I have to fire thirty rounds at this from twenty-five yards. Each bullet has a possible value of five points. See how the target has different point values depending on where you hit it?"

"Yeah," Phil replied as he looked at the target.

"There's a possible hundred and fifty points. My total score has to be at least one-hundred and five to qualify," Tommy advised.

"Well, big brother, let's see if you still got it," Judy teased. Tommy was a good shot. He took his service revolver and a box of shells out of a small zippered carrying case. He ran a target out to twenty-five yards on the overhead cable. He loaded his gun and started to shoot. Tommy continued to fire, reload, and fire until he had fired the required thirty rounds. He pulled the target back and handed it to Judy. "Here, Sis, add this up for me."

Judy held the target at arm's length and angled it toward the lights.

"Not bad, Tommy. A bunch of ten's, some nine's, and one eight. That adds up to one-hundred and twenty-eight," she said.

"Damn, Tommy, that's really good," Phil offered.

"It's qualifying. If you want to see good, wait until she shoots. Come on, Sis, take out that little pop-gun you carry all the time and show Phil how to do it." Tommy said.

Judy went into her purse and pulled out her gun. It was a .32 caliber semi-automatic. She hung a target on the pulley system and ran it out to twenty-five yards. She fired five of her shots, pulled her target back and handed it to Phil.

"Holy Shit! My God, Tommy, look at this. All five holes are dead center, and all the holes are touching this X in the center. Son-of-a-bitch, tomboy. You're one hell of a shot!" Phil stated.

"Enough about me. Let's get you set up with that Luger. I'm dying to see how it shoots."

Judy put a target on Phil's overhead and took it out to twenty-five yards. Phil took the Luger out of his coat pocket and the magazine from a different pocket. He loaded the gun, cocked the toggle, and started firing *I'm a decent shot. Nothing like Judy, but I think I'll pretend I don't know what I'm doing. I don't want them to know I've had training,* Phil thought to himself.

"Shit, Phil. You completely missed the whole target with five shots, and got two seven's and an eight," Judy said when she pulled the target back to look at it. "Load five shots in the clip for me." Judy ran the target back out to the twenty-five-yard marker.

"That's a nice gun, but it shoots about an inch high and one inch right," she observed when she took the target down.

"Mind if I try your Kraut gun, Phil?" Tommy asked.

"Not at all. Here, let me fill the clip for you," Phil replied.

"Aim an inch left and an inch down, Tommy," Judy advised.

Tommy fired eight shots and retrieved the target.

"Boy, that really has some smooth action, Phil," Tommy said.

"Head hunting this time, huh? You got four hits in the head region and four just outside of it," Judy commented. She got another target from the table and ran it out to fifteen yards for Phil.

"Okay, Phil, I think we need to work on your aiming," Tommy said. He then proceeded to teach Phil how to aim properly. "You need to see the front blade in the middle of that notched sight in the back. Then hold that image over where you want the bullet to go."

Phil continued to fire until his cartridges were gone. Tommy thought the scores improved because of his teaching. The reality of it was that Phil was trying to miss with some shots. They finished shooting, cleaned up their brass and left.

"Say, Tommy, do you think we could stop by that White Castle place for lunch? I'll buy," Phil said as they were going up the stairs to the first floor.

"Ha, ha! See, I told you! Pretty damn good, huh?" was Tommy's reply.

***

"Here ya go," Tommy said as he handed Judy and Phil beers and sat down at the Nowicki kitchen table with one for himself. Tommy opened a tackle box that contained his gun cleaning equipment.

"Isn't Phil's 9mm Luger about the same size as your .38 caliber?" Judy asked Tommy.

"Yeah, pretty much. Phil can use the .38 brushes and stuff. Do you guys mind if I go first? I want to listen to the last part of the game on the radio," Tommy advised.

"No, go right ahead, brother," said Judy.

Tommy cleaned his service revolver, went into the living room, and turned on the radio.

"Do you want another beer, Phil?" Judy asked.

"No, thanks, I'm good. Tommy said you carried that little gun in your purse all the time. Why is that?" Phil asked.

"Detroit is a wonderful city, but I work downtown and sometimes ride the bus. There's a bit of a seedy element in the downtown area. A girl just can't be too careful nowadays. Tommy got me a permit to carry a concealed gun, so it's all legal and everything," she said.

"I sure would pity the poor S.O.B. that messed with you, tomboy," Phil joked.

"You'd like to mess around with me, wouldn't you?"

"Yes, ma'am. But Tommy is home, and I saw the Ford in my driveway. That means Chris is home, too," he said.

"Maybe we could meet late tonight?" she asked.

"Damn, cutie. Much as I'd like to, I need to turn in early tonight. I start those double shifts tomorrow, remember?"

***

The alarm clock on Phil's night stand went off. Phil rolled over and turned it off. He held it close to his face. The clock read three o'clock. Phil got out of bed and got dressed. He left the house through the side door just off of the kitchen. Standing behind the Ford, he could see that none of the houses had any lights on.

Perfect. Nobody's up yet. I'll just be very quiet and get the stuff out of the car, he thought to himself. Phil retrieved the backpacks from the back seat, being careful to close the door as quietly as he could. Standing by the open car trunk, he stuffed the plastique into the backpacks. He grabbed the detonator the general had given him. He closed the trunk slowly and quietly and took the backpacks into the house.

Down in the basement, Phil wired eight ten-pound blocks of the plastique ready to explode independently of each other. He put four of the plastique blocks into each backpack. A pair of wire cutters and a roll of black electrician's tape went into the backpack that he was going to carry. Phil put the detonator on the work bench. He twisted the handle. He repeated this six more times. Each time the detonator worked perfectly.

I think I'll make one little adjustment, put this stuff in the trunk of the car and go back to bed, he thought.

Chapter Thirty

"Are we all set for tonight?" Hagen asked as he was driving to the Packard plant Monday morning.

Phil was in the middle of lighting a cigarette. He touched the flame of a match to his cigarette. He sucked the smoke in and blew it back out, then blew the match out and tossed it into the ash tray of the Ford.

"Yeah. I got up early this morning and put everything together. All the stuff is in the trunk," Phil advised.

"How long do you think it will take to wire the bridge?"

"Maybe a half-hour, unless we run into problems."

"What kind of problems?"

"It's the middle of winter. If there's ice and snow on those support beams, we'll have to take it slow."

"Yeah, you're right, Phil. I don't want to take a three-hundred-foot plunge into that river."

"No shit. So what time are you planning on leaving the plant tonight?" Phil asked.

"Well, I was thinking of nine o'clock. What do you think?"

"The bridge is a half-hour out of town. That gives us well over an hour to wire the bridge, run out the five-hundred feet of line into those trees south of the river, and set up the detonator. Nine o'clock will be fine," Phil said.

"You know what bothers me about this mission?" Chris asked.

"No, what?"

"We're going to be putting in a lot of overtime this week. Once you blow the plant up and we haul ass to Mexico, how are we going to get those big-ass paychecks?"

"Have Packard forward them to Germany, care of Adolph Hitler," Phil joked.

The two Nazis had a good laugh at Phil's joke as they pulled into the plant parking lot.

**

"**B**ill Shore wants to have a quick meeting before the shift starts," Eddie McKay informed Chris and Phil as they walked into Building #10. "Put your shit away and meet in the center of the building."

"Sure thing, Eddie," Phil said. Walking to the locker room, they passed the boxcar that everyone had decorated the day before Thanksgiving. "There she is, ready to be loaded with engines," he remarked.

The shift had assembled in the middle of the building. Bill Shore climbed onto a work bench to address them, as he always did.

"Good morning, everyone," he started. The crowd mumbled back their greetings. "You all look good and rested after the four-day weekend. Some of you look like you put on a few pounds from Thanksgiving. I know I sure as hell did." The group laughed at Bill's joke. "Let me get to the point so I don't keep you too long. The overtime is going to be unlimited for the next month. There's one exception, and I'll get to that in a minute. Starting today, you can pull double shifts and even work on Saturdays and Sundays. Work as many hours as you want to. Now the union has advised me that because this is all voluntary, you also don't have to put in any overtime if you don't want to. Or if you only want to work an extra four or five hours a day, that's fine. The only exception is that you can only work eight hours of overtime on any given day. That's a state safety regulation. Any questions? Good. Now, your area supervisors will be coming around every morning and asking you how many hours you're going to work that day.

Okay? Let's kick some ass and make some serious money for Christmas."

Bill Shore got a clapping and whistling ovation when he finished addressing the workers. People then moved away and headed to their workstations. When Phil got to his machine, he poured himself a cup of coffee from his thermos. He took a couple of sips and began to set up to run his first crankshaft of the day.

"Hey, Phil, how you doing?"

"I'm fine, Eddie. How are you?" Phil returned.

"Good, good. I'm here to find out how many hours you plan on working today," Eddie said.

"I got a real hot date tonight, Eddie. But, I can stay until nine o'clock," Phil replied.

"Okay, that's great. I'll put you down for an extra four hours," Eddie remarked.

***

Phil wanted to finish up his coffee before he started his machine up. Suddenly a loud boom echoed through the building, and the floor vibrated. Phil was taken aback by what just happened.

Son-of-a-bitch! I wasn't expecting that. Sounds like they're going to run the 100-ton hydraulic press today. I still feel bad about pushing that poor bastard into it. Guess I'm going to be reminded of it all day today, Phil thought.

***

The hydraulic press stopped pounding shortly after the regular shift ended. Eddie McKay was walking by Phil's work area.

"Hey, Eddie," Phil called out.

"Yeah, Phil," Eddie replied as he walked toward Phil.

"I'm going to go outside and grab a smoke to clear my head. That fucking press pounding all day has driven me about half nuts."

"Yeah sure, Phil. Take your time. You might want to bring some cotton balls for your ears tomorrow. They sure help," Eddie commented, pointing to the cotton in his own ears.

"Good idea, I'll do that," Phil replied.

***

Leaning against the building and smoking his cigarette, Phil noticed one of the MP guards walking in his direction. The guard shined his flashlight into Phil's face.

Aw shit, I wonder what this is going to be about?

"Hey, Mac. You got an extra one of those?" the MP asked, pointing to Phil's cigarette.

"Sure, pal." Phil took a smoke out of the pack and handed it to the MP. He then struck a match and held it cupped between his hands. The soldier lit his cigarette from the flame and took a long deep drag.

"Thanks, Mac," he said.

"No problem. You wouldn't have the time, would you soldier?" Phil asked.

The guard held his Thompson under his left arm and pulled his heavy coat sleeve back to look at his watch.

"It's twenty minutes past five," the soldier said.

"Thanks, pal," Phil replied.

The two of them stood in silence as they watched the yard engine position the boxcars.

Good. Goddess Nike is the lead car, followed by three other boxcars. That means eighty engines, Phil thought. He finished his cigarette and threw the butt down onto the snow.

"Well, back to the salt mine," he said to the soldier.

"No shit, huh?"

***

Phil met Chris in the locker room at nine o'clock.

"You about ready?" Phil asked.

"About as ready as I can be," Chris replied.

***

Hagen lit a fresh cigarette off of the butt of the one he just finished. He reached over and stubbed the butt out in the ashtray.

"Are you nervous, Chris?" Phil asked.

"Why do you ask?"

"That's the third cigarette you've had, one right after the other. You usually don't smoke that much," Phil answered.

"Yeah, I guess I'm a little nervous," he replied.

"Why?" Phil asked.

"I'm not real keen on high places. Thinking about that fucking bridge is making me worry about falling off," Chris confessed.

"Don't worry. Just move slowly and don't look down."

Hagen drove on the highway bridge over the river. He turned left on a dirt road a ways down and parked the car in a group of trees.

"This is a good spot. I don't think we can be seen from the highway," Phil observed.

"Let's go," Chris said, and they both got out of the car.

"This backpack is yours," Phil said as he handed Chris his backpack from the trunk. Then he put on his backpack.

"Thanks. You wouldn't have a parachute in there, would you?" Chris asked.

Phil didn't answer. He lifted the heavy spool of wire out of the trunk and sat it on the ground. After he had unrolled a few feet of wire, Phil tied the end to the bumper of the Ford.

"You're not going to be able to carry that wire by yourself," Chris said. Phil reached into the trunk and took out a four-foot section of steel water pipe. After he inserted the pipe into the hole in the center of the spool he said,

"I know. You're going to help me," he said.

"What about the detonator?" Chris asked.

"We've got to come back here to use it. We might as well leave it here. Go ahead and lock the trunk," Phil said.

The two Nazis started trekking across the open field. The spool of wire, suspended between them, unrolled as they walked.

"Shit! I didn't even think about how deep the snow would be in this field," Chris said, breathing hard.

"The next time we blow up a bridge in the middle of winter, try to remember some fucking snowshoes, would you?" Phil cracked. "Let's hunker down for a couple of minutes. I need to catch my breath," Chris said.

Kneeling in the snow, Phil said, "I wonder where our next assignment will be?"

"Someplace warm, I hope," Chris offered.

"That pretty well rules out the Russian Front, doesn't it?" Phil joked.

"How are you going to deal with leaving Judy?" Chris asked.

"I don't know. She's an easy person to love, and I'm afraid she'll be impossible to forget."

"Maybe after this fucking war is over, you can look her up?"

"That's a nice thought. Hang on to that for me. Come on, let's get going," Phil returned.

***

"Fuck, that's a long way down!" Chris exclaimed as they reached the bridge and he looked over the edge.

"Don't think about it. Come on, help me unroll the last of the wire off of the spool," Phil said. Phil tied the end of the wire to his belt and said, "Okay, let's go."

The two saboteurs walked on the wooden ties until they reached the first set of concrete supports. Phil hung from the tracks and swung himself onto the concrete cross-member that connected the two upright pillars. The cross-member formed a "U" shape with the pillars about five feet below the bottom of the railroad tracks. They had good footing in the snow on top of the cross-member, but they had to stand in a bent-over position. Chris swung down and joined Phil.

"What do I do?" Chris asked, hugging the concrete support.

"Can you let go of the column?" Phil asked.

"I think so," was Chris' reply.

"Okay. Take one of the blocks of plastique out of your backpack," Phil said as he did the same thing he was telling Chris to do. "Now look up. See where this heavy steel beam above us connects to the concrete column?"

"Yeah, okay," Chris replied.

"Now reach up and push the plastique onto that connection. Make sure the wires are facing out," Phil said.

The first two charges were now in place. Phil pulled the slack in on the wire he had tied to his belt. He cut the wire and, holding the end of the wire attached to his belt in his teeth, he wrapped the end coming from the field around a railroad tie. Phil stripped the ends of both wires and attached them to the wires coming out of the plastique. The electrician's tape went around the connections, and the first leg of his daisy-chain of destruction was complete.

Phil moved to the other column. Chris was hugging the column again.

"I'll need some room to work here, Chris," Phil said because of the cramped space.

"There isn't enough room to get by you!" Chris exclaimed.

"Okay, calm down. Climb back up to the top and wait for me," Phil said in an effort to calm Chris down.

"Alright," Chris said as he reached out to pull himself up to the top. Chris' hand slipped from its hold. "Ahhh!" he screamed.

Phil had his left arm wrapped around the steel beam above his head. He quickly grabbed the front of Chris' coat, preventing Chris from falling to a certain death below. Looking at Chris, Phil saw the absolute horror of a man certain he was about to die. Phil was straining with everything he had to hold Chris up. Chris was at the end of Phil's arm, flailing his arms and legs and screaming.

"Stop moving and climb up here!" Phil yelled down to Chris, trying to get through to him.

Chris was able to hook his leg over the top of the concrete cross-member. Grabbing Phil's legs, he was able to pull himself to the top of the cross-member. Chris lay on top of the cross-member, straddling it with his legs and hugging it for dear life.

"*Fuck. Jesus Christ,*" Chris moaned. He turned his head over the side and vomited. After he had regained a little composure, he sat up and said, "Many thanks, my friend. I owe you my life!"

"Are you okay to move, Chris? We need to get out of here."

"Nothing I'd like better," Chris replied.

"Okay, give me your backpack." Phil took Chris' backpack and threw it up onto the railroad tracks. "Now, I'm going up first, and then I'll help you get up."

Phil lay on his stomach and helped Chris up by pulling on the back of his coat as he ascended.

"You go to the end of the bridge and wait for me. I'll finish this up," Phil said, looking at Chris and seeing that he was wide-eyed and staring out into the distance with fear in his eyes.

"Are you sure?" Chris asked.

"Yes, now go."

Phil finished the next three supports. Finally he had all eight blocks of plastique daisy-chained together. He jogged to the end of the bridge where he found Chris hiding in some bushes. Chris was smoking a cigarette, his hands visibly shaking.

"Okay, Chris. Let's get the hell out of here," Phil said as he extended his hand to help Chris to his feet.

Phil untied the wire from the car bumper and connected the ends to the terminals on the detonator.

"What time you got, Chris?"

"Ten-thirty," Chris said after he looked at his wristwatch.

"That gives us a half-an-hour until the train comes. Let's sit in the car and stay warm."

"I'm all for that," Chris said, unlocking the driver's side door. He sat in the Ford and leaned over to unlock the passenger side door for Phil.

"Do you have a light, Phil?" Chris asked.

Phil took his pack of cigarettes out of his pocket and put one in his lips. He struck a match and cupped it in his hands, holding the light in Chris' direction. The glow of the match illuminated Chris' face. Phil could see that Chris just wasn't right yet.

"You going to be okay, pal?" Phil asked.

"Yeah, but it'll take a while. I meant what I said out there. You saved my life, and I take that very seriously. But can we talk about something else?"

"Okay. You never told me about your encounter with Sally," Phil said.

"Ha! I got to tell you, she is one wild girl. I lost count on how many times we did it. It was at least seven times. Crazy, huh?"

"Captain, you're a fucking stud!"

"Thank you. She was just a passing fling. Because you're my friend, I really think that you leaving Judy is going to screw you up. Why don't you ask her to go with us?"

"I have thought about that. I just don't think I could talk her into going to Germany. I'm afraid I'm just going to break her heart. I hope she meets someone nice."

Chris and Phil didn't have much else to say to each other. They sat quietly smoking and watching the railroad bridge.

***

"Hey, Phil. I hear a train whistle! Get ready."

"You got your binoculars?"

"Yeah, right here under the seat."

"You watch the train, and let me know when our cars are at the bridge."

Phil got out of the car. He knelt down beside the detonator, twisting the handle into the ready position.

"Get ready, Phil!" Chris shouted. "Any second now. NOW, NOW, NOW!" he shouted as loud as he could.

Phil twisted the handle on the detonator. Nothing happened. Phil twisted it again. Nothing happened.

"Son-of-a-bitch!" he yelled as he twisted the handle for the third time. Now Phil was mad. He twisted the handle several times, shouting cuss words the whole time. Finally, he threw it down into a snow bank and put his head through the open passenger side window.

"That fucking General gave us a defective detonator. The motherfucker doesn't work!"

"It's too late now, the whole train has crossed the bridge," Chris related as he was looking ahead through his binoculars.

"Shit, now what do we do?" Phil asked.

"Get in the car. Let's talk about it," Chris said. Once Phil took a seat in the car Chris said, "Are you sure you wired everything correctly?"

"Come on, captain. With all the training and practice I've had? This was just a simple daisy-chain. Yes! I'm sure it was wired correctly. It's the detonator, I'm telling you," Phil said, appearing insulted.

"Okay, what should we do now?" Chris asked.

"We should take the detonator back to the fucking general and get one that works. We can leave the charges for another time. I'll cut the lead wire and hide the ends in the snow," Phil said.

"Okay, great."

Phil threw the detonator in the trunk and took off across the field toward the bridge. Chris sat in the car and thought, *He was sent on this mission because he is an explosives expert. I know he has had all the training and a lot of experience. I'm no expert but, I think if I were I would have checked out that detonator very thoroughly before we tried to use it.*

***

"Are you hungry?" Phil asked as they were driving back toward Detroit.

"Yeah, I could eat something," was Chris' reply.

"If that White Castle up there is still open, pull in there," Phil said.

"What's White Castle?"

"Your next addiction," Phil joked.

"Okay, I'm game."

"Are you going to radio the General when we get back to the house?" Phil asked.

"I think it'll be too late. I'll radio him in the morning."

Chapter Thirty-One

Tuesday morning at six o'clock, Chris was sitting on the floor in the attic. He was coding his message to the general. Phil walked up the stairs.

"I brought you a cup of coffee," Phil said.

"Great. Sit down," Chris replied.

"What are you going to tell the old bastard?" Phil said as he sat down with his back against the wall. He put his coffee on the floor between his legs and lit a cigarette.

Chris stopped writing, took a sip of his coffee, and lit a cigarette, too.

"I'm going to tell him the truth. Everything was wired properly, but his detonator was defective."

"He doesn't strike me as the kind of guy who likes to hear that something didn't work out," Phil said.

"No, he isn't," Chris answered.

"You said you worked for him before. What more can you tell me about him?"

"General Arensdorf is a carry-over from the Great War, and I've heard that he wasn't worth a shit as a combat officer. Lots of our men got killed due to his inept decisions. The only reason he's still in the army is because his family is rich and they made huge contributions to the Nazi Party. The SS got stuck with him, so Himmler put him in charge of small operations like this one and sent him away to other countries."

"Does he have any idea what he's doing?" Phil asked.

"Probably not. But what general does?" Hagen cracked.

Phil laughed. "You could be right about that, Chris," he offered.

"A word to the wise. Don't take the general lightly. He's an aristocratic old asshole who's also mean, sadistic and vindictive," Chris offered.

"Thanks, I'll keep it in mind."

***

Chris finished coding his message and sent it. The pair sat drinking their coffee, waiting for a reply. When it came, Chris decoded it.

"What does it say?" Phil asked.

"Here, I'll read it to you. '*Leave the bridge for another time. Have Richter meet Hans at the railroad yard tonight at midnight...signed Arensdorf.*'"

"Sounds like tonight's the night you're going to wire the boxcar to blow up the plant," Chris offered.

"Yeah."

***

The top floor of the Penobscot Building was scrambling, trying to get a fix on the Nazi radio traffic.

"This is weird. These guys never broadcast in the daytime," one of the Army operators said. "It's going to be hard to pick this one out."

"Why is that?" the duty sergeant asked.

"Sun spots. It makes it sound like they're piggybacking on the Willow Run Airport frequency," said the operator.

"Do the best you can," the sergeant replied.

"Here's all I can tell you. A message originated from the west side of Detroit and a reply came out of Windsor. Nothing more. It was too weak to pinpoint anything," the operator said.

"Keep listening. I'll call the FBI."

The sergeant dialed the FBI direct line and listened to the phone ring several times.

"Shit, it must be too early for the G-Men. Anyone know what time those guys show up in the morning?" the sergeant asked.

"Around eight o'clock, Sergeant," a voice in the background offered.

***

"Steele here," is how Ron answered the direct line in the FBI office. He had heard the phone ring as he was unlocking the door and ran to answer it.

"Yeah, Agent Steele. We thought you guys would like to know that the radio frequency you guys wanted us to monitor was active at six o'clock this morning."

"You're right, that is good information. Did you get a fix?"

"No, too much atmospheric interference to pinpoint it. Same basic areas, though. Origination on the west side and the response came from across the river."

"Okay, thanks. Keep us posted. Will you?"

"Sure thing."

Agents Nick Stark and Steve Johnson walked into the office at the same time. Ron Steele hung up the phone and said, "In my office, fellas." The three FBI men sat in Steele's office. During the process of Steele lighting his first cigar for the day, he said, "I just got off the phone with the top floor. They picked up radio traffic from that suspicious radio on the west side at six o'clock this morning."

"Son-of-a-bitch! Nick and I were in a triangulation truck on the west side until four o'clock this morning. The other two trucks were stationed around the city. Shit! Those assholes never transmit around that time. That's why I ended the detail at four o'clock," Steve Johnson said.

"Yeah, it's pretty obvious that we'll have to man those trucks around the clock now if we're going to catch those pricks," Steele offered.

"Yeah, so I guess you want us to head back out there?" Stark asked.

"I'm afraid so, fellas. I'll call Washington and get some help sent over. Look for your relief to come around five or six tonight."

"Okay, boss," Johnson said and he and Stark left the room.

During the elevator ride down to the ground floor Stark said, "Let's stop somewhere and pick up every newspaper we can and a deck of cards. I got this feeling that today all we're going to see is that damn scope going around and around."

"I have to agree with you on that one, partner."

***

"Phil, you're awfully quiet today," Eddie McKay said at the lunch table.

"I guess I'm a little under the weather today," Phil replied. He looked around the table to see all the men he had made friends with since he arrived at Packard. Most of them were engaged in lighthearted conversation. Groups broke out into laughter from time-to-time. Some of the men were talking about their wives and children.

Tomorrow is the day. I wish I could set that boxcar to go off at lunchtime. At least these guys could be out of harm's way at that time. Hans said the boxcar will be inside at ten o'clock and out of the building by eleven o'clock. The death of these guys is going to be hard to live with when the mission is over. But it's all in the name of the Fatherland, Phil thought.

***

Home at the end of the workday, Phil was pacing the floor and drinking beer.

"Why don't you go next door and talk to Judy for a while? This pacing you're doing is driving me nuts," Chris said, looking over the top of his newspaper from his easy chair.

"That's a damn good idea," Phil said. He finished his beer, put on his coat and left.

"Hey, cutie. Are you up for some company?" Phil said when Judy opened her front door.

"Phil! Of course I am. I didn't see you all day yesterday. I missed you," she offered right before she kissed him on the lips.

"What's with the big apron, cutie?" Phil asked.

"I'm doing some baking. Come on in the kitchen and keep me company."

Phil took off his coat and put it on the back of the chair before he sat down.

"Coffee or beer, darling?"

"I could really use a beer tonight, cutie."

"They're in the fridge. Open me one, too, would you?"

Phil opened two beers, gave Judy one and sat back down. Judy continued to work at the counter with her back to Phil.

"What are you making?" Phil asked.

"I've already made some cookies for your lunches, now I'm going to bake a cake," she replied.

"Cake? What's the occasion?"

"Oh, nothing. I just felt like baking a cake," she said

Judy needed to get some flour out of the kitchen cupboard. She opened the door and saw it was on the top shelf. She stood on her toes reaching out for it, but the five-pound bag of flour slipped out of her hands, hitting her directly on the top of her head and bursting open. The flour exploded everywhere once the bag broke. A smoke-like cloud of dust filled the air. She turned and looked at Phil. Phil almost doubled over in laughter. "God damn, that's funny!"

"Oh, Phil," Judy said, starting to blubber. Phil could see that Judy's tears were making paths through the flour on her face. He got up and rushed to her. He gave her a big hug and got covered with flour himself. He tried to reassure her that it was okay. He could feel her body heave as she continued to cry. He tried to console her, but every time he patted her on the back, a puff of flour arose, causing him to giggle.

"Come on, Aunt Jemima, sit down and I'll clean this up for you," Phil said.

Judy laughed at Phil's joke and said, "I guess I do look pretty God damn silly, don't I?"

"You'll always look beautiful to me."

"Aw, how sweet of you to say that. But, now I'm mad. That was the last bag of flour I had."

"I'll finish cleaning this up. While you're in the shower, I'll go get you some more flour. Okay, my little ghost?"

"Oh, thank you, honey. I would so appreciate that," Judy said as she left the room. The flour came billowing off of her in clouds that formed as she walked. He brushed the flour off himself that he picked up when he hugged Judy. Phil finished cleaning the kitchen, giggling to himself. He then took the Ford to the market.

***

"That is a hell of a lot of flour, pal," the guy at the market said.

"All I know is that she said to get flour, so I'm getting flour. The last thing I want to do is not get enough," Phil said.

"Spoken like a married man, pal."

By the time Phil returned to Judy's house, she had showered and changed into her bathrobe.

"Here is your five-pound bag of flour, cutie," Phil said.

"Thank you, Phil. You are such a nice man. Get yourself another beer." Judy proceeded to mix the cake.

When she was done, she poured it into two round baking pans and placed them in the oven.

"There. It'll be a while before those are done," Judy said as she held her robe open, revealing her supple naked body to Phil. "Want to go upstairs and kill a few minutes?" she said.

"Oh, I have such a bad headache from work today, I really don't think so. Besides, we never just take a few minutes. I'd be afraid your house might burn down. I think I'll just finish this beer and go home to get some rest."

"Are you sure? Can we spend some time together tomorrow?"

"Of course."

***

Phil lay on his bed, waiting for the time to leave for the railroad yard. *I hope she bought that headache story. Tonight would have been our last time. That should have been special. How can I make it special without telling her I'm leaving? The last thing I want her to think is one last fuck for fucking's sake before I split on her. She deserves better than that.*

***

Chris walked into Phil's room and shook him awake from his nap.

"Time to go, pal. Do you want me to go with you?"

"No, I'll take care of this," Phil replied. He put his boots and coat on and left for the railroad yard in the Ford.

Phil drove into the railyard and pulled up in front of a three-story wooden structure. It was the yard house, from which Hans controlled all the tracks and engines within the yard. Hans zigzagged down the three flights of wooden stairs on the outside of the building and went to the driver's side window of the Ford.

"Here's a map of where to go," Hans said as Phil was rolling down the window. "You're going to be way back in the far corner of the yard. There shouldn't be anybody around." Hans reached in his pocket and handed Phil a key. "This will fit the locks on both sides of the boxcar. Everything you need is inside it. Don't forget to lock it back up when you leave," Hans instructed.

"Thank you, Hans. I guess this will be the last time I see you," Phil said as he held his hand out of the window for Hans to shake.

"Good luck," Hans said as he shook Phil's hand.

***

Phil followed the map and within minutes, he parked in front of a Burlington-Northern boxcar. He turned off the headlights and got out of the car. He was surprised how dark it was in this part of the yard, but he got a tool bag and a flashlight out of the trunk. He unlocked the boxcar door and rolled it back. Inside the boxcar was a thousand pounds of dynamite and a twenty-pound block of plastique. He climbed into the boxcar and went to work. After setting the alarm clock for ten-thirty, he jumped down. He rolled the boxcar door closed and locked it with a lock he had brought from home. Circling around the boxcar, he replaced the lock on the other door with one of his own. Phil then crawled under the boxcar and from his tool bag, set small charges of plastique at all four corners. He wired everything to his own alarm clock and set it to go off at ten-thirty, too.

Chapter Thirty-Two

Chris Hagen was sitting in his easy chair when Phil walked into the living room and sat on the couch. "Phil, you look like shit today. What's wrong?" Chris asked.

"I'm not surprised that I look like shit. I couldn't sleep last night, and my stomach is tied in knots."

"What time did you set the timer to go off this morning?" Chris asked.

"Things will go boom at ten-thirty."

"Blowing up the factory is probably what's bothering you, huh?"

"I'm sure of that. Lots of people's lives will be changed forever by ten-thirty-one this morning."

"I'm going to call in sick for the both of us in a few minutes."

"You should probably send a message to that prick, General Arensdorf, too, Chris."

Hagen went back to reading the newspaper while Brown just stared at the wall across the room.

***

Ron Steele walked out of his office and stood in front of Agent Johnson's desk.

"Guess you guys didn't get any hits yesterday," he said.

"No, boss, nothing. We just sat in that truck and watched the dial go round and round, all frickin' day," Johnson replied.

"The guys on night shift didn't get any hits last night, either. Maybe things will change today, fellas," Ron said.

"We sure hope so, boss," Nick Stark offered as he and Johnson headed out the door to start their shift in the triangulation truck.

***

"Hello, Personnel Department," a female voice said into the telephone.

"Yeah, hello. My roommate and I work in Building #10, and we're calling in sick today," Hagen replied.

"What are your names?"

"I'm Chris Hagen and my roommate is Phil Brown."

"Nature of your illnesses?"

"Upset stomachs. Guess we had too many White Castle burgers last night."

"Oh, that'll do it for sure," the voice said with a giggle. "Okay, I'll notify your department."

"Great. Thank you," Chris said as he hung up the phone. "Okay, that takes care of that."

"I'm going next door to see Judy. I don't know what I'm going to say to her. All I know is I need to see her one last time," Phil said.

"While you're gone, I'll radio General Arensdorf."

***

"Phil, you look like shit," Judy said as she opened her door for him.

"You're the second person to tell me that this morning," he replied.

"What's wrong, sweetie?"

"My stomach is all messed up today. Chris, too, that's why we called in sick today."

"You guys didn't eat White Castle last night, did you?"

"No. I was over here last night, remember?" Phil said.

"Oh, yeah. Can I get you some coffee and something to eat?"

"God, no. I think a glass of milk might be the best thing."

"Sure, sweetie. Come on into the kitchen and sit down. I'll get you some milk," she replied.

Phil sat and drank his milk and just looked at Judy. He wanted to say something to her. His thoughts of how she was going to react made him feel even worse. It got so bad that he ran out of the room, down the hall to the bathroom and vomited into the toilet. He returned to the kitchen a few minutes later.

"I don't have anything here for upset stomachs. Come on, Phil, let's go to the drug store and get you something," Judy said.

Phil remembered that he still had the Ford keys in his pocket from the night before. He took them out and handed them to Judy.

"Would you mind driving?" he asked.

"Sure, sweetie."

***

The attic of the safe house found Hager sitting on the floor again. He was coding a message to transmit to General Arensdorf. The message read, *Plant scheduled to blow up at ten-thirty this morning. Signed, Smoltz.*

Chris lit a cigarette and leaned against the wall, waiting for a response. When it came, he decoded each letter. When he was done, the message read,

Well done, Captain. Kill Richter and leave his body in the basement for disposal. Proceed to extraction point in Mexico."

No, no, that can't be. I'll decode it again," Chris said to himself aloud. The second decoding read exactly the same as the first. "That son-of-a-bitch!" He coded the following message and sent it to General Arensdorf: *Why? He has done everything we have asked of him ."*Now what, you piece of shit?"

The return message read, *That is an order, captain. Follow the order or you will face severe reprisals.*

"Okay, asshole. One more time. See how you like this message." *General, you are asking me to kill my best friend and the man who saved my life two nights ago. I can't do it, sir.*

The return message simply read, *Follow your orders, captain.*

"You're going to love this one, you fat piece of shit," still talking aloud. Chris transmitted, *Screw you, General. If you want him dead, kill him yourself.* Chris leaned back against the wall and thought about what he had just done. "I'm a dead man," he thought. "General Arensdorf will see to it that I face a firing squad or worse. Either way, I'm dead. Well, fuck him. There's no turning back now."

***

"Truck two, truck one," Nick Stark said into the microphone of the FBI radio.

"This is truck two, go," was Agent Michael Kushner's reply.

"Michael, are you guys picking up a broadcast on the frequency we're monitoring?" Stark asked.

"Like a searchlight down Woodward Avenue," Michael replied.

"Truck three, truck one," Stark sent.

"This is truck three. We got it too, Nick. Five by five."

"Get the compass directions from the other trucks, Nick and I'll plot it on the map," Steve Johnson yelled from a small desk in the back of the truck.

"Truck two. What's the compass bearing on the frequency you're picking up?" Stark asked.

"We have it real strong coming to us from the southwest at 225°, Nick," Michael relayed.

"Truck three. What direction are you picking it up from?" Stark asked.

"Nick, we also have it strong out of our northwest at 295°."

"Stand by guys, Steve is plotting this out on the map," Stark broadcast.

"Okay. From truck two's location at 225°," Johnson said aloud as he plotted on the map with a ruler and a pencil. Then truck three has it at 295° from where they are at," still talking out loud. He then plotted a line on the map. "Okay, we're here, and we have him from almost due east at 89°." Plotting the third line, Johnson circled where the three lines intersected. "We got him! Nick, tell trucks two and three to meet us on Pelkey Street, right off of Eight Mile Road."

"Trucks two and three, meet us on Pelkey Street, right off of Eight Mile Road," Stark broadcast.

"Hey, that's my street!" Michael put out over the air.

"I hope it's not your wife, Michael," Stark joked.

"Funny, real funny," was Michael's response.

***

The truck three team stationed themselves behind 2067 Pelkey, in the alley. Both agents were behind cover and training their Thompson submachine guns on the back of the house. Michael took cover and trained his Thompson on the right side of the house. George covered the left side of the house from the Nowicki front porch.

"Are you ready, partner?" Stark asked Johnson as they stood on either side of the front door at the house, their .38's drawn.

"Yeah, let's go!"

They both threw their shoulders into the front door. The door burst open, and the two agents ran inside, yelling, "Don't move! FBI!"

"Hi, fellas. I've been expecting you," Chris Hagen, seated in his easy chair, said calmly.

"Down on the floor, Mister. Down on the floor!" Stark yelled.

Chris put his cigarette out in an ashtray and got facedown on the floor. Stark covered him with while Johnson handcuffed him. "Anybody else in the house?" Stark asked.

"No, just me," Chris replied.

"Search him for weapons. Then get Michael and George in here to check the rest of the house," Stark instructed.

***

"Fuck me! Nick, you've got to see this!" Johnson yelled from the kitchen.

"Tell me. What is it?" Stark yelled back.

"I got two Thompsons, two Colts, enough ammunition to start a war, some of that plastique, blasting caps, and timers. Right here on the kitchen table," Johnson called out.

"I guess you're going to want to talk to me about all those washing machines that blew up a few days ago, huh?" Chris said.

"Nick," Michael Kushner said as he walked up. "I found the radio in the attic, and guess what,"

"What, Michael?" Stark said.

"The wire on the microphone was wrapped around it. It held the mike in the open position all this time."

***

Stark and Johnson helped Chris to his feet.

"Guys, could I have my coat and hat? They're on the couch over there," Chris said.

Johnson picked up the coat and squeezed all the material checking for weapons. Not finding any, he draped the coat over Chris' shoulders and put his hat on his head.

Agents Stark and Johnson were on either side of Chris, leading him down the walkway to their truck. Out of the corner of his eye, Chris saw the Ford coming down the street.

Shit! Chris thought. *These two guys don't know the Ford, but if Kushner spots it, they'll get Phil too.*

Kushner was standing about ten feet away, with his back to the street. Chris broke away from Johnson and Stark, ran up to Kushner and buried his lowered head in the agent's stomach.

"What the hell is going on, Phil?" Judy asked.

"Never mind, just keep driving," Phil snapped back.

"I have to stop, Phil."

"You stop and I'll kill you!" Phil yelled as he held his switchblade to Judy's throat.

The Ford passed by unnoticed because all the agents were in a pile, trying to pull Chris off of Kushner.

Chapter Thirty-Two

"What the hell is going on, Phil?" Judy asked.

"Just shut up and drive. I have to think. Oh, yeah, I'll take this little popgun out of your purse," Phil said as he took Judy's gun and pointed it at her side. *I guess I had better get out of town and lay low for a while,* he thought. "Drive to your cabin," he ordered.

"What are you going to do to me?" Judy asked nervously.

"You won't get hurt if you do what I tell you to do," Phil replied.

***

"So, this is our Nazi saboteur, huh?" Ron Steele asked as he walked into the interrogation room of the FBI office. Chris was seated on a metal chair in front of a small metal table. Another metal chair was directly across from Chris. Ron Steele sat in the empty chair. Stark and Johnson were leaning against the wall a short distance away.

"That Identification badge on your coat says your name is Chris Hagen and you work at Packard. Is that right?" Steele asked.

"Smoltz, Eric. Captain. Serial number SS751559," was Chris' reply.

"Tell me about the guns and explosives we found in your house."

"Smoltz, Eric. captain. Serial number SS751559."

"Name, rank, and serial number, huh? Okay, I get it. Where's the other guy who lives in the house?" Chris remained silent. Steele turned and asked Johnson, "Do we have a name for the other guy that lives in that house?"

"Yeah, Michael actually met the guy. He said his name was Phil Brown," Johnson related.

"Who's Phil Brown?" Steele asked Chris.

"He's a nobody. I answered his 'roommate wanted' ad when I came to Detroit," Chris answered.

"How did you plant that bomb in the rail yard the other day?" Chris didn't say anything. "Did Brown help you blow up that boxcar?" Again, Chris made no reply.

"Okay, boys. It looks like Captain Smoltz here doesn't want to answer any questions. Put him in the holding tank. I'm going to contact the Army. Maybe they can beat something out of him," Steele said to Johnson and Stark.

***

"Are you going to leave the handcuffs on me in here?" Chris asked when Johnson led him into the holding cell.

"Naw, I guess not. Turn around," Johnson said. Johnson removed his handcuffs and put them into the case he had on his belt. He closed the cell door and locked it.

The phone rang in Ron Steele's office.

"Special Agent Steele," Ron said when he answered it. "Holy shit!" Ron belted out. "Yeah, I got two agents right here. I'll send them over immediately," Ron said to the person who called. "Stark, Johnson, get in here now!" Ron yelled out the door.

"What is it, boss?" Stark asked.

"A bomb went off at the Packard plant! You two get over there right now!"

***

Phil stood behind Judy as she unlocked the cabin door. Phil had the .32 pistol trained at her back.

"Shit, it's just as cold in here as it is outside," Phil said as the vapor escaped from his mouth. "Let's go get some firewood."

Outside the cabin, Judy put pieces of firewood against his chest and he held them in place with his left arm, all the time holding the .32 in his right hand. Back in the cabin, he threw the wood onto the hearth.

"Okay, go ahead and light a fire," he said as he stepped back.

As the room warmed up, Phil took off his coat and put Judy's gun in his waistband, behind his back.

"Okay, cutie, let's talk," he said.

"Phil, whatever's going on, we can work things out."

"No, we can't, Judy. I'm a...,"

"Nazi spy!" General Arensdorf bellowed as he burst through the cabin door. The general had his pistol trained on the two of them.

"General, what do you want?" Phil asked as he moved to stand next to Judy.

"I want all the loose ends of this mission wrapped up. Hagen has been arrested, so that leaves just the two of you. I think I'll start with her," General Arensdorf said as he took aim at Judy.

Phil watched Arensdorf slowly pull the trigger on his Mauser pistol. Phil jumped in front of Judy. Two shots rang out. Phil was hit in the head and shoulder and he went to the ground. General Arensdorf squeezed the trigger a third time. His World War One-issue Mauser had jammed. He squeezed the trigger again and nothing happened.

Judy knelt down beside Phil. She pulled her gun from Phil's waistband and fired once. The bullet struck General Arensdorf directly between his eyes. His head jerked back and he fell to the floor.

"Judy! Judy!" a voice from outside the open cabin door yelled.

"Who is it?" Judy yelled back as she trained her gun to shoot anyone who came through the door.

"It's me, Hans!" the voice yelled back.

"Come on in, Hans," Judy said, lowering her gun.

Hans walked into the cabin with his hands held up to show that he wasn't a threat.

"Good going. I'm glad to see that fat fucking prick dead. How's Phil?"

"He's still alive. The bullet only grazed the side of his head. The one in his shoulder is pretty bad, though. Help me get him into the bedroom."

***

Judy treated Phil's head wound. Using Phil's switchblade and a fork, she dug the bullet out of Phil's shoulder. Phil remained unconscious as she bandaged him up.

"What are we going to do with this piece of shit?" Hans asked as he pointed to the general when Judy came into the room.

"Here are the keys to that Ford. Drive it down to the lake and tow my ice fishing shanty up as close to the cabin as you can get it," Judy said.

Hans left the cabin and Judy stepped over General Arensdorf to get some more firewood. By the time Hans returned, Judy had made a fire in the kitchen woodstove and made a pot of coffee.

"Now what are we going to do?" Hans asked when he returned to the cabin.

"First, I'm going to finish this cup of coffee. Then we're going to dispose of Arensdorf. Do you want a cup of coffee?" Judy said.

"Yeah, that sounds good," Hans said.

Hans poured himself a cup of coffee and sat down at the kitchen table, across from Judy.

"How is it you happened to be here, Hans?" Judy asked.

"I heard some radio traffic this morning that General Arensdorf wanted Chris to kill Phil. Chris told the general to go fuck himself, he wasn't going to do it. I figured the shit was about to hit the fan, so I was driving to your house to warn you. That's when I saw Arensdorf tailing you guys, so I tailed him," Hans explained.

"Well thanks, Hans. Now we need to load the general into the shanty and take him out on the lake."

***

"You got anything to weight him down with?" Hans asked as Judy was driving the Ford back toward the lake.

"Sure do," Judy replied. She stopped just before going onto the ice. Off to her left was her rowboat, turned upside down on a pair of sawhorses. Under the boat were two concrete blocks with a length of rope tied to each one. They were what Judy used as anchors when she took the boat out fishing.

"Get those two cinderblocks from under the rowboat and put them in the shanty with the general," Judy told Hans.

"Are you sure we aren't going to go through this ice?" Hans nervously asked as Judy started to drive onto the lake.

"Yeah, I'm sure," Judy said as she proceeded to drive on the ice. She continued until they were over the deepest part of the lake. "Okay, here we are," she said as she stopped the car. "Let's chip a hole in the ice, and we better make it a wide one."

When they finished the hole, Judy pulled the car ahead until the shanty was over the top of it.

"Hans, tie those anchor ropes to his feet. I'll go through his pockets," Judy said once they were inside the shanty with the general.

"There. He's all tied up. How long do you think these will keep him on the bottom?" Hans said.

"It doesn't matter. This thick ice isn't going to melt until late March or April. There won't be much left of him by the time the catfish feast on him," Judy said.

"Fish food, huh? I couldn't think of a better ending for you, you fat fuck," Hans exclaimed as he spit on the general's body.

"Holy shit!" Judy exclaimed. She had pulled a wad of cash from the general's coat pocket.

"I think the motherfucker was going to pocket the money left over from financing the mission," Hans offered.

"There must be ten thousand dollars here. Here, you take it," Judy said as she held the money toward Hans.

"No. You keep it. You might need it to help Phil. Did you find any information on him?"

"Just this," Judy said as she unfolded a small map. "This must be where they were going to be picked up by a U-Boat off of the Mexican coast. I'll have to pass this along to the Navy," Judy said.

Hans dropped the concrete blocks into the hole. The two of them then pushed, shoved, and dragged the generals body until it went into the hole after them. He sank rather quickly among a torrent of bubbles.

"You want this?" Judy asked as she held the general's Mauser.

"No, not really," Hans replied.

Judy threw the Mauser into the hole in the ice. It went *plunk* and sunk out of sight.

***

Back on shore, Hans disconnected the shanty and Judy drove back up to the cabin.

"Hans, take some of this money, go into town and bring me back some provisions for a week or two," Judy said.

"Anything else?"

"Yeah, you better get me some bandages and tell Tommy, and *only* Tommy, where I am. Take your car. They're probably looking for this Ford by now," she said.

"You got it."

"Thank you, Hans."

***

Johnson and Stark returned to the FBI office in the late afternoon.

"Well, what happened?" Ron Steele asked as he greeted them.

"There was a bomb, and it made one hell of a mess. Nick'll fill you in on what happened and the cover story, boss. I want to talk to Captain Smoltz," Johnson said. He went down the hall to the holding cell. Chris was lying on the cot with his back toward the door.

"Hey! Wake up, I want to talk to you," Johnson yelled. Chris didn't move. Johnson unlocked the cell and went in. He shook Chris, but he still didn't move. Johnson rolled Chris onto his back.

"Aw, you stupid fuck!" Johnson yelled. Chris' eyes were wide open and there was a white foam around his mouth. Chris had gnawed the cyanide capsule from the lining of his hat and swallowed it.

***

Darkness had come by the time Hans arrived back at the cabin.

"What took you so long, Hans?" Judy asked when he brought in the first load of supplies.

"The bombing at the Packard plant today. It's all over the radio. I waited for the afternoon edition of the newspaper to come out so you could read about it. Here," Hans said as he handed the newspaper to Judy. Hans went back outside to get more provisions. Judy opened the paper.

Bombing at Packard

The FBI reported that a bomb went off at the Packard plant today (pictures on page 2). Agent Steve Johnson reported it was all part of a training exercise put on by the FBI and the US Army to create alertness against possible saboteurs. At ten-thirty this morning, small charges blew open ten-pound bags of flour at each corner of a boxcar that was parked inside Building #10 of the factory. The flour was used to simulate what might happen if a bomb were to actually go off inside the plant. "It sure made a big mess." Agent Johnson was quoted as saying. Bill Shore, a Packard supervisor, told reporters, "We used this exercise to test our security and evacuation procedures. Some of our employees didn't know about the exercise, and it scared the hell out of them. We may never get the flour dust out of the rafters." Continued on page 2.

Phil Brown, you loveable asshole, Judy thought as she put the newspaper down.

Chapter Thirty-Three

"Good morning, sunshine," Judy said from the chair she'd pulled up next to Phil's bed. It took Phil a few moments to fully wake, and when he went to move, he groaned loudly from the pain in his shoulder. He reached up with his left hand and felt the bandage around his head.

"So what happened here wasn't all a bad dream, I take it," he said quietly.

"No, it really happened," Judy said.

"How long have I been out?" Phil asked as he was rubbing his head.

"About three days," Judy replied.

"What happened to Arensdorf?"

"You do remember that he's the one who shot you, don't you?"

"All I remember is that my last thought was trying to keep you safe."

"And you did, Phil. Arensdorf's gun jammed after he shot you. So I got my gun from your waistband and put one between the general's running lights," Judy advised.

"Where is he now?"

"At the bottom of the lake."

"How did you get that fat fucker out there?"

"Hans stopped by to help me."

"Hans? The Hans from the railroad yard? How the fuck do you know Hans?" Phil demanded to know.

Judy took two cigarettes out of a pack, lit them both and handed Phil one.

"I think it's time we told each other the truth. I want you to remember that the most important thing I'm about to tell you is that I love you. That is the God's honest truth."

"I love you, too, Judy," Phil said.

"I know that, Phil, I don't think you'd step in front of a bullet for any other reason. Anyway, you remember the album I showed you on Thanksgiving?"

"Yeah, sure."

"Remember a photo of my dad and his commanding officer from the first World War?"

"Yeah. You said it was William Donovan, the director of the Office of Strategic Services. Am I right?"

"You're right. But, I left out the fact that he's my Uncle Bill."

"What? Holy Christ, I'm going to burn in hell for sure," Phil said.

"Hold on, cowboy, let me finish."

"Please do," Phil said.

"When Uncle Bill formed the OSS, he realized that a lot of the women agents were going to have to be taught how to shoot. He thought they might be less intimidated by a woman instructor. He came to me and asked me to take the job. Well, I jumped at the chance to do it."

"So, you're a shooting instructor for the OSS?" Phil asked.

"I was at first. Then the agency got wind of Germans coming to Detroit to sabotage our Arsenal of Democracy. So Uncle Bill made me an operative. Because Tommy is a cop and I'm his niece, Uncle Bill made special arrangements with J. Edgar Hoover because we live right next door. I had to report to the FBI brass as well as Uncle Bill."

"You mean the woman I love is a spy?"

"So's the man I love, Phil."

"Fuck me. I never saw that coming. How do you know Hans out of all this mess?"

"Hans was my first assignment. Hans and his partner were led to believe that the house next door to me was a

Nazi safe house. I was assigned to watch whoever was in the house and figure out why they were here."

"I guess I was an assignment, too, then. Shit, did you make love to him too?"

"It wasn't like that. I've never even kissed Hans. The only reason I slept with you is because I fell in love with you, you big dummy!" Judy yelled in anger.

"Okay, okay. I'm sorry. So tell me what happened."

"I got information that they were going to blow up a train full of tanks outside of the Chrysler plant. I set a trap for them, but shooting started and I killed Hans' partner. Hans was given the choice of facing a firing squad at dawn or becoming a double agent for us. I'm now his handler."

"Son-of-a-bitch, cutie. Never in a million years would I have guessed any of the things you just told me," Phil said. "Is that firing squad or double agent my fate as well?"

"No, not really. I love you too much to turn you in. In fact, I have over ten thousand dollars, courtesy of the general, that you can have if you just want to disappear," Judy said.

"No, I can't do that. My stomach was so churned up the other day at the thought of leaving you, all I wanted to do was puke."

"You sure say the sweetest things, you Nazi bastard," Judy replied, laughing.

"I'm no Nazi anymore. That Nazi general was going to kill me. I can't be a party to that shit anymore."

"What are you going to do, Phil?"

"I'm going to turn myself in and take the consequences."

"You may not have to do that," Judy said.

"No, I have to. I've killed too many people."

"We've all killed people, Phil. That's what happens in war."

"Judy, I'm not the person you think I am."

"I know that you're Adolph Richter, and you came here to destroy our ability to make the Rolls-Royce Merlin engines. Please don't ask me to call you Adolph. You'll always be Phil to me. Now, you must be famished. Do you think you could hold some soup down?"

"Yeah, but do you think I could have another cigarette first?"

Judy put a cigarette between Phil's lips, struck a match and held it out for him. Phil leaned forward to light his smoke but grimaced in pain. Judy took the smoke from Phil's mouth, lit it and put it back in his lips.

"I'll bring you something for the pain, too," Judy said, and she left the room.

***

Minutes later Judy came back into the bedroom carrying a tray. She put the tray down on the nightstand.

"Something smells good," Phil commented.

"Yep, Campbell's Chicken Noodle Soup. Guaranteed to cure what ails you."

"I wish it were that easy," Phil bemoaned.

"Here, take this first," Judy said as she put the pill into Phil's mouth and handed him a glass of water. Phil took a drink of water, swallowed the pill, and handed the glass back to Judy. Judy pulled her chair closer to the bed and began feeding Phil his soup.

"I talked to Uncle Bill about you a couple of days ago, and I have some good news," Judy said as she spooned the soup into Phil's mouth.

"What's that? I'm only going to prison for the rest of my life."

"No, silly. Uncle Bill was very impressed with the way you wired that bridge to explode."

"Shit, you knew about that too?"

"Of course we do, just like we know about the way you fixed the detonator so it wouldn't work. Oh, and he told me to tell you that the bags of flour at the Packard plant was genius, sheer genius."

"Glad he liked it. I guess General Arensdorf didn't much care for it," Phil said with a wry smile on his face.

"No shit. But anyway, Uncle Bill said he'd like to have you teach new operatives how to wire explosives the way you do. If you agree, he'll tell the FBI that you were a double agent working for the OSS the whole time."

"That sounds like a pretty good deal. What kind of offer is he going to make Chris?"

Phil had finished his soup. Judy put the bowl back on the tray. She took Phil's left hand into both of hers and said, "Phil, darling, Chris is dead."

"Oh, no. How?"

"Tommy came by yesterday. He said that he went to the FBI office and talked to an Agent Stark. Apparently that ruckus we saw in your front yard the other day was Chris creating a diversion so you could escape. When they interrogated him, he told them you had nothing to do with anything. He told them you were just some guy that worked at Packard who needed a roommate. When they left him alone, he took a cyanide capsule that he had hidden in his hat."

"Damn. The poor bastard. What a waste."

"It wasn't a waste. Your friend gave up his life so you could start a new one."

"Yeah. You're right. Tell your uncle that I'll take his deal." Phil said as he reached out and hugged Judy with his good left arm.

Epilogue

Christmas had come and gone, and it was now the spring of 1944. Adolph Richter found himself standing in front of a Judge's bench in the Superior Court of Wayne County, in downtown Detroit. He was there for two reasons.

"Mister Richter, I have read your explanation of facts and your application. Is there anyone in the courtroom who will vouch for Mister Richter's character?"

"I will, Your Honor."

"Thank you, General Donovan. I am signing the application and declaring that this man will now and forever more be known as Phillip Brown. As for the second matter, all parties join me in my chambers." the Judge stated.

***

Several people followed the Judge into his chambers. "Who among you will be the official witnesses?" the Judge asked.

"It will be our honor, Your Honor."

"Please identify yourselves for the record."

"Yes, we are Tommy and Linda Nowicki."

At the end of a very brief civil ceremony, the Judge announced, "Ladies and gentlemen, may I now present to you Phillip and Judy Brown."

***

"Judy, can I steal your hubby away from you for a couple of minutes?"

"Sure, Uncle Bill," Judy said.

Phil and Uncle Bill sat at a quiet booth in the back corner of the bar in the restaurant where the wedding reception was being held.

"Nobody from across the river has contacted you, have they?" Bill asked.

"No, sir. Not a peep," Phil replied.

"With any luck, this damn war will come to an end in a year or so. I want you to stay at Packard when you're not teaching my people and wait for them to contact you again."

***

Phil was never contacted again. The war ended in 1945, after which Phil and Judy were discharged from the OSS. With their ten-thousand-dollar nest egg, they opened an elegant restaurant in Grosse Point, an upscale suburb of Detroit they called Merlin's. In 1947, they had one son, whom they named Christopher.

About Chuck Beach:

I was born in Detroit, MI and spent my teenage years in San Jose, CA. After high school I went to West Valley College and San Jose State University, but wasn't real serious about school at the time. I thought I would rather be making money, so I dropped out. I had a bunch of nowhere jobs. I did work at the San Jose Mercury-News for a few years. That was cool. Craving some excitement and adventure I joined the CHP in 1973. Long story short I got hurt on the job and was medically retired after almost ten years (damn knees). The doctor said I needed to find a line of work that would allow me to sit on my ass. So, I went back to school and got a degree in accounting. I worked for a lot of companies, and ran my own practice for 20+ years. I got tired of sitting behind a computer screen. In the midst of my mid-life crisis I came to the realization that I only had a few more years of working, so why not do something I always wanted to do - teaching. Back to school I went and got my teaching credential and a master's degree in Special Education at Azusa Pacific University. I taught math to special ed. kids for ten years. I totally loved it. So when people ask me about my past I tell them that I have had three careers. One very exciting. One very boring, and one really fun career. Away from work I have been married for 34 years. We have three great kids who are all grown up. One grandson, who is the light of my life.

Acknowledgements:

More thanks that I can possibly express to Jane Lowrey for her suggestions and editing talents.

Thank you to my friend, Ty Brown for his technical contributions.

Thank you to my Facebook friends. Without their comments and encouragements this book would have not been possible.

If you enjoyed this story, check out these other Solstice Publishing books by Chuck Beach:

High Tension Murders

This is a fictional story that takes place in Southern California. It involves police corruption, deceit, and serial killing at the highest level. Ben Maloney was a highly respected and decorated homicide detective in Los Angeles County. Setup on phony charges by the evil sheriff, Ben is forced to resign. He takes a job with the Kern County Sheriff's Department, and is assigned to the small desert community of Ridgecrest. The small Sheriff's Department is nicknamed "the outpost," because of its remote location.

A serial killer is depositing the naked, mutilated bodies of Los Angeles hookers outside of town. The bodies are suspended 100 feet of the ground on the high tension power lines that run through the desert. Ben must determine how the bodies got there without any clues. Then he has to find out who is responsible for the grizzly ritualistic killings.

http://bookgoodies.com/a/B01J97ESOI

www.ingramcontent.com/pod-product-compliance
Lightning Source LLC
Chambersburg PA
CBHW070909180626
46817CB00003B/982